THE LOOKING HUT

ABOUT THE AUTHOR

Alan Vaughan grew up in a small village which nestles at the foot of the North Downs in Kent. From an early age within this rural idyll around him, he learnt the lore of the countryside and developed a life-long passion for nature in all its forms.

As a result he often uses the villages of the North Downs as the backdrop for his novels, often weaving in the local rural crafts and traditions, many of which are now sadly destined to the history books.

Proud to be a Man of Kent, Alan still lives close to where he was born with his wife Vivienne. They have a son and daughter and four grandsons.

BY THE SAME AUTHOR

THE LONG JOURNEY HOME

The dark clouds of war gathered when a line of men marched out of a small Kentish village to join the thousands of others who were already dug deep and dying in the clinging mud of the Somme.

Twenty-five years later another war had erupted across the world and the decision to fight or to join the retreat to the beaches of Dunkirk was to be Tom's alone.

Later, whilst vengeance and hate burned deep in his heart, thousands of miles away the flame of a candle flickered in a cottage window to welcome him home.

"A brilliant and harrowing tale of family love and war"

"What a great read, I couldn't put the book down".

"This is a book which everybody should read"

"The story moved me so much and gave me cause to reflect on the strength of the human spirit"

This is a fictional work based in part on actual events. Any resemblance to persons living or dead, except in the case of historical fact, is purely coincidental.

All rights reserved. No part of this publication may be reproduced, stored in a retrieval system, or transmitted in any form or by means, electronic, mechanical, photocopying, recording or otherwise, without prior permission of the publishers.

Copyright © Alan Vaughan

THE LOOKING HUT

By Alan Vaughan

The book is dedicated to my wife Vivienne, who together with our son and daughter and four grandsons, has Huguenot blood running through her veins.

THE LOOKING HUT

INDEX

Map of Spitalfield

Map of Southwell

Part One

1755

1   *Weaver's Loft*
2   *The Parsonage*
3   *The Smithy*
4   *The Looking Hut*
5   *The Eternity Box*
6   *Unexpected Visitors*

Part Two

1765

7   *The Speckled Monster*

1798

8   *Where The Mind Goes*
9   *The Greenless Tree*
10 *The Judge's Lodgings*

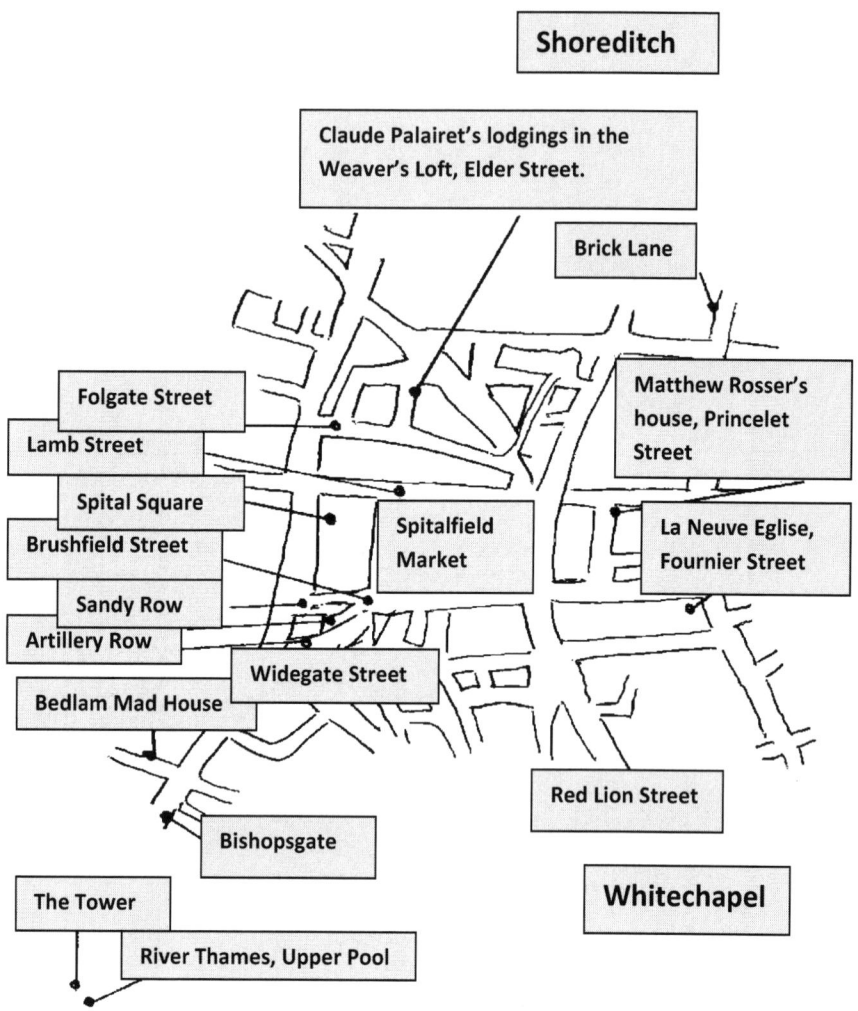

SPITALFIELD-1755

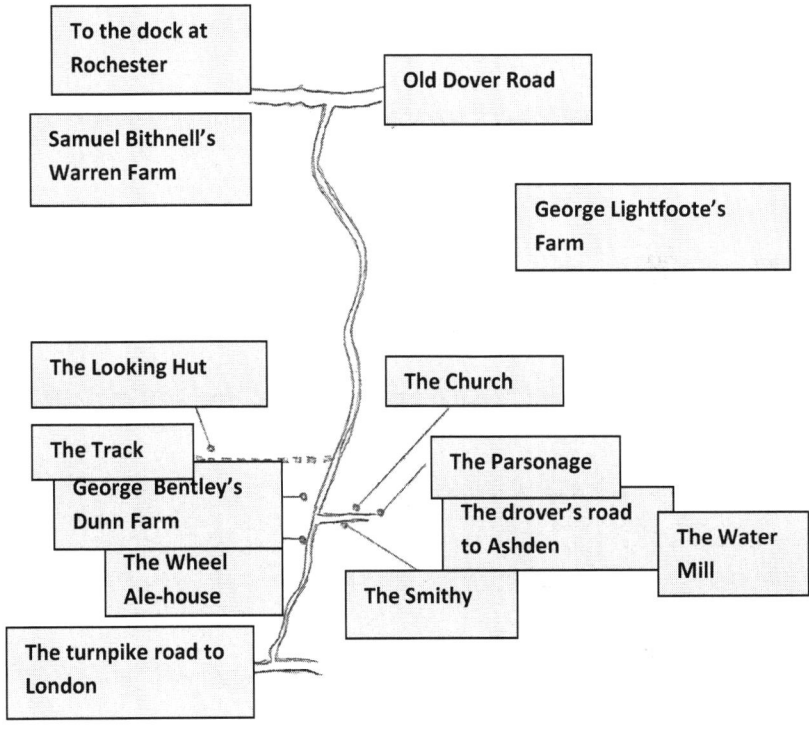

SOUTHWELL, KENT-1755

PART ONE

"Most people are born good and will always fight off evil. Others are born into light and fall into darkness, whilst a few are born into darkness and will never see the light"

1

Weaver's Loft-1755

The sky above *La Neuve Eglise* was a pure shade of cobalt blue and the bright midday sun was casting a bold shadow onto the flat face of the sun dial fixed on the south wall of the Huguenot church. It was barely twelve years since the church had been built by the French Huguenot community in this part of London's east end and the towering red brickwork of the church was still in pristine condition. It rose like a beacon amongst the weavers' houses which clustered in the streets around it, whilst alongside the unfathomable jumble of narrow passageways stood lines of crumbling buildings and houses where only the very poor and the thieves and foot-pads lived. Beyond this labyrinth of humanity lay the marshes and green fields of Shoreditch and above it all, plumes of smoke, tainted by the nearby river, rose limply into the fetid air from the many bake houses and workshop chimneys nearby.

Despite the noise of the lusty voices singing the final hymn of the morning service which resonated from deep inside the church, the sounds from the river Thames could also be clearly heard. Wooden-hulled barges were clanking impatiently at their mooring chains, pulled to and fro by the lapping tide and the cries of the hawkers selling the wriggling eels which languished in the bottom of their round, wicker baskets, pierced the sultry air. Outside, the eye-watering stink of the animal waste and offal left rotting amongst the butchers' stalls which were bunched in the streets around the ancient Tower, hung heavy overhead.

Most of the church's congregation lived around Spitalfield, plying their trades as gold and silversmiths, clock and lace makers and silk weavers. Although for most of them, their families had lived here for three generations, ever since their forebears had fled from France escaping the horrors of religious persecution, the sound of the occasional French voice could still be heard as they spilled out from their two hours of song and prayer.

Claude Palairet and Matthew Rosser were the last to leave the church and as they stood under the curved arch of its white-painted front door, they both blinked as they adjusted their eyes to the bright sun which was rising above the four-storey houses which stood opposite.

Claude looked up at the clock and read the inscription carved above it, "*Umbra Sumus*, we are shadows".

Matthew thought for a moment before replying, "*Puluis et umbra sumus*, we are but dust and shadows. It's a quote from Horace's odes".

Claude grinned at his friend's superior knowledge and said, "Enough of this morbid quotation, *tis* the day which the Lord *hath* made and we will rejoice and be glad of it".

Matthew Rosser smiled and answered, "*aye*", at his friend's remark.

Like many of the Huguenots, his family had adapted their French name of Rozier to one more suited to their adopted country and was amused that Claude still hung on to the old ways and to his family's old name.

The two men couldn't have looked more different in their appearance. Matthew was smartly attired, tall and solidly built with soft, well bred features. His family had prospered in England whilst Claude Palairet's family had remained poor. When he had arrived in England, Claude's grandfather, who had been a struggling lawyer, did not have the language to practice his profession nor the skills to flourish in the many workshops and weaving houses which had become established around Spitalfield. Claude was thirty-nine years of age but looked older with his pallid skin and purple ringed eyes. Shorter by about six inches than his friend, his second-hand clothes, purchased from the rag market on Tower Hill, hung loosely on his bony frame. His throat tightened and he coughed as he felt the familiar pain rising from deep down in his chest.

Matthew waited for Claude's sudden coughing fit to cease before replying but it was his friend who spoke first.

"*Tis* the foul stench coming from the murky river which is full of all manner of defilement that is *provoking* my cough", he explained as he tried to clear his throat. "I fear I may have caught the *ague*", he added unconvincingly, as he wiped his tear-filled eyes with a piece of cloth which he had hastily retrieved from his pocket.

Matthew Rosser nodded noncommittally and suggested a walk down Brick Lane to take the air in the market gardens where the old brick fields once were in Shoreditch and where the air was fresh and clean. His friend's cough had persisted for some months now. At first, he thought Claude had caught a chill during the prolonged winter, when the snow had laid deep on the streets and even the shallows of the Thames had frozen over, but now he wasn't so sure.

Claude waited for his coughing to wane and then thought for a moment, before saying, "If *thee* don't mind *Mathis*, I will walk up to the market and buy Sarah and Jabez a rosy pippin each as a Sunday treat for them".

The two men shook hands and went their separate ways. Claude Palairet turned left, walked past the weavers' houses lining both sides of Fournier Street which was less than a stone's throw from the rambling market place at Spitalfield. Despite the dry weather, putrid mud and human waste still collected in puddles on the cobbled streets and with his 'kerchief pressed to his mouth, Claude picked his steps carefully through the mess. At the end of the short street and with the market in sight, he stopped to catch his breath outside Christ Church, one of the grandest churches in all of London, its towering spire was like a giant finger pointing to the heavens above.

Matthew had turned into Wilkes Street before passing his own house in Princelet Street and then, minutes later when he had only walked a dozen or so paces down Brick Lane, he became increasingly concerned about Claude. He turned round and traced his steps back in an attempt to find his friend but despite his efforts, Claude had already disappeared into the crowds of people milling about in the market place.

As Matthew turned for home somewhere in the distance a gin seller was hollering, "Drunk for a penny, dead drunk for *tuppence*, straw for nothing". It filled him with disgust. There was a gin shop on every decrepit street corner and drinking dens flourished in the bowels of their stinking cellars. He hated the vomit churning drink but knew it offered some relief from the winter's bone-chilling cold and *sated* the desperate hunger for many of the desperately poor who were mixed amongst the throngs of people around him, it was a blessed relief from the brutal drudgery of their lives and he gave thanks to God that he had no need of the *hell froth*.

His house was closer to the market than the one where Claude and his family lodged but regrettably it caught the markets' foul smells whenever the westerly wind blew. It was similar to all the other houses surrounding it. Either side of the wide front door, with its carved, flat canopy above, were two sets of windows made deliberately large to encourage as much light as possible to enter, particularly on the weaving floors. The ground floor, which served as Matthew's shop where he traded the silk cloths and ribbons woven on looms on the two floors above, had ornate plaster mouldings decorating the ceiling and door frames, never failing to impress the many customers who entered. Matthew lived very comfortably above the weaving floors, in four large rooms on the fourth floor, each with an ornate iron fireplace, whilst in the loft space above, lodged his weavers and their *draw-boys*.

Meanwhile, Claude had weaved his way through the crowds, peering at the array of goods and food piled high on the lines of mongers' barrows. He paused to look at the sheep's flesh marooned in pools of blood and at some scrawny looking fowls which were lying alongside rows of sad-looking fish with dull-staring eyes. Those in the crowds with empty pockets looked on enviously, whilst the few who had money in their pockets pushed their way through to the front, anxious to view what was being offered on the Sabbath day. In the eastern corner of the market Claude found a barrow with the pink and red-flecked apples he had been looking for and started his search to find three of the ripest fruit without the evidence of any burrowing maggots.

"Those *be* called the *king's fruit*. Fresh up on the cart from the orchards of Kent this morning", the old costermonger said cheerfully, anxious to sell his perishable wares.

Claude smiled as he carefully selected three of the choicest fruits. *King's fruit* indeed, I know a pippin when I see one, he thought as he handed over a shiny penny with the face of old King George, looking regally up at him.

The family's humble lodgings up in the weavers loft in Elder Street were no more than ten minutes walk away and Claude turned down Rose Lane which bordered the market and into Folgate Street as he headed as briskly as he could for home, leaving the smiling costermonger with the *copper* already buried safely in his leather pouch.

Sarah Palairet looked lovingly across the sparsely furnished room in the loft at her son as he sat reading a book trying to catch what light he could coming through the dirty window. There was no luxury to be found here. The accommodation consisted of two scruffy rooms at the top of the four story building which were generously provided to them by the master weaver in return for the fetching and carrying jobs Claude was able to do around the silk weaving looms spread around the floors below.

Claude was a softly spoken man who spoke ill of no one and certainly didn't begrudge the master weaver of his wealth, nor that he lived close by in a grand house in Spital Square. In fact, he had always been grateful for the Christian charity the man had so generously given them.

During the twenty-five years they had lived in the loft, Claude frequently marvelled at the skills of the weavers and the *journeymen* as they worked at their wooden-framed looms. The weaving looms on the second floor were smaller than those on the floor above and made silk ribbons and trimmings in a myriad of different colours. One shuttle weaver, with his feet pushing down on the wooden treadles to lift the *heddles*, was all it took to make the narrow widths of cloth.

When Claude had first seen the larger looms on the third floor, he thought they looked not dissimilar to four post bedsteads, with their rectangular frames and square oak supporting posts. It was on these towering machines the weavers and their *draw boys* wove the heavy silk and elegantly designed damasks and brocades, with raised patterns in expensive gold and silver threads. Claude often watched the slow and tedious business when the weavers set up the draw looms which could take weeks before they were ready to use. It was not unusual whilst he was working around these machines to hear the weavers complaining that they would earn nothing whilst setting up but still had to keep their *draw boys* in pay and *victuals*. Claude always sympathised with their predicament, although he knew the job of the *draw boy* was not easy, standing on top of the towering looms and lifting the heavy reeds every time his master called out his instructions. He knew they earned their pittance, weaving the lengths of dazzling coloured cloth, row by row at less than a yard a day.

Claude and Sarah's only child, Jabez, was small in stature and quite thin and frail. He was a quiet and studious young man who became totally absorbed in whatever book he was reading. He seemed older than his twenty years and was never happier than when he was discussing with his father the need for the freedom of religious and political thought or was teaching himself Greek and Latin from one of the many books piled high on the dusty window shelf.

Sarah eyes strayed across the sparse room and into the bed chamber. Two wooden bedsteads, which had seen better days, stood side by side, whilst a battered settle nestled against the foot of the larger bed, its coverings little more than a pile of rags. In the corner of the room was the cupboard where the family stored most of their worldly goods, standing precariously on the uneven wooden-planked floor. Sarah hardly noticed the family's privation, she had all she had ever wanted with the love of a fine man and a son she was proud of.

She had a gentle and generous soul and as she gazed at her son, she was thinking that although they were poor in *chattels* and the like, they somehow managed to survive with their heads held high and their dignity intact. Despite everything, Claude, her darling Claude, had always found a way to buy the books their son craved for, allowing him to progress with his studies unhindered.

Jabez raised his head from his book and smiled at his mother, their mutual love for each other was plain to see.

It was her who chose the name of Jabez for their only child. It came from the Old Testament and it meant pain. Not just the life-sapping pain she had suffered during his birth but much more importantly to her and Claude, it also meant someone who was at the centre of learning, someone who would achieve greatness in life.

Sarah's thoughts were interrupted as the door creaked open and her bright blue eyes immediately lit up like the sun spangling on crystal clear water, as her husband walked in.

"Oh Claude, you're back earlier than I expected. I thought you would go for a stroll with Matthew Rosser", she said in her quiet voice, as she embraced her husband warmly. As she did so she could not help noticing how drained he looked, his skin blanched by the malady which had afflicted him for some weeks past.

Although he had stopped to rest on each of the three landings, he was still out of breath after walking up the never-ending flights of wooden stairs.

"Indeed, *Mathis* invited me to do so but I thought I would walk to the market to buy these" he panted, as he extricated himself from Sarah's firm hold and held the juicy apples aloft.,

"They're pippins", she gushed, as she recognised the familiar fruit, "Kentish pippins".

He smiled as he began to catch his breath.

"I knew you would like them, especially having apples like these growing in the orchards on your father's farm. Can *thee* remember when………?"

Claude paused knowing his wife's mind was elsewhere. Perhaps, he thought wistfully, he shouldn't have bought them, particularly with all the painful memories Sarah would associate with the fruit.

She sat down heavily on one of the three bent-wood chairs clustered round a wobbly table. The room was almost devoid of furniture, apart from an aged oak *aumesbury* where they kept what little food they had, together with some second-hand cutlery and a few bone beakers and pewter plates. In the corner, a soot-blackened, three-legged cooking pot was bubbling on a pot-bellied stove, its chimney disappearing through the wooden lathes of the loft's roof. Piled alongside in a neat stack, were a dozen or so split hornbeam logs which Sarah bought from a merchant in the market on one of the rare occasions they had arrived in any quantity from the Sussex woods. In the dark winter nights, the fire burning in the stove provided enough light to brighten the room thus saving the price of a candle, unless Jabez wanted to read and then one would be lit without further thought or worry about its cost.

She looked wistfully at the pippins as her thoughts turned to her childhood at Dunn Farm which nestled in the folds of the chalk Downs and the flower-filled grasslands around the Kentish village of Southwell. Thirty years evaporated as she was *struck* by the memory, and she was a six year old child again.

Straddled between the chestnut tree which stood in splendour on the village green with centuries of history trapped within its massive trunk was the old alehouse curiously called the Wheel, whilst on the other side of the ancient tree was the brick-built school-house with its red-tiled roof. Laughter seeped from its windows as the few lucky children who were taught there and whose parents could afford the few coppers the school master charged, lifted the lids of their ink-stained desks and quickly placed their books inside as they prepared to leave for home. Sarah did not have far to go and she stopped to pick a posy of yellow-faced celandines for her mother. Her memory came back to the present and she could remember how her father refused to pay the meagre amount for her schooling, shouting that girls should bend their backs working in the fields and how her mother had somehow found enough money to pay the elderly teacher for her tuition.

Claude coughed loudly but it was not sufficient to interrupt his wife's childhood memories.

She did not have far to go home, ten minutes at most, and she skipped up the narrow lane to give her mother the flowers she had picked. She was an only child and soon, with the long days of summer coming, Sarah remembered how, with her mother, she would search the grass verges for the patches of wild strawberries which grew in profusion there and for the more elusive brown canes of the wild raspberries and the elusive honey-sweet fruit which hung from them. Sarah absentmindedly shone one of the pippins on her sleeve as she recalled how her mother had playfully scolded her once for eating the small fruits, telling her they were not for eating and were being picked to make the conserve. It was only when Sarah had turned round, did she notice the crimson juice of the berries was also running down her mother's chin. Sarah could hear the sound of their laughter. How, hand in hand they would run through the blazing colour of the bluebell woods, delighting in the sweet scent as it was flung like wafts of perfume through the spring air. The hours spent cooking together in the large farmhouse kitchen, smells of fresh bread and how they raised the pastry cases for the mutton pies. Winter evenings spent sitting together in the hollows of the cavernous inglenook fireplace, roasting their legs in front of the logs burning in the huge grate. She shivered as she remembered how the vicious draughts blew under the doors and the howling gales outside which the windows had tried in vain to stop coming in.

Unknowingly, Sarah smiled as she recalled how her mother had taught her all the different embroidery stitches when she made her sampler during those long winter evenings. The cross stitches and the tent stitches, how they chose the pastel coloured silks together and the pride she had felt when she finally stitched her name, Sarah Bentley and the date 1730, onto the finished linen.

It was the shared happiness with her mother that Sarah thought would never end.

But it did, four years later. She was just sixteen when her mother died.

Claude could see his wife was becoming increasingly melancholy and said, quite deliberately to break her daydream, "Sarah, is that ox-tail stew I can smell cooking on the stove?"

His wife looked up and said, as a heart-warming smile returned to her pretty face, "Yes dear, it's Sunday".

She always bought an ox tail in the shambles on a Saturday afternoon in readiness to cook it as a stew on the following day. It was a recipe the original Huguenots had brought to the country generations ago and now even the locals were enjoying it. So much so, the huge ox tails on the butchers' chopping blocks were in such demand, that on some days, none could be found anywhere, either on the market stalls or in the shambles by the Tower, both for the locals and Huguenots alike.

Her eyes followed her husband as he walked across to the window to see what book Jabez was studying. He was sitting hunched up, totally immersed in his reading and almost oblivious to what was going on around him when Claude peered across his shoulder and saw the book was titled, "*The Freedom of Man*".

Jabez looked up at his father, his brilliant blue eyes sparkled as he said earnestly, "It's interesting father, it really is".

Claude nodded his head knowingly but remained silent lest his cough returned and walked away with a proud paternal smile on his pale face.

Although there was still some light left outside, there was not sufficient coming through the grubby windows and Sarah decided to light the solitary tallow candle on the table before she served supper. The windows were always kept firmly shut to keep out the foul smells and the evil of *consumption* which abounded in the city air, afflicting both rich and poor without distinction. She walked across to the stove and lit a fat-coated taper before holding its flickering flame to the candle's blackend wick. She was thankful she did not have to strike the flint into the tinder box and carefully nourish the spark to make it grow into something which would become a useful flame.

Her nose screwed up as the rank odour coming from the sooty flame drifted in the air. Candles made from the fat of cooked mutton or beef smelt less rancid but at nearly two shillings a dozen, she always bought the cheapest ones made from pig's fat and had lost count of the number of times she had wished they could afford the sweet - smelling beeswax candles the gentry and the clerics bought.

The small family assembled and sat at the table eager to start the meal Sarah was serving. With the appetizing steam of the oxtail wafting up from their pewter plates, they bowed their heads and clasped their hands together as Claude began to say grace.

"As we prepare to eat our food we must remember that the generosity of God is lively within each of us, Amen", Claude recited.

Sarah and Jabez repeated in unison, "Amen".

"Father", Jabez said, as he eagerly lifted a spoonful of his mother's stew to his mouth, "You have told me often about the desperate flight of the French Huguenots and those from the low countries but you have never told me about your grandfather and how he escaped".

Claude rested his spoon on his plate, wondering if his son's unexpected request had something to do with the book he had been reading and after a few minutes of reflection, he said, "We must finish the meal your mother has cooked for us and then I will".

"He came here from Paris in 1685", he began, seemingly forgetting what he had just said, as he scraped his spoon round his platter to savour the rich gravy.

"Was he a Frenchman?" Jabez interrupted, with his own spoon hovering in front of his mouth

"Yes", his father answered, "he was a lawyer, married with a young wife".

"Why did they leave France and come to live in London?"

"Did they have to flee from the persecution?" The questions were coming thick and fast.

Claude cleared his chest before saying, "I think first we had better finish your mother's delicious stew, for it is going to be a long story".

He raised his rag *'kerchief* to his mouth in anticipation of an oncoming cough and eventually, as he lowered the crumpled rag, he glanced at its contents.

It was not un-noticed by Sarah as she cleared the finished plates from the table whilst Claude settled himself once more in his chair and prepared to tell his story. She turned her head to look back at her husband, his illness concerning her greatly.

"Were they Huguenots, like us?" the impatient young man asked.

His father nodded. "The story of our family begins over two hundred years ago in 1535, when the King of France issued an order for the extermination of all the Huguenots in his country unless they gave up their faith and returned to the Catholic Church".

"Did they?" his son questioned, with a look of disbelief in his voice as he reflected on the word, *extermination.*

"Perhaps a few did, but hundreds of thousands didn't and for the next sixty years there was much persecution, torture and slaughter", Claude said quietly, as he glanced across at his wife.

"What happened next?" Jabez asked, wide-eyed in horror.

"There was a new king on the French throne by then and he issued a proclamation that was called the Edict of Nantes, it granted the Huguenots religious freedom and for the next eighty-seven years we were safe and allowed to practice our faith in peace".

The expression on Jabez's face showed he was following the story intently and seemed relieved at what his father had just said, unaware of what was to come.

Claude waited until his next bout of coughing subsided before continuing with his story, "In 1685 when my grandfather was thirty years old and was already a practising *avocet* in the courts".

Claude used the French term for attorney before he continued with his story.

"The edict was revoked, torn up and the Huguenots were in peril once more and the horror began all over again". He paused, weighing up the implications of the words he had just spoken. "Men, hundreds and hundreds of men who were caught were executed or sent in heavy chains to the French fleet for a lifetime of slavery".

Claude corrected himself, "in fact for a very short lifetime, as manacled galley slaves. Women were killed and their children sent all over France into Catholic convents. All Huguenot churches were destroyed. The persecution of our people was unremitting. It was at this time that many started to flee across *La Manche* into the welcoming arms of England".

"So it was at this time your grandparents, my great-grandparents, came to England?" the studious young man asked, increasingly inspired by the story.

His father left the table and walked across the small room to face the window and staring into the blackness, he said solemnly, "No, things were to get a lot worse, much, much, worse. It happened seven years later in Paris where my grandparents were living at the time and is remembered as the Saint Bartholomew's Massacre. The slaughter in Paris continued for several weeks before spreading like a wild fire across the cities of France. The dreaded dragoons roamed the streets pillaging our shops and houses, murdering the occupants. Many women chose to kill themselves rather than submit to the evil of the soldier's lust, which they knew would be forced time and time again upon them".

Claude paused for breath and for a fleeting moment he was in France with his grandparents and a shiver of fear went down his spine.

Sarah cast another look of concern at him.

"Come back to the table and rest awhile", she pleaded.

"There was mob violence", Claude continued to stare into the blackness outside seemingly unaware of his wife's plea. "Men, women and children were hunted down like animals. Over a million innocent human beings were brutally murdered. Their bodies were piled high in the streets and thrown in the river *Seinne*. Blood flowed freely in the gutters and the rivers of France were so full of corpses, that for many months no fish could be eaten".

"Claude. I beseech thee. This is not a story for anyone's ears, let alone for Jabez at this time of night", Sarah remonstrated as she took his arm and led him back to the table.

A look of annoyance flooded over Jabez's face. "I am a man of twenty years and not a child", he rebuked his mother.

"Sarah, this is not *just* a story", Claude replied sternly. "It is Jabez's legacy, passed from father and son and down the line until it came to me. Someday, when our good Lord *calleth* me and I am in His place, it will be through the telling of this *story,* our son will inherit the knowledge of the suffering, hate and intolerance that was inflicted on those who could not defend themselves."

Neither Sarah nor Jabez spoke as they digested his words. They realised he was ill but never, even in their darkest moments, did they think that he would die. Jabez looked at his mother and saw the haunted look that had come over her face, leaving it pinched and afraid.

Jabez broke the silence which followed, saying softly, "What happened to my great-grandparents?"

A weak smile touched his father's face, pleased that his son was eager to hear the end of the story.

"They fled to the safety of the woods, thickets and copses where the trees were thickly leafed and gave them cover from the worst of the weather. They lived on bitter tasting berries and the mushrooms and fungus which grew there and their bellies aching with the pains of hunger, they tried to find whatever shelter they could".

Claude gave Sarah a loving look as if to say, "Forgive me" as he carried on.

"It was after many weeks of hiding, always scared they would be discovered and killed or at the best, parted forever, when, on one particularly dark night, with the heavy clouds obscuring the moon, they set off on their perilous journey. The weather was atrocious and they decided to head for a seaport called *Le Havre,* a distance of over one hundred and fifty miles".

"Why?" Jabez asked.

"They had had little choice If they had stayed they would have succumbed in the cold driving rain".

The young man nodded his head: he had heard of the place called *Le Havre*, he had read once it was one of largest ports in France.

Claude coughed again. "For days they trudged across wet fields and quagmires, clambering through thick undergrowth and fields of vines. Many nights were spent huddled together, cold and wet, fearful for their lives or of being betrayed. When they could, they searched the streams and rivers for tiny, bone-filled fish, anything to quell their pangs of hunger".

Hardly believing what his ears were hearing, Jabez said quietly, "It's difficult to imagine their months of suffering".

Sarah got up and went to the earthenware jug on the old, oak aumesbury and poured a beaker of thin ale before returning to hold it to her husband's lips.

Claude took a sip as his breath came in ragged, shallow bursts.

"My dear one, please take a rest" she pleaded, "continue with your story in the morning". Her hands held the beaker steady as she looked into her husband's eyes with growing concern.

The embedded wick of the candle stub had almost burnt down to the bottom and its fat was running low: its weak flame *guttered* for a few moments before it finally surrendered, casting the room to its familiar gloom.

Claude sipped the ale and thanked his wife for her kindness before clearing the phlegm in his throat and saying breathlessly, "It is nearly finished".

His voice was barely audible between the hacking, painful coughs. His chest rattled as he tried to take a deep breath.

"They finally reached the shore at the French port but the boats were full, crammed with other refugees and ever fearful for their lives, they hid in the town and with *naught* to do, other than pray, they had to wait for another three months before they tried again. Can *thee* imagine what it was like?" he asked his son.

Jabez nodded silently and slid his thin hand across the table and took his father's cold fingers into his own.

"They didn't mind where the boats were going; escape was the only thing which mattered. Eventually they found a fisherman who would take them to England The wind and tide took the boat to Rye, a small cinque port in Sussex. The crossing was fraught with danger and the turbulent sea caused much sickness amongst the thirty or so people crammed onboard the small fishing boat, laying on the deck with the waves crashing over them. When at last they were landed on a shingle beach, south of a small, hill-top town, they lay in rolling surf totally exhausted but safe and thanking God they were alive. Wet and cold and not knowing which direction they should head for, they waded and crawled across the salt marshes and the mud flats, past the ruins of Winchelsea castle, until they found a road which would lead them to London and a new life in England".

Sarah sighed with relief that the story was finished, almost paralysed with fear for her husband's health.

"Your great-grandparents came here with nothing, other than the rags on their backs and sadness in their hearts but with their faith intact", Claude concluded as he started coughing once more.

"Jabez, perhaps with the story now finished and the candle burnt out, it's best that you go to your bed and let your father rest", Sarah quietly suggested to her son.

"Father", Jabez said quietly as he rose from the table, "I will never forget what you have just told me". His face *set serious* and unsmiling.

"I know you won't".

Claude Palairet's coughing erupted again and he quickly retrieved the *'kerchief* from his pocket and put it to his mouth.

Sarah waited anxiously.

Claude slowly lowered the cloth from his mouth and peered in to it. He already knew what to expect.

Mixed amongst the phlegm was blood, crimson red blood.

Sarah had seen it too and cried out in horror.

"My darling, I'm…." he whispered, "I'm afraid my life is drawing to a close".

Her heart was already breaking as she stared into his eyes, praying what she was seeing wasn't true. "Shush, shush", she repeated.

Claude reached across the table and clasped her hands into his own and said softly, "My darling, I am persuaded that neither death nor life shall be able to separate us from the love of God".

Sarah put her arm under his and lifted him from the chair. He coughed again, but more gently this time. Taking his weight, she half-carried him to their bedstead and propped his head up on the straw-filled *bolster*.

Jabez, awake and aware of what was happening, turned his head and in the darkness, looked towards where his father was laying.

Sarah reached out for Claude's weak hand and gripped it tightly as his breathing faltered and stared at him with unblinking eyes. His breathing re-emerged again but more faintly than before.

Death wasn't kind and it came in slow, rattling gasps as he exhaled his last. In a few moments he had passed on, his soul bound for the Lord.

His death came too quick and too unexpectedly for Sarah to cope with and as tears rolled down her pale cheeks, she shook her head in disbelief that the life which had dwelt within her dead husband for thirty-nine years had gone. His death had ripped away a part of her, the part that was most precious and as she sat staring into the darkness, her face was already sunken and haunted.

Grief flooded her mind and her body froze as her husband's final words lingered inside her. Still gripping his hand, she pressed her wet cheek against his already cold face and as she did so, she suddenly felt bewildered that he could cling to his faith to the bitter end. A Huguenot faith, so strong, it had survived for generations.

Slowly, as her emotions calmed, she thought she would willingly give herself to God if there was something, anything, she could do to bring him back to her.

Slowly she released his lifeless hand as grief overwhelmed her and nothingness took over and held her soul.

Behind her, in the shadows, Jabez slowly swung his legs from over the side of his bedstead. He had been watching their final parting with horror etched on his face and tears in his eyes. Slowly and quietly he walked across to his mother and held her into his arms.

2

The Parsonage

Although the candle's flame was strong, it *guttered* wildly as a stray draught found its way through the gaps in the warped and twisted floor boards of the loft. Sarah remained sitting at the table until the flame settled, quill in hand and staring at the blank sheet of paper in front of her. Her face was taunt and devoid of all emotion. The draught would burn the cheap tallow candle out in half the time and it was careless of her not to move it to a less draughty place knowing she could ill afford another candle. Although her thoughts were on other matters, she could almost hear her mother's words ringing in her ears when the same thing happened in her childhood home, "It may only be but a pound a year dearest, but it is money wasted", her mother had scolded her.

She could not blame the master weaver for what he had said to her that day. He was a kind man and his face had shown the dilemma he had faced in making the decision. Nobody could have done more for them over the past three months since Claude's death but the man needed the accommodation for an additional journeyman and his family to work on one of the looms below.

How could it have come to this, she thought, having to write this awful letter? The words had been conceived in her mind long before the need had arisen to light the tallow candle and even before Jabez had retired to his bedstead but having to commit the words to paper and bring them to life….. It's been over twenty years, she thought sadly, as she stared at the blank sheet of paper lying forlornly on the table.

Suddenly her face screwed up, not with a physical pain but because it was heart wrenching in having to write the letter. Her eyes narrowed and her brow furrowed not unlike a child's face when they are given an unpleasant infusion for a malady. Sarah had decided the only option they had now was for her to write the letter and as she took a deep breath and quickly scribbled the words on the paper, the only sound in the candle-lit room was the scratching of her quill pen on the coarse white paper.

"There it is done", she said decisively, as she held the letter up to the candle's flickering light and breathing out, she began to read the words she had committed to paper.

"Dearest father,

My husband has died of a dreadful apoplexy in the lobe of his lungs. The apothecary sayeth it was likely caused by the cold and dampness of our accommodation here in Spitalfield.

It is very difficult to get alms now because there are so many poor people seeking it. I have little money with Claude now in his grave and food is hand to mouth. I do not want to be dependent on thee as no doubt thou have costs of your own.

If I might return home with my son Jabez, I will pick up the stones on the fields from dawn to dusk to help earn our keep. I will do any work, hop tying, seed sowing, cleaning out the beasts in their byres, anything that so pleases thee my father.

I wish I could find another way out of my troubles. It is but a worry to me. Please believe me.

I remain your affectionate daughter

Sarah"

Against her better nature she had addressed her father as *dearest father* and had used the words *affectionate daughter* as a salutation because she thought, she hoped and even prayed, her father may have changed.

She placed the letter back on the table and for a few minutes she was alone in her thoughts.

With the letter read for a second time, Sarah carefully folded it into two equal parts and then into another smaller part to create a flap and tilted the candle slightly towards a small block of sealing wax she was holding. She watched *dolefully* as some of the molten red wax dribbled onto the paper flap and sealed the letter. Quickly turning it over and dipping the quill into the small pot of black ink, she scribbled the familiar address….

George Bentley Esquire

Dunn Farm

Southwell, Kent

Outside, the quarter moon was drowned in heavy clouds and with the flame of the candle pinched out, Sarah sat in the darkness and let her mind drift back to the time her mother had died and the day she had left home.

She remembered how her father, who had always been an unpleasant man, turned vile and hateful towards her after her mother's death. Perhaps it was the drink which made him treat her the way he did or could it have been the loss of his wife, my mother, Sarah thought charitably? Although there was nobody to see it, her head shook vigorously from side to side at the thought. No it was not that. Could she forget so easily the daily misery the man caused to her beloved mother?

She moved uncomfortably on the hard chair as his final words rang in her ears when she had packed her bag to come to London.

"*Thee* are dead to me now. You were nothing to me when your mother lived and *thou* are less than nothing now", he had shouted. Even in the dark loft Sarah could almost feel his spittle spraying into her face and smell his repugnant breath. He had often beat her as a child for what he considered to be her misbehaviour but as his anger boiled and his shouting turned to screaming, Sarah recalled how she had thought on this final occasion she would be killed by the hand of her own father.

His volley of execrable oaths rang in her ears as she recalled her last walk down the tree-bordered lane, strewn as it was with wild flowers. Past the schoolhouse, then across the green and past her father's nightly haunt, the alehouse called the Wheel and then with a quickening pace, on to where Joe Haycock's farm cart was waiting for her. Sarah's flight from home lasted less than twenty minutes but nevertheless, she left without so much as a backwards glance.

She shook her head as she fought off the memories. What was done, was done, she thought sadly.

Sarah rose wearily from the chair and took to her bed and as she lay wide-awake on her straw-stuffed mattress looking at the shafts of moonlight coming through the cracked tiles on the roof, she thought with just a degree of amusement, her father never knew she had climbed in the back of the farm cart and had sat amongst the load of Kentish pippins it was carrying; her father's Kentish pippins.

He never knew how she had climbed onboard the sailing barge which was moored at the wharf in Rochester that would take the sweet smelling apples the rest of the way to London.

Her father never knew she would beg a lift on the wagon that would take the pippins on their final journey from the docks in London's Upper Pool, to the costermonger's barrows at Spitalfield market.

She was wrong.

He knew how she got to London.

He knew she met a Huguenot in the silk weaving workshop in Elder Street.

He knew they had married and had a son of twenty-years they had named Jabez Palairet and since that time, nobody in Southwell could begin to count the number of times George Bentley had spat venom and had called the boy, "That bastard son of the Huguenot".

Early the next morning, as soon as the sun had fully awakened, Sarah reached for her shawl off the peg on the back of the door and made her way to the market with the letter clutched in her hand. It had rained heavily during the night and the air was filled with the stench of wet horses and the *night soil* coming from the many chamber pots which had been empted since the early hours, their contents running freely in a fetid open sewer down the street. Sarah jumped to one side when she heard the clatter of a horse-drawn carriage approaching over the cobblestones with its iron-rimmed wheels splashing through the foul smelling puddles and watched it go on its journey down Red Lion Street towards Whitechapel. She had lost count of the number of times she had wondered what it would be like to be a lady in a carriage, powdered and sweet smelling, with liveried footmen attending to her every need.

Although it was only a short distance to the costermonger's barrow she was seeking, she kept to Folgate Street rather than risk cutting through the cat's cradle of alleyways where thieves and pickpockets lurked. All around, the shrill cries of children *hawking* their wares began ringing down the streets as the city awakened. "Mussels *a penny* a quart…, new sprats all large and *alive o, tuppence* a plate…, pineapples a *ha'penny* a slice….sweet singing songbirds, linnets and finches".

Sarah had already worked out how to get the letter back to her father but if it did reach its destination, would he bother to answer it and if he did, would his reply be favourable and even if it was, would the letter eventually find its way back to Sarah? So many *ifs,* she thought nervously.

"When will the next cart-load of vegetables come up from Kent?" she anxiously asked the costermonger whom she had heard the other men refer to as *Spuddy,* having earned himself a reputation for selling bad potatoes.

The man glanced at the letter in Sarah's hand and half-guessed what she had in mind and stood looking her up and down for some minutes before answering. "Expecting a load of *tatters* and *nips,* in the next few days", he said, not too unkindly.

"Could you give the wagon man this to pass on to the barge-master and ask him if he would kindly to pass on to the man called Joe Haycock, when brings up the next cart load of vegetables from Southwell?"

Spuddy recognised the look of urgency in Sarah's eyes and replied, *"Tis* a lot to ask but I can do that much for *thou* but…….." He shrugged his shoulders and indicated how unlikely it all seemed, by repeating, "I will give the waggoner your letter. Best come back in a week or so to see if there's been a reply".

The time dripped by slowly as Sarah's situation at the loft became increasingly desperate. They had only ten days left before they would have to leave the modest accommodation to make way for the journeyman and then what would they do? The thought of her and her son having to creep into one of the many derelict houses in Widegate Street, amongst the thieves and beggars who were packed in them like herrings in a barrel, had kept her awake for many nights past. She shuddered at the thought of sleeping amongst those lice-ridden people, laying in the filth on rotten floor boards with the black rats which abounded as they scurried about in the claustrophobic darkness.

×

The parsonage garden was alive with the fragrance of the *woodbine* flowers as the creeper entwined itself amongst the thorny stems of the rambling *noisette* rose. The wild abandon of the rose's blush-pink blooms complemented the bright yellow flowers of the *woodbine* perfectly.

Tobias Lamb breathed in deeply, relishing the aromatic scent as he sat on his secluded seat beneath the graceful arches of the rose arbour and surveyed his pride and joy which was the garden.

"Good day, Reverend", Thomas Brown mumbled gruffly, tugging the forelock of grey hair hanging limply over his forehead, as he trudged with his swan-necked hoe towards the flower beds.

The old gardener was a man of few words, who, together with his wife, Hester, were the only servants the Parson employed. The couple had served him faithfully ever since he had taken the cloth and had arrived at Southwell, a village which was so old, it blended perfectly with its surroundings

The cleric returned the compliments of the day and as he did so, his eyes lifted up towards the heavens. The sun had become hidden behind thickening clouds and as the sky turned increasingly grey, a chilly wind began to strengthen from the East. Buttoning his singled-breasted frock coat to its top button, he slowly rose from his seat, deciding he would take some exercise and walk round the garden.

Oblique cordons of apple and pear trees were wired against the brick wall running round the garden's perimeter and at its base Thomas had planted gooseberry and blackcurrant bushes at regular intervals. Large sprawling fig trees stood pressed against each of the far corners of the wall, with their thick-trunked stems anchored deep into the richly manured earth. The Parson was fastidious in his taste for tidiness and simplicity in the garden. Expanses of tulips, lily of the valley, sweet-smelling stocks and large-headed peonies had been planted in neat groups, with exposed areas of bare earth between them. It was important to the Parson's well organised mind that each variety of plant was kept distinct from its neighbour.

Either side of the rolled gravel path were freshly-clipped, low hedges of yew and holly laid out in geometric shapes. Within each of the shapes were growing culinary and medicinal herbs, bergamot, sage, mint, camomile and thyme. The cleric leaned on his stick and paused to watch the browsing honey bees which had ignored the cloudy sky and continued to seek out the yellow pollen hidden in the ragged, red flowers of the bergamot plants.

"Charming", he muttered, as his thoughts turned to the amount of honey the bees would produce.

With his exercise over, the Parson decided to return to the rambling parsonage and was pleased when he saw puffs of white, wood smoke billowing from one of its tall chimneys

"Good, Hannah *hath* lit the fire in my *withdrawing* room", he murmured to himself, "It will warm the chamber nicely".

Before stepping over the parsonage's *threshold*, he paused to smell the large, light crimson blooms of the *apothecary's* rose growing in profusion over the oak front door, marvelling how the petals had opened to release its fragrance and the golden yellow stamens which reached out to welcome any visiting insect to within its midst.

Tobias Lamb lifted the iron latch and entered the large stone-flagged hall. When he first saw the parsonage, the expansive hall was the main living area of the large dwelling, full of hustle and bustle and the place where the clergy of years past had taken their meals with their servants. That was from Queen Bess's reign and time had moved on and much to Hannah and Thomas's initial disquiet, the Parson decided he had wanted more privacy and separation from his servants. His preference was to use the many chambers within the house as places where he could either dine alone or with visiting guests. Chambers, where he could study or write his sermons in solitude and have a private place where he could maintain the parish registers and church accounts.

Rising in front of him was a wide, carved-oak staircase, wide at its base like a fish tail, before ascending to the first floor, leading on to a narrow passageway which in turn, led first to the private bed chambers and then on to the smaller servants accommodation beyond. Off the hall, to his left, was a long, dark lonely corridor leading to the parlour and then through to the kitchen, pantry and buttery. The pantry was Mistress Brown's province where the meat and other foodstuffs were kept, along with the shining pewter platters, all of which diplayed the patina of constant use and the collection of fine china which was brought out on the rare occasions when the Bishop visited. Whilst the Parson was happy for his servant to have this chamber as her domain, the buttery was certainly his. It was in here the oak butts of ale stood under the wide wooden shelves upon which the neatly placed rows of wine bottles were arranged, each according to their age, colour and the region whence they came. The cleric felt the chill in the cold hall; the inglenook fireplace, with its ancient rack irons and hooks was seldom used now and he opened the adjacent door and walked along the dark passageway to his favourite chamber where there was a cheery fire burning in the hearth.

×

Jabez could almost smell the impending violence in the stale London air as he made his daily search for food or alms through the narrow, wiggling streets which had grown up on what was once King Henry's artillery field. After he had been *deprived* of his father, the generosity of the master weavers could have been relied upon, not all of them, but enough to provide some food and charity but the mood had changed and now a small army of desperate and hungry people were all doing the same thing, searching for something to fill their bellys or clothes to put on their backs. He was on the point of returning after walking as far as the butcher's shops in the shambles by the Tower and was feeling despondent with *nought* to show for his efforts, when, with his eyes downcast, he spotted a penny broadsheet laying discarded in the gutter. Reaching down and picking it up, he smoothed out the creases and like all written matter which came his way, he started to read it, intrigued by the ink-smudged words.

"*In the ages of Old*

We traded for Gold

Our Merchants were Thriving and Wealthy

Warm Wool for our Poor

And Medicines for the Sicke and Unhealthy"

"To Neglect their own Works

Employ Pagans and Turks

And let Foreign trumpet over Them

Shut Up their Own Door

And Starve Out their Poore

For the Tawdry Madam"

He was still thinking what the verse meant and was, unknowingly, at the bottom of Artillery Lane when a disorderly tide of people swept round the corner, much like the Thames in flood. The mood of the crowd swirled in unseen currents beneath the dark surfaces of their angry faces. Leading them was a small group of men and women who were beating a variety of pots and pans with sticks and spoons in a crude attempt to create some form of music to rally the mob on. Behind the raucous *band*, Jabez could see a terrified-looking man with fear *set* in his eyes, seated backwards on a donkey. His hands were *lashed* behind his back and judging by the cuts and bruises on his face, it was evident he had been beaten before he had been manhandled and placed onto the beast's back.

Jabez hardly had time to think what was happening before he began to be swept along in the midst of the crowd towards Brushfield Street despite strenuous attempts to disentangle himself from the mob which was moving like a serpent, whooping, hollering and shouting as it went. The crowd was more than a hundred strong and within it, there wasn't a single smile or even an expression of doubt that Jabez could see.

"What's happening?" he asked a sullen looking man, who was pressed hard against him.

The man nodded his head towards the poor wretch on the donkey, "He's a journeyman who's agreed to work for below the agreed rate. It's no wonder we are all starving with traitors like that about. He should be strung up".

Jabaz chose to ignore what had been said, and queried "Where are you heading for?"

"We're taking him to the house of the silk master who employs him, in Spital Square", the rough looking man replied, with anger spilling over in his voice.

"Then what?" Jabez questioned.

Before the man the man could answer, the tide of people pushed and shoved their way along Lamb Street before slowing and coming to an untidy stop as they reached one of the grandest houses bordering Spital Square. The dwellings were some of the finest in the area, having been built thirty years previously on the site of the ancient Saint Augustine's hospital, hence the square's abbreviated name.

Jabez saw some of the men had armed themselves with clubs and heavy sticks. He shuddered when he noticed the ringleaders were flourishing long-pointed *sharps*, their curved blades flashing in the weak sunlight.

At the first the mob just milled around with their fists waving and shouting abuse at the rows of sash windows which lined the house's facade. The noise had started like a low snarling of many voices but it grew louder and louder and had now become a sullen, deafening roar.

"This is the house of the man who would see us starve, rather than pay us a decent wage", a rabble-rouser screamed out to the *rout*.

"He would rather employ the Turks and the Irish than us", shouted another.

Another hoarse voice from someone hidden deep in the milling crowd, added, "I'd rather swing than stand by and do nothing",

Jabez could hear more and more voices ringing out above the general mutterings of the mob.

Emboldened by the shouts and threats, the crowd pushed forward in waves and began to besiege the house. Jabez looked up at one of the rectangular-paned windows and saw the damask curtains move slightly in one of the bedchambers.

There is someone in there, he thought.

Stones began to fly through the air. With the cheers of the mob ringing out, some of the largest and angriest men grouped together and started to push over the blue-painted iron railings which separated the house from the road, which up until that point, had separated the mob from the silk master. Others were tearing up the neatly laid flagstone steps leading up to the wide, front door of the house. The *rough music* stopped and was quickly replaced with the crash of breaking glass as someone hurled a stone. A volley of more stones and rotten fruit followed, smashing more panes and raining down in showers against the grand dwelling place.

In the corner of his eye Jabez saw the flames of burning torches being held aloft by some of the mob and he had no doubt their blood lust would not be *sated* until the house was completely destroyed. He wanted no part of it and shoved and elbowed his way to the outer edge of the baying rabble.

As he turned his back on the destruction of the house, with the cries of jubilation ringing in his ears, he suddenly remembered that the silk master who had let them live in the loft of his weaving shed and who had been so kind to them, also lived in the square and a shudder of concern ran down his spine for the man's safety.

"Don't judge them too harshly", Jabez heard a voice say. It belonged to a journeyman who worked on one of the draw looms on the floor beneath the loft.

"They are committing felony to persons and property", Jabez said earnestly, as he shook the man's hand.

The journeyman nodded his head in agreement before adding, "We have every right to be angry; we cannot survive on the wages we are now being paid. There were food riots last week in Shoreditch and two journeymen were *scragged* outside the Salmon and Ball Inn in Hare Street, two days ago".

"Hung!" Jabez gasped in astonishment.

The man nodded solemnly. "They both swore their innocence before the judge but the silk master told the *wig* that the men had broken into his silk shed and destroyed his looms".

"Were they innocent?" Jabez asked.

"Yes", was the man's quick reply. "The silk master paid a *snitch* to testify he had seen them do it. Their statements were ignored and they were found guilty and a gallows was quickly erected outside the Inn. With their necks stretched, they left the poor souls swinging for a full fifty minutes with their wives and children looking on......the silk master said it would put the fear of God into the rest of us. He paused before adding with heavy cynicism in his voice, "Remember Jabez, judges are there to ensure the guilty are convicted and the innocent are hung".

Jabez was wide-eyed as he stared in disbelief at what the journeyman had just said.

As the two men shook hands and bade their farewells, the journeymans' eyes lingered on Jabez, as he said, "This is only the start of things to come my young friend. You and your mother will be best out of it".

×

The Parson leant back in his chair and relished the divine warmth of the crackling fire. His grey, horse-hair wig sat firmly on his balding head and his white collar was still tied round his neck, the two white bands which hung from it, dangled down to his chest. Save for his black frock coat which he had left in the hall, he was as always, clerically dressed. He was a genial man, round and short with ruddy cheeks, glazed red by his love of the outdoors, though some of his flock would say, it was due to his equal love of good food and wine.

The bottom of his white cotton gown with its balloon sleeves and gathered cuffs lapped over his black breeches which were tightly buttoned over his white stockings, just below his knees. There was a crack from the fire as an ember flew from the log burning low in the grate causing him to withdraw his black, buckled shoes quickly from the rim of the hearth he was resting them on.

"Chestnut", he muttered disparagingly to himself, "it always spits".

He smiled when he thought how he could still tell the difference between the woods stacked up in the side of the grate and knew what was a good burning log and those which would only smoulder and spit. He was a countryman at heart and for many years had ministered to his parishioners whilst enjoying the pursuits of a country gentleman. How he had loved hearing the black and tan hounds barking in their iron-framed kennels and following them in the chase, but the fall, he thought ruefully, if only the nag hadn't thrown him over that stiff hedge. He was lucky he could still ride, albeit in a fashion and fortunate that he could easily out-walk any man of his age or younger, even with his limp.

The twisted-stemmed glass he was holding had already been filled for a second time from the bottle of fine claret on his desk. He had his sermon to write for the Sunday service but it could wait, it normally did.

He took another deep draught of the ruby-coloured elixir and relished its flavour and aroma. It was a good wine but due to his sweet tooth, it began to taste raw as yet another gulp slipped down his throat. His nose wrinkled slightly as he rose from the comfort of his chair to add a spoonful of the honey kept in a clay pot on the oak dresser. He nodded his head in approval as the sweetened wine slipped easily down his throat.

He was over forty-four years of age and the most energetic thing he did now, apart from collecting his tithes, was to tend to the dozen bee hives he kept in the glebe field, the church land which lay behind the parsonage's sweeping garden. That is, as well as keeping an experienced eye on his six hardy down-land sheep grazing on the rich grass behind the church in the graveyard. The thought of the sweet-tasting honey from the hives excited his appetite and he turned his head to look at the hands on the long case clock standing in the corner of the dark-panelled room in the hope his housekeeper would serve supper on time.

Whilst he waited his mind wandered back to that bleak February morning when long fingers of ice hung from the eaves of the parsonage and the fields glittered with the hoar frost which decorated the bare branches in the trees. The sun had just gloriously risen and the frozen landscape was full of red light as if it was on fire. The contented rooks cawed overhead, safe in the knowledge that their breakfast would be forthcoming as soon as the land had thawed a bit and the teams of plough horses and oxen had done their work. It had been a particularly energetic chase through brush and cover and open ground and the cold had sunk its teeth into his bones. Even now he shivered at the thought of it. Charlie had broken from his earth and the hounds' muzzles were fixed firmly to the ground until they caught his scent and were off, yelping and barking with joy. He smiled as he thought how the horses and riders had given chase to the fox on that cold and crisp morning.

"Oh, the joy of the hunt", Tobias Lamb murmured to himself as he leant back and nestled himself in his leather chair and relished the memory with the glass of sweetened wine still clasped in his hand.

His mind filled with the image of the chase as if it was yesterday.

He was on his fine mare, following in full cry and could see the black tip of the fox's brush as the animal used all its stealth to out-run the pack of baying hounds. The bitter wind was blowing from the north and was stinging his face. He spurred the mare on, first ducking under the low spreading branches of the oak trees which brushed his face and then jumping over the remains of rotten boughs which had crashed down on the frosted ground during the winter gales. He dug his heels into the mare's muscular flanks and flicked the reins urging the animal on, quickly turning in his saddle to see if the rest of the hunt were following the pursuit. Charlie was cunning. First running on and then doubling back, *legging on* through brooks and streams and thick brush to evade his pursuers but the clamour of the hounds told him the final chase was on.

Tobias Lamb could still remember how his heart hammered and how the blood ran hot in his veins.

The thorn hedge was not the highest he had jumped that morning but it came up quick, too dammed quick. He had leant back, *scant* in his saddle, ready to jump it. His brown leather boots pushed hard into the stirrups. He pulled back on the reins but the mare breasted the hedge and over the top he went in a sickening fall.

"*Damn your bloods*", he had cursed, as he lay in the frost-crusted mud, his fine, green velvet coat ruined and his leg snapped.

His faced winched with the pain he had felt that day as the village bone-setter had pulled and reset the leg but despite the smith's best efforts, the leg became shorter and he was left with this infernal limp.

Something settled on his nose and as he brushed it away he was brought back to the present. He raised his glass to his lips and drained it before resting his head back into his chair as the memories of the hunt faded. Within minutes his head started nodding and as his chin dropped to rest on his chest he obediently allowed his heavy eyelids to slowly close. His grip loosened and the glass fell to the floor. Somewhere in the room he could hear the frantic buzz of a bluebottle. It was a sleep inducing sound and he drifted to the edge of consciousness before submitting to a deeper state of slumber.

Southwell, tucked beneath the folds of the North Downs, was a small, straggled parish with only a hundred or so inhabitants but with the tithes the Parson was able to collect, it provided him a good living and a comfortable residence. Whilst most of the villagers were poor, there were a few good quality farmhouses inhabited by wealthy farmers. Scattered throughout the back alleys and the village *twittens* were also a number of flourishing businesses, amongst them was a tanner, a baker and two brew-houses, whilst standing on the edge of the village green, opposite the church, was a smithy. Heading eastwards on the drover's road towards the market town of Ashden, stood the watermill, its wheel groaning as it was driven round by the fast flowing current of the mill race whose watery expanse glittered like polished silver whenever the sun was high in the sky. It was indeed a good village to *reside* in.

The old parsonage had stood in the shadow of the Norman church for over a hundred years and over that time the iron latch on the study door had gradually been pulled loose from its fixing screws and as the house-keeper knocked softly on the door and lifted the latch, it rattled on the door frame.

The click and the creak of the door woke the Parson from his slumber and he quickly adjusted his half-moon spectacles which had slipped down to the tip of his imposing nose.

"Begging your pardon sir but supper will be served in ten minutes", her voice was soft and low and with the country lilt of generations past.

Hester Brown had been the Parson's maid and house-servant for nearly twenty years, soon after the clergyman had arrived at the parsonage and despite the fact she had just cooked his meal, her long apron and mop cap were without blemish and were as white as driven winter snow.

"May I enquire what I am about to eat this evening?" the genial man asked. He was somebody who greatly enjoyed his food and it was his habit on occasion to discuss the food his maid had cooked and how she had prepared it.

Hester smiled before answering. The Parson was a confirmed bachelor and it gave her much pleasure to know he appreciated her efforts.

"I've stewed a dozen oysters for you sir, in white wine with some shreds of anchovy and grated nutmeg. I thought I would serve them on toasted bread *snippets*", she said with evident pride in her voice.

"And to follow?" the clergyman prompted, already savouring the taste of the oysters in his mouth.

"A platter of mutton collars from the breast and neck of one of the graveyard sheep which was butchered *but* last week. Before I bound the collars I rolled them in the white of three fresh eggs".

She paused before adding, "I hard boiled the yolks to add to the sauce made from the meat juices. I knew you would appreciate it. I also sprinkled in some thyme and parsley together with a generous knob of butter". She concluded the detailed explanation, hoping the Parson would appreciate the amount of care she had taken in preparing his supper.

"I will waste no more time Hester and come to the table without any delay", the Parson said, as he rose from his chair and threw another, but more carefully chosen log on the fire. "Could you put a bottle of claret on the table so I can do justice to the fine meal it would appear that you have cooked for me?" he quickly added as an after-thought.

With the meal concluded, the Parson had the look of a man who had just enjoyed a hearty meal when Hester entered the parlour to clear the dishes. She ignored the belch which emanated from deep inside her master's wide girth and asked if he required anything further.

"Thanking *thee*, but no", he replied, lightly patting his ample belly to indicate he was indeed full. I think I'll retire to the *withdrawing* room to write my sermon and perhaps partake of a bowl of tobacco".

Try as he might, he could not quite manage to walk in a straight line as he made his way along the long corridor from the parlour, across the large hall and towards his favourite room in the house. In the flickering yellow light of his candle, the shapes of the equally-spaced chairs were hardly discernible and he stubbed his foot heavily on one as he stumbled along towards the chamber. Even the normally vibrant colours of the oil paintings hanging along the walls, appeared almost grey in the dim light of the candle and could only be really appreciated in the bright light of day.

With a sigh of relief he sank down heavily into his chair in front of the red-hot embers which still smouldered in the fire and reached for his long-stemmed clay pipe and tobacco pouch. Sucking hard, he held a burning spill to the pipe and not stopping till his cheeks were fit to burst, he exhaled a billow of the sweet-smelling smoke with a sigh of relief and thanked the Lord of Heaven and Earth for this laudable of pleasures.

In his state of contentment and by the light of the remaining embers, he began to think, and not for the first time, the life of a country parson was one which many would desire, but for him, it had not been his first choice.

"Primogenitor", he scowled to himself, the damned law where only the first born son would inherit the family estate and the second son received nothing other than a modest bequest. Had it not been for that, he would be a farmer now and not a Parson, full from his supper and enjoying a pipe-full of rich tobacco. He remembered how he realised as a very young man he would have to make his own way in life but what profession befitting a gentleman he had questioned on many occasions? Would he choose the law or medicine? He decided he would choose the one which would provide a living, a regular income and a home for the span of his life. He chose the church.

He studied in the halls of Cambridge and obtained a degree together with a testimonial vouching his fitness for the ministry which he had presented to the Bishop.

"A family friend", he muttered under his breath, with a broad grin spreading across his face.

The Parson recalled how he had demonstrated his knowledge of the scriptures to the Bishop, together with his competence in spoken and written Latin and then at twenty-four years of age, he was ordained and ready to be in charge of a parish.

"Yes", he said, rather smugly to himself, "I chose the church and what a comfortable, worldly living it has proved to be".

He had a residence with a large garden which suited him well, together with a small additional income on the occasions he taught the scriptures at the village school, not to mention the tithes he collected annually from the farmers and tenants alike, coin or kind. From those whom he judged could ill afford the tithes, he would collect a goose or two, or the side of a hog but others, like George Bentley and Percival Lightfoote, he would insist on full payment, to be paid precisely on Michaelmas day and would delight in seeing their sour faces and hearing their unseemly oaths, as they reluctantly counted the coins into his open hand.

The image of the two men sitting in their box pews, either side of the church aisle filled him with distaste and subconsciously he drew in rather more smoke from the pipe's bowl than he intended to and as a result, broke into a coughing fit.

He wiped the tears from his eyes on the large, silk *'kerchief* he took from his pocket and emptied his nose with a long and resounding trumpet, before deciding he would not allow the distasteful thoughts of George Bentley and Percival Lightfoote to invade his mind again and spoil his evening.

The sermon, he remembered reluctantly, oh yes, the sermon; but there was not enough light left in the room to read, let alone to write, he decided.

Perhaps tomorrow, he thought, as he closed his eyes.

3

The Smithy

From deep inside the smithy the rhythmic sound of metal being hammered on an anvil rang out like the church bell calling the village faithful to worship. In the gloom of the smithy burning sparks traced snake-like patterns and flew in all directions as the bar of glowing iron took shape with every measured blow of Gideon Larkin's heavy hammer. Eventually the thud of the hammer blows stopped and the blacksmith appeared in the doorway wiping his sweating brow with the sleeve of his button-less linen shirt. A thick leather apron, reaching down to his knees covered his broad chest, protecting him from the forge's scorching heat and the sparks coming from the red-hot metal he fashioned daily.

Outside, his son, eighteen year old Nathan Larkin was day-dreaming as he sucked on a stalk of *bedstraw* blown in from the neighbouring poppy-splashed barley field. He was aimlessly watching the *eaves swallows* as they collected the mud from under the stone horse trough which stood outside the smithy. Whilst the horses waited to be shod, they often shook their large heads after taking gulps of the cool water, causing it to overflow and to be churned into mud by the shuffling of their heavy hooves.

The young man watched as the black and white birds collected the rich-black mud in their beaks to plaster their cup-shaped nests clinging to the eaves of the ancient dwelling, until his restless eyes strayed to a rusty horse shoe that had been nailed to the wall of the ancient smithy generations ago.

"*Feyther*, why is the horse shoe on the wall?" he asked curiously, as he turned towards his father, his tongue having the Kentish drawl.

Gideon Larkin ran his fingers through his sweat-soaked, jet black hair and with a wide grin on his bronze-coloured face, replied. "Is this the first time in eighteen years that you've noticed it lad?"

"It's the first time I've wondered why it's there", his son countered. Despite his age, he was now a *man grown*, very personable, tall and broad in the shoulder with a *well knit* body like his father.

With a mocking seriousness in his voice, Gideon started to explain, "The devil once asked Saint Dunstan to nail a shoe on his horse but instead, the Saint nailed the shoe on the devils foot which caused great pain. The devil, which had the horns of a ram and the ears and fur of a goat howled with pain and begged for the shoe to be removed. The Saint agreed to remove it but only after the devil promised he would never enter any dwelling place which had a horseshoe nailed to its door".

"Oh", said the young man, noncommittally.

"The old school master doesn't *learn* that to the young scholars who are chalking on their slates in the school house and being *showed* how to read and write and *reckon up*", the blacksmith mocked, with a trace of humour in his voice.

Nathan nodded his head in agreement. He would have no use for those things now he was apprenticed to his father, nor in years to come, when he would eventually become the village smith.

A thoughtful look then came over the young man's frowning face as he quizzed his father once more, "If the horse shoe on the wall has its toes pointing up to keep the devil away, why are the toes on the horse shoe over the door inside the smithy, pointing down?"

His father's laugh was like a low, rumbling boom, "This one on the wall holds onto the luck whilst the one inside the smithy pours the luck over the heads of everyone who enters, even the horses when they are brought in to be shod in the winter". Then enjoying the joke, he added as an afterthought, "Believe me lad, those horses will need all the luck they can get when *thee* start shoeing them".

Nathan smiled as his father's laughter began to wane, almost like a peal of thunder rumbling away in the distance and then as Gideon turned and headed back into the dark smithy, he called back to his son, who was already a younger reflection of himself, "George Carter wants to collect his stone chisel after noon and it won't *be making* itself".

Gideon paused to look at his son and realised, almost un-noticed, what a strapping young man he had become and his mind drifted back to the time when he was Nathan's age.

He too had been apprenticed to his father at the forge, as had his father before him. Times past, even before his grandfather's time, what went on in the darkness of the smithy was a mystery to the people in the village and elsewhere. It had been kept that way during the three generations of the Larkins as they shod the heavy cart and plough horses and the lighter and more nimble steeds the wealthy rode. Compared with many village folk who often had to seek poor relief, the Larkins enjoyed a regular income which put food on the family's table and warmth in their chambers. Yes, Gideon thought, his family had prospered for three generations thanks to the four-legged beasts.

His thoughts were disturbed by a series of low guttural sounds coming from the backyard where his large, mud-covered hog was standing on his hind quarters, grunting as it looked over the door of its stye at the chickens scratching for worms amongst the rows of well-tended vegetables, its morning sleep having been disturbed by the noise of Nathan shovelling coal into a bucket.

Gideon looked towards his son as he heaved the coal up onto the forge's hearth and said, "One thing is for certain, nothing will ever replace the horse and the plough and if *thee* master the skills and protect our secrets, you'll always be able to enjoy a plate of cold meat and a quart of ale under the roof of your dwelling".

Nathan smiled at his father.

It was not the first time he had been told that and he knew it wouldn't be the last. For over a century, all manner of things had been made and repaired in the smithy. Nails and hinges for the carpenters, sickles and flails for the men who laboured in the fields and fire-irons and harrows for the farmers who employed them.

The *brightsmiths* in their London workshops could make pretty trinkets for the gentry in gold and silver but it was only the blacksmiths with their mastery of iron, who could make the much-needed bands wrapped round the wheels of their carriages and could fashion bars of iron into whatever the yeomen and labourers needed. It was only the blacksmiths who knew the secrets of making swords and axes hard enough to keep their edge or how to forge the tips of a harrow that would neither shatter nor blunt when they hit a flint. They knew how to forge gate hinges which were soft enough so they wouldn't snap if the gate flapped open in an autumn gale. Indeed they had the range of skills to make virtually anything else which was required to work the land or use in the village dwellings.

The smithy snuggled against the end of the blacksmith's modest cottage and at its heart, within its gloomy interior, was the square, stone-built forge where Gideon, as did his forebears before him, nursed the fire and heated the bars of iron in its roaring flames. Around the forge's base and scattered in untidy piles, were stacks of horseshoes of varying shapes and sizes, ready to be finally forged and fitted to whatever horse or donkey was led hobbling into the smithy. Some of the shoes had been there so long they had rusted with age whilst others were fresh from the forge and still had the flaking black-scale clinging to them.

Gideon watched as Nathan carefully placed some lumps of coal around the outer edge of the forge's fire.

"Managing the fire is the most important part of our craft", he counselled his son.

Without looking up, Nathan nodded, as he continued arranging the coal.

"It is always changing", his father continued, "and must be looked after constantly. We can get the fire up to its best heat by pumping air into the back of it with the bellows but whilst the fire maintains its heat for a while, it soon begins to cool and we have to start all over again". His laugh was loud and throaty as he *jested,* "Much like a woman *methinks*".

Nathan's eyes sparkled with the eagerness of his age as he watched his father rake forward the coal which had been turned into coke by the fire's heat and as he did so, wisps of smoke curled and twisted their way up the smithy's wide, stone chimney.

To most eyes, the inside of the smithy would have appeared to be crowded and chaotic. Wooden racks, overflowing with fresh hay lined the back wall, ready to feed the horses whilst they waited to be shod, keeping them content and placid which lessened the chance of the blacksmith being kicked by an irritable nag. Under the hay racks, stacked on shelves and hanging from rows of rusty nails were different sized callipers, rasps and hammers of every shape and size imaginable. There was a rack fixed to the front of the forge and hanging from it were dozens of pairs of tongs and swages, each one designed for a particular purpose. Flat jaws, box jaws, pointed jaws, hollow bits, hot and cold bits, fuller swages…names and uses, some of which the watching apprentice still had to learn. Tall conical mandrels stood on the brick floor, ready when different sized rings were needed to be hammered round them. Within easy reach on the other side of the forge was a tall leg-vice bolted to a sturdy work bench whilst bristled headed brooms and a collection of long-handled shovels leant against an adjacent treadle-operated whetstone. In fact, despite the appearance, everything within the smithy's gloomy interior had a place and a purpose and it had been that way for over a hundred years.

A smile which had started in Gideon's eyes gradually spread across his face as he lifted a pair of box tongs from the rack and handed them to his surprised son, saying, "Let's see what you're like at in making a mason's chisel".

Nathan nervously took them and after adjusting his grip to ensure the crude lump of iron was being held firmly, pushed it into the roaring fire. Soon, under his father's eagle-eyed instruction, he began to turn the glowing metal into the mason's chisel, hard and sharp enough to cleave through the hardest of rock.

"Push it into the heart of the fire", Gideon shouted over the roar of the bellows he was pumping, "and keep turning it….make sure you heat it evenly and wait 'till it gets white-hot before you take it to the anvil. That way it will take the properties from the fire so that we can make it hard enough to keep its edge".

Nathan grinned, realising his father was at last, beginning to share the deeply-held secrets of the forge with him. It had taken six years but at last it was beginning to happen.

"Keep it white but don't let the metal burn", his father ordered, "I'll get the powder".

Gideon turned away from the forge and quickly walked across to his work bench. Bending on one knee, he reached under the bench and dragged out a small wooden box. His face was red and sweating as he plunged his massive hand into the box and started to spread a fist-full of the fine black powder it contained, over the face of the anvil.

Nathan removed the iron bar, glowing dazzling white from the heat of the fire and quickly carried it across to the anvil, knowing speed was essential. The anvil, which was raised to knee height on a section of a tree trunk, was exactly one pace from the forge and stood to the right of it, because both Nathan and his father were right-handed.

"Quick lad, hammer it into the powder….keep turning it over and over and beating it until all the powder has been worked into the iron".

Sparks, flying like chaff in the wind were coming off the white-hot metal as Nathan followed his father's instructions.

Gideon, who was watching intently, suddenly shouted, "Stop" as the metal began to lose its heat. "Put it back into the fire and once all the powder has been beaten in, you can begin to start shaping it into the chisel".

The blacksmith had started to move back to the fire and was raking fresh coke into the flames when he sensed someone had entered the smithy.

A large man in a mud-stained frock coat with a dirty wig askew on his head was striding into the forge with the arrogance of someone who was used to getting his own way. His mouth was wide, not unlike that of a frog's and quite out of proportion with his round snub nose and his little pig-like eyes which were almost lost in the mountains of flesh that made up his bloated face.

Gideon turned to confront the man and took a step forward to stop him coming any further into his workplace. Nobody entered the smithy without his say so.

"Good day Mr Lightfoote", he greeted the man in a flat, expressionless voice, not bothering to raise his index finger to his temple, as was his usual practice to rich and poor alike.

"My nag *hath* thrown a shoe", the raw-looking man said bluntly, his odious voice bristled with malevolence. For a reason best known to the man, he had taken *a set against* Gideon and the blacksmith took a degree of pleasure in returning it.

Gideon took half a pace forward, forcing Percival Lightfoote to quickly step back. Gideon looked beyond the irate man and saw his sullen-looking son was standing behind him, holding the reins of two horses, one of which was lifting a foot. The fool has been riding it hard without a shoe, the blacksmith observed. His distaste of the man was evident.

"I haven't time to waste", blood *suffused* the man's face as he snapped impatiently.

With his hands placed firmly on his hips, Gideon remained calm and said evenly, "Sorry but we are forming a chisel".

He looked towards his son who had continued to forge the chisel and was pleased when he noticed it was beginning to take on its long tapering shape.

"Tether the nag to the ring set into the wall and I'll attend to it later", he said sharply to the agitated man.

Lightfoote exploded with anger at the blacksmith's insolence towards him and with his nose almost touching Gideon's, spluttered, "I will do no such thing. You will do it now".

Gideon could see the red flush on the man's face growing in intensity and his eyes narrowed as he said with a degree of finality in his voice, "I will shoe your nag when the mason's chisel is finished".

Lightfoote's anger sharpened as his fists clenched and he felt his chest tighten into a knot as his rage rose at the man facing him. "How do you expect me to get home?"

He spat the words out.

There was almost a sardonic grin on Gideon's face as he replied, "On *shanks mare*".

"Walk!" Lightfoote screeched in fury at Gideon's reply as his fingers curled and uncurled round the whip he was grasping. He wanted to strike the man for his impertinence and beat him into the ground. He was feared by virtually every man and woman in the village and would have done it to every single one of them, except to the person standing defiantly in front of him.

Gideon stood his ground with the confidence of a man who was treated with respect throughout the village. His father had also been the village magistrate and the church warden whilst his grandfather had been the village bone setter, undertaker and animal physician. Gideon did not have the need to hold such offices and was content to concentrate on the demands of the smithy. He had the measure of the loathsome man fuming in front of him who was nothing more than a thug and bully who ruled through fear and violence. It was only by the chance of birth that he owned a few hundred acres of farmland bordering the Downs to the south of the village and styled himself as the local Squire.

Nathan had finished forging the chisel and as he waited for Gideon to be done with Percival Lightfoote, he marvelled at his father's composure. Never had a father and son been so different in that respect. Nathan was quick tempered and easy to anger and as he watched Lightfoote's tantrums, he couldn't help thinking if it had been him confronting the man, he would have probably smashed his fist into the arrogant man's face without thought of the consequence. He knew it was sinful to wish evil on others and remained silent, as if his jaw had been wired shut.

Defeated, the hostile man turned to his sullen-looking son, snapping angrily, "Abel, tether the nag to the ring".

"That'll be one shilling and six pence, if *thee* please sir", Gideon said calmly.

Lightfoote ignored him and turning his back, started to mount his son's horse.

"I would be obliged for payment before the nag is shod". Gideon knew Lightfoote never paid his debts, preferring to let his friend, the corrupt magistrate, decide the matter in his favour, before the two of them invariably departed to one of the alehouses and taverns.

"*By the blood of Christ,* I will not", fumed Lightfoote, as he awkwardly removed his foot from the stirrup and turned to confront Gideon once more.

He paced back into the smithy, red-faced with his fists clenched ready for a fight.

Gideon could see the pulsing veins in the man's forehead and stood his ground, with his swarthy arms folded, unimpressed by the man's resurging anger. "Then *thee* best unhitch the nag and let it hobble back *whence thee* came", he said, as calm as ever.

Percival Lightfoote was at breaking point as he reached into the pocket of his mud-stained breeches and pulled out a pouch of fine kidskin. "*God blind you*", he mouthed as his fingers searched the pouch.

The man's threats and curses were now being spat out with so much ferocity they seemed to rattle the walls of the old smithy.

Gideon remained still and unblinking against the onslaught of venom as three silver coins were dropped into his open palm.

Lighfoote's voice was barely human as he growled, "The day will come Larkin when you and your bloody son will pay dearly for this".

Gideon watched impassively as once again the scowling man jabbed his boot into the stirrup and swung up into the saddle. With a sharp yank on the horse's reins, Lightfoote pulled its head round and as he did so, he looked down at Gideon and said menacingly, "One day *smug*", he used the word for an unskilled blacksmith, *"the devil will flay your hide"*. The metal bit cut into the side of the horse's mouth and it raised its head in pain. Lightfoote yanked on the rein once more to turn the beast round as his anger rose with the flood of bile from his overfull belly.

The blacksmith stood with his jaw fixed as the man lashed the horse's flank with his whip and kicked it into a canter. As Gideon shook his head in dismay at the horse's suffering, his son could not resist a smile when he saw the look on Abel Lightfoote's face as he trudged behind in the cloud of dust his father was leaving behind him. As the pair rounded the corner past the church and *bore their way* up the old drover's road towards Ashden, Gideon turned to Nathan and said with a broad grin spreading across face, "We had better finish the chisel you've forged; enough time has been wasted on that *horse's arse* of a man".

Nathan grinned on hearing his father's rare profanity and rather unwisely ventured one of his own, "A fart in his face, eh feyther".

Gideon ignored his son's attempt at coarseness and taking the chisel, he inspected it intently, nodding his head with satisfaction at Nathan's workmanship.

"Once we've ground a sharp edge on it we can start to harden it to meet the mason's need", Gideon said as he walked across to the whetstone and amidst a shower of sparks and with a practised eye, he began to sharpen the chisel on the spinning wheel.

Nathan watched as his father ran his thumb along the chisel's blade, checking the bevelled edge was to his liking.

"There are a number of secrets a blacksmith must keep close to his heart to ensure we keep our mastery of iron", Gideon told his lad as he closed the double doors of the smithy. He lowered his voice as he continued, "How we build and maintain our fire and the way we turn the coal into coke are some of the secrets. Another is how we make the black powder I keep in the wooden box".

Nathan interrupted him, mischievously asking "How do you make the powder?" He deliberately emphasised the word *you*.

A grin lifted the corners of his father's mouth, "Not so fast, lad. I'm going to tell you some of my secrets today but not all of them".

Gideon handed the sharpened chisel back to his son, whilst he explained, "When you were forging this and I told you to push it into the heart of the fire, it was so the iron absorbed the carbons hidden in the burning coke and when I told you to hammer some of the powder into it whilst it was white-hot, it was so we can now turn this chisel into a tool any mason would be proud of". He walked across to the forge and taking the chisel back from Nathans' hands he gripped it firmly in the box tongs and said, "Jump on the bellows and get the fire to roar, we need to heat the point of the chisel up to red-heat, just red-heat...no more". He watched as the fire became hotter and the chisel slowly turned from black-heat to cherry-red. Swinging round quickly and taking one stride back, he plunged the glowing chisel into the water-filled cooling trough, sending a cloud of hot, wet steam up to disperse amongst the forges roof timbers.

He held the still-warm chisel up for his son to see, explaining, "What I have done is to turn a soft iron chisel into something which is as hard as glass. The only problem is that if the mason was to use it now, it would probably shatter and take his eye with it".

Nathan retrieved the chisel back from his father and examined it with a curious eye and as he stroked it lightly with one of his blackened fingers, he said, "It almost feels hard to the touch".

His father beamed. "Good, you're beginning to feel what we have put into the metal....only a true blacksmith can do that".

"What we need to do now is to soften it slightly so it will do the job it's intended for...." Gideon stopped in mid-sentence and asked strangely, "Do you know why there are no windows in the smithy?"

Nathan shook his head at the curious question as he handed the chisel back.

"*Tis* so I can see the colours of the iron when it's heated. Different colours for different things and different tools, lad", Gideon continued to explain.

Nathan stared intently as his father heated the middle of the chisel to a very dull red-heat and watched as rainbow colours began to travel along its length to the tip. It was a simple and straightforward procedure for Gideon but as he watched, the apprentice was absorbed in everything his father was showing him.

"Light straw", his father shouted as the colour reached the end. "Dark straw", the colours were travelling so quickly along the chisel Nathan's eyes were struggling to keep up with the speed they were changing.

Gideon spun and roughly pushed his son to one side as he quickly plunged the tool into the water again. "Dark straw, that's the colour for a mason's chisel. If I hadn't cooled it quickly it would have become too soft. Dark blue is for hoof picks and the like, light blue for scrapers, light straw for swords and axes and dark straw for things like this". He held the finished chisel aloft. "We call that *tempering*. You'll soon get the hang of it as long as you remember, quick is the word and sharp is the action", he said with the resounding laugh of craftsman to his inexperienced apprentice.

✕

All around Spitalfield market there was the usual throng of people jostling with each other, some eager to sell their wares whilst others were eager to buy them and mingling amongst them all were the usual pickpockets and thieves.

"*Comealong, comealong*", the traders were chanting their sing song cries. Their *hallooing* grew louder and their voices became hoarser as each one tried fervently to entice the market goers away from the other barrows and stalls.

The horse-drawn carriages of the rich silk traders and master weavers were fewer now with the rioters roaming the streets and threaded their way cautiously through the populous, leaving a trail of grasping beggars and ragamuffins following in their wake. The carriage windows were tightly shut and their finely clothed occupants pressed sweet-smelling nose-gays tightly to their faces in an attempt to dispel the noxious odours that *abounded* the place.

Sarah and Jabez had *broken their fast* with some bread crusts and two small herrings and as Jabez left the table, he noticed the wistful look which had come over his mother's face and saw the evidence of the tears which were beginning to well up in her blue eyes. Her eyes had lost their sparkle since his father's death and as every day passed since she had left the letter with the costermonger, she was becoming more withdrawn and pensive.

"Mother, I have been thinking", he said as brightly as he could in an attempt to give his mother some cheer, "when we go to live with my grandfather, I'm sure our circumstances will improve and perhaps I will even find work to do on the farm".

Sarah smiled thinly and remained silent, alone in her thoughts. Several minutes passed before she suddenly snapped out of her melancholy and getting up, said, "Let's get my shawl and your coat and go see if my father has replied to the letter. It's been *neer* two weeks now and I'm sure we will get his answer soon".

With Jabez following behind, Sarah quickened her pace and made her way through the jostling crowds to the lines of costermongers' stalls and donkey barrows which were crowded around the market, hoping against hope, the wagon had arrived and with it, the reply to the letter she had left with the man they called Spuddy.

✕

Outside the smithy Percival Lightfoote's horse was shaking its head and pounding the dirt with a hoof causing the frayed rope attached to its filthy halter to tug mercilessly against the iron ring fixed into the wall.

"He's getting impatient", Gideon said, as he walked towards the mud-crusted gelding. It saw him and holding his head up high, snorted loudly as it stared at the blacksmith, sensing that once again it may be in danger.

"*Whoa* boy". The blacksmith stroked the nervous horse reassuringly, running his fingers through the long hair on its neck, as he tried to calm the frightened animal.

The gelding swung it's long, skinny neck towards Gideon and looked at him dully with its sad looking eyes.

Nathan joined his father, dismayed as he saw the horse's condition. Its jutting hips and rib cage were plainly visible under its sweat-drenched, coat. Turning to his father, he said, conclusively "Lightfoote has treated the beast badly".

Gideon stoked the gelding's huge head and nodding in agreement, said sadly, "I daresay, it's the same way as he treats every other living thing. Get the poor beast a bucket of oats from the stable whilst I give it a quick rub down before I begin to get my tools together".

"He's got a good temperament, despite everything he's been through", Gideon said, as ran his hand down the horse's leg before squeezing the tendon just above its ankle. Slowly he began to lift the gelding's leg between his own until the sole of its hoof was facing upwards.

Nathan saw the gelding shift its weight onto its other three legs.

"Good boy, good boy", his father was saying as the horse pushed its nose deeper into the bucket of oats. "Horses don't stand still and they kick out if they are annoyed", his father advised his son, as he carried on talking softly to the beast.

Nathan knew exactly what he meant as he remembered what had happened to Henry Prinn. Prinn was a simple-minded *clod* with a vacant look who followed Abel Lightfoote about, much like a *well-broked* dog which was subservient to its master. The pair of them swaggered round the village day and night threatening violence and abuse on whoever they so pleased, without fear of any consequences from the magistrate and the village constable, Abel Lightfoote's father saw to that. Often, when the pair of them were drunk in the alehouse, it was not unusual for them to try to pick a fight with any unfortunate traveller who was unaware of their reputation and ill-fitting *countenance*.

It had been some years previous when Prinn had been walking behind a grazing stallion and decided for no good reason, other than to cause the animal pain, to stab it in the rump with a sharpened stick. The beast reared up giving Prinn a hefty kick, breaking his leg and leaving him crying in agony. The bones were set badly leaving him with a hobble and a spayed left foot. Nathan smiled as he thought that everybody except stupid Henry Prinn, knew horses kicked out if they are abused.

Gideon picked up his short stone pick and started to clean out the muck and stones from the sole of the gelding's hoof, carefully checking it wasn't cut or damaged, particularly after the way Percival Lightfoote had ridden the poor animal. Using the hoof knife he had forged when he was his son's age, he deftly cut away the sole's hard outer layer to reveal a white, softer layer underneath. Without raising his head, he worked quickly to trim the edge of the hoof with his nippers and then, using the inside of his knee to push out the horse's leg out slightly, he finally levelled the hoof with his sharp-toothed rasp.

"That's the difficult part of the job done", he joked to his watching son as he gently lowered the gelding's foot to the ground "*tis* about time you learnt how to nail a shoe on".

Nathan's mouth dropped open as he croaked in surprise, "Me"

After giving his son a few minutes to recover from the shock, Gideon said, "Go and find a shoe you think will fit" and as Nathan disappeared into the smithy, he shouted after him, "and don't forget that the front and hind feet of this old nag will be different shapes".

Gingerly, Nathan began to lift the horse's leg to size the shoe he had chosen against its raised hoof.

As Gideon watched intently, he barked out instructions to his apprehensive apprentice. "Squeeze its tendon", he urged "keep the nag calm".

Despite his nervousness, Nathan had watched his father shoe many horses over years he had been apprenticed to him and he proceeded with a confidence which only comes with youth.

Gideon watched as his son heated the horseshoe to red-heat and then with beats of his hammer, he shaped it over the beak of the anvil until it fitted perfectly round the edge of the horse's hoof. He smiled knowingly when he noticed the sweat running off the boy's face and falling like spatters of rain onto the smithy's uneven brick floor.

Nathan lifted the gelding's foot as he gently lowered the hot shoe onto its freshly cleaned hoof, creating a smooth surface between the shoe and hoof. Gideon leant forward and peered through the smoke billowing from the burning hoof to ensure the fit met with his approval and on seeing it did, Nathan cooled the still hot shoe into the murky water in the plunge trough.

There was naked pride on Gideon's face as his son began to secure the shoe onto the horse's heavy hoof. With the blows of his driving hammer, the youth drove eight nails, four on each side, at an outward angle through the holes he had punched in the horseshoe and into the gelding's hoof wall.

He was out of breath as he clinched the nail tips by bending them over and snipping them off and then with the job completed, he gently lowered the horse's leg to the ground.

Gideon slapped his son soundly on his back and with a broad grin spreading across his glowing face, he turned to Nathan and said, "If the shoe hasn't been fitted properly and this old beast throws his rider, then Praise be to God it will be Percival Lightfoote"

The two men were still laughing as they sat on the edge of the smithy's water trough, each enjoying a jug of home-brewed ale..

Gideon drained his tankard before commenting that shoeing a horse always gave a man a good thirst. He was wiping the ale's foam from his mouth as he rose and disappeared through the door which led into the cottage. Minutes later; he re-appeared holding something in his huge hands.

"My father gave me this after I had shod my first horse and so I think the time has come for me to pass it on to you" he said to his son, with a proud smile on his face.

Nathan recognised it immediately and took the small box into his open hands. It was his father's tinder box with its carved, sliding lid.

"It originally belonged to my grandfather who fashioned it himself out of a solid block of oak", Gideon explained as his son traced the outline of the horse shoe which had been carved deeply into the lid. "You'll never find another one like that. It's a tinder box made by a blacksmith for a blacksmith", he said with evident pride of his grandfather's work.

His son slid back the lid and lifted the lead damper plate to reveal the contents. Nestled in the bed of dry tinder was a small piece of iron and a jagged flint

"That's the best tinder you'll find hereabouts, your mother makes it from dry moss and the remnants of the rags she *chars* by the fire.

"A blacksmith's box full of a blacksmith's wife's tinder", he laughed as he slapped his ham-sized hand soundly on his son's broad back.

4

The Looking Hut

"Another fine morning, mistress, is it not?" Spuddy greeted Sarah jovially as she approached his coster's barrow and cracking a toothless smile he reached inside his grubby jacket,

Days of worry surged from Sarah's body and she breathed a huge sigh of relief as she took the letter the shabbily dressed man had produced and stared open eyed at the name which had been untidily scrawled on it in jet-black ink. Jabez anxiously looked on and could tell by the look on his mother's face something was wrong.

"Sarah Bentley", his mother read sadly, as she turned to Jabez, "he did not even have the courtesy to address me by the name your dear departed father bestowed on me".

Anxiety was etched on her face as she turned the letter over and stared at the blobs of red wax which had been carelessly dropped on it. She paused, not daring to break the seal, fearful of what she would read inside.

Several minutes passed before she tentatively put her finger under the flap and slowly began to break the wax and open the fateful letter. Sarah was ashen faced as she looked blankly at the cold words written on the crumpled paper.

"I told thee when thou saw fit to leave that thou were nothing to me and nothing has changed since", she read in a trembling, broken voice.

"The very presence of thee and the Huguenot's child would offend my eyes.

Your dead mother found joy in thee and for that reason and that reason alone thee can have the Looking Hut as an abode.

Expect nothing else for nothing else will ever be offered to thee or given".

For some minutes she stared at the letter not believing what she had just read. "Oh my God, your grandfather has chosen to give us no charity other than granting us the use of the Looking Hut", she cried, as her heart sank and a gripping fear took hold.

As the blood in her veins turned to ice she turned to Jabez and questioned, "How could we have been brought so low?"

Jabez had never seen his mother look so despondent and wondered if she was going to break down in tears. He took her hand and squeezing it tightly, asked, with growing concern evident in his voice, "What's the Looking Hut?"

She remained silent and without letting go of her son's hand, she steered him towards the far corner of the market, close to where the old charnel house stood and where she could speak to him away from the hubbub and raucous noise around them. She glanced around and as she did so, she became aware of a small group of unsavoury looking men leering at them and she increased her pace accordingly. Elsewhere, people were elbowing and pushing their way through the bustle of the market. A street vendor was calling out "Hot *taters*". Other cries rang out selling pigs' fries and spiced ale and mint cakes. Close by an elderly woman had lit a fire getting ready to cook a huge pot of *hasty pudding*. Children, no more than five or six years of age and dressed in rags, wove their way through the throng, hawking gingerbread and brightly-coloured ribbons. Raised voices around the barrows haggled over the prices as the hoarse-voiced mongers continually hustled the crowds to buy their wares.

Sarah with Jabez in tow ignored them all and pushed her way through until they reached the edge of the market where it was relatively quiet and where they could talk undisturbed.

"It's a hovel, Jabez, nothing more than a mud hut in the woods". Sarah looked deep into her son's eyes and said mournfully, "What will become of us?" Her voice was faltering and Jabez began to feel a deep foreboding.

Minutes passed and neither mother nor son said a word before Sarah realised how distressed Jabez looked. She forced a smile and explained in an attempt to put his mind at rest, "It was built many years ago by an old shepherd called Gabriel Taylor out of woven hazel wattles and furze. He used it as a place to shelter from the cold north winds when they blew across the low ridge of chalk hills called the Downs and as somewhere to keep the early April lambs warm and dry. It stands in a small glade speckled with more wild flowers than you could count, where the sunlight dapples though the leaves of the ancient oak and ash trees which surround it.

Sarah's mood lifted slightly as she continued, "He cut the sods for the roof from the down-land turf and when the warm spring showers fell on it, it became a carpet of golden yellow trefoil flowers. The children called them granny's toe nails", she said, as youthful memories began to return.

Jabez was listening intently, enthralled by what he was being told.

"The little flowers are as bright as the feathers you will see on the breast of the yellow hammers which sing their sweet songs in the whitethorn hedges that abound", Sarah explained, as her mood became brighter by the minute. "In the spring there were violets growing in the *wood-ways* which I used to pull for the market and daffodils grew under the ivy hedges and in the orchards the tight pink buds on the apple trees were so big they looked like the clenched fists of a new-born baby".

"The hut is sheltered in the folds of the Downs and stands on the edge of thirty acres of pasture we called Fairfoin Rowens which is flush with meadow buttercups and white ox-eye daisies all summer long. All around, the fields and woods of Kent spread out for miles in the untainted air. Overhead the larks rise high in the sky, singing their sweet songs before falling like stones to the ground, ready to return to their secret nests of neatly woven grass. When the summer breeze blows softly off the rolling hills, you can even smell the wild thyme and marjoram plants which grow in abundance there and you can marvel at the clouds of the little blue butterflies which feed upon them.

Jabez's attention was interrupted as his nose caught the nauseating stench of the nearby hog pens and slaughter houses and his glowing vision of the Looking Hut evaporated. Instead of the sweet scent of the wild herbs his mother had described, all he could smell now were the piles of rotting food cast amongst the market stalls and costers' barrows. His eyes caught something in the sky and glancing up, he saw black kites circling with their heads held down and their amber eyes steely focussed, ready to swoop down to rip open the carcass of the next dead animal they saw lying in the filthy streets.

"There is a babbling chalk stream running close to the Looking Hut", Sarah continued, unaware of her son's unpleasant distractions, "no more drinking the *mawkish* river water which is full of all manner of things and the crowds of unsavoury people who *habit* these streets.".

Despite his mother's glowing description of the place they would now be calling home, he could detect the worry in her eyes and wrapping his arm round her thin waist, he said softly, "Mother, I'm sure everything is going to be alright", he hesitated before asking cautiously, "can I take my books?".

"Yes, I am sure everything will turn out for the best and of course you will take your books", she said, trying to feel more optimistic about their future in Southwell.

A sharp evening wind chilled their faces as the pair hurried their way down Sandy Row to their lodgings in the loft, both pleased to be clear of the place before darkness finally fell. Already, in the alleys and narrow lanes, they could see the light coming from some cooking braziers and the odd candle lanterns.

Jabez remained silent as his mother lit a candle and read her father's letter for one last time. In the dim light he looked into his mother's eyes and tried to read them as she slowly held the edge of the letter to the candle's flickering flame and watched as the paper suddenly burst into flames. Nothing was said as fragments of black ash fluttered down on her bowed head.

A week had passed slowly since Sarah had made the arrangements with the costermonger for her journey back to Southwell and during that time their situation at the loft had became even more desperate. They had only ten days left before they would have to leave the modest accommodation above the weaving floors and make way for the journeyman but then what would they do? The thought of them having to creep into one of the derelict houses crowded around Artillery Passage, crammed full of felons and the ne'er-do-wells of Spitalfield, had haunted for many nights past.

The dawn had beckoned the arrival of another day as once again, Sarah made her way to the market in the hope of seeing the wagon delivering the turnips and potatoes which had come up from Southwell but, as on all of the previous days, there was no sign of the wagon or the driver.

Some days, she would pass the time of day *tattling* with the costermonger whilst on others, she would just look on from a distance through the ever present crowds of people, hoping to see the man sitting high on the wooden wagon. London's dark heart of the East End had become overcrowded with beggars and thieves and was riddled with crime which even the ever increasing public hangings did little to stem. Sarah could remember when she had first arrived, there were some open fields nearby to enjoy, and small hamlets to visit but now, all around the market it was densely settled, not least by the tens of thousands of Huguenots and other migrants who had arrived seeking safety. Even these numbers were now being swelled by foreign workers who would ask less to weave the silk and as a result, growing ranks of unemployed weavers and their journeymen, whose families had been here for three generations, were beginning to fill the streets in the vain hope of finding some work or food and when it was not forthcoming, they looked for any Irishmen or anyone else, they could pick a fight with.

"Mistress, Mistress", it was the sound of Spuddy's harsh voice cutting across the clamour of the marketplace and on a day when Sarah was beginning to think that all was lost.

Sarah hurried towards him and as she got closer, she saw to her horror, the man's barrow was already piled up with newly delivered white-skinned turnips and a jumbled heap of potatoes which still had thick loam of Kent clinging obstinately to them.

"The wagoner said he would be back within the hour to take you to the Upper Pool where it has been arranged you can take the next barge to Rochester. They came in on the tide and with the water running fast will leave as soon as it ebbs. If you are not here, the wagon will go on without you", the costermonger said, with a hint of warning in his voice. "Time and tide *waiteth* for no one".

Sarah stared at the man not believing her plans to return home were at last coming to fruition.

It was then the panic started to race through her mind as she realised she had to go back to fetch Jabez and pack what little belongings they had and return before the wagon left. She decided to save time and regardless of the risk, she would go back to the loft through the airless and stinking alleyways which lay between Spital Square and Folgate Street, where menace was around every corner. She had already started running as she turned her head and shouted back to the costermonger, "Thank you sir, I'll be back with my son as soon as I can, thank you, thank you".

She was breathless with nerves as taunt as an archer's bow string when she reached Elder Street and racing up the wooden stairs she burst into the loft.

"Jabez, pack your books into a bundle". Her son looked at his breathless mother in surprise. "We're leaving now. Hurry, I'll gather up what belongings we will be able to carry.......we need to get to the market where the waggoner will take us to the barge which sails to Rochester".

Half running and half walking the pair, clutching their scant possessions tied up in the rags which were their bed-coverings, turned their backs on the weaver's loft for the last time and hurried up Rose Lane towards the market..

On reaching the market Sarah froze. Spuddy and his barrow were not there, neither was the *roots* wagon.

The other costers shrugged their shoulders when she asked if they knew where he was or if they had seen the waggoner. She turned round looking through the throngs of people in the hope she would see them but despite the babble of noise around them, it was he son's calm voice she heard.

"Mother", he said, "*tis* best now that we walk and trust we can reach the dock in time".

Jabez's bundle of books was heavy on his weak arms and his pace slowed until he eventually paused and rested it on the ground as they reached Gun Street, just up from where the old St Mary's hospital once stood.

"Hurry son, we must hurry", his mother chided when she realised he was not keeping up with her fast pace as they headed into Artillery Passage.

The words had hardly left Sarah's mouth when without warning, the sound of a huge crash echoed down the narrow alley, growing in volume as it rumbled towards them,. A thick gust of brick dust followed the noise covering the pair so much so, it left them coughing and choking.

Somewhere in the thick dust cloud ahead of them, Sarah could hear the shrill cries of terrified people.

Her nerves had been frayed and on edge ever since she had written to her father, in fact, ever since Claude had died and their very existence had become so precarious. Her heart pounded and without a thought other than they must keep hurrying, she picked up her bundle and as her legs tensed into action, she started to run through the dust in her urgent flight to the dock.

"**Come on Jabez**", she was shouting, "**hurry**".

Faces contorted with fear started appearing through the dust. "**What's happened**?" Sarah shouted hoarsely to a group of wide-eyed people who were running blindly towards them. The passage was barely the width of three people standing shoulder abreast and within seconds, mother and son were being roughly jostled aside by the panic-stricken mob.

"A shop sign has crashed down. It was whipped by the wind and brought down part of the dwelling it was hanging from", a dust-covered man croaked back as he pushed past her. "There are people trapped beneath it all".

She listened and through the dust she could hear people wailing.

Instinctively Sarah looked up either side of her at the huge, pendulous signs overhead, protruding over the shop fronts on large iron brackets and noticed the broken and crumbling brickwork they were all precariously fixed to.

"**Quickly**", she urged Jabez, as she grabbed his arm and started once again to push through the melee in the direction of the dock.

"**Can't go that** way", the dust-covered man shouted back above the noise, the passage is blocked. He saw the look of panic on Sarah's face and asked with concern as his voice drained back to a level of normality, "Where's *thee* heading for?"

"The Upper Pool", Sarah replied quickly.

The man thought for a moment before saying, "You'll have to turn around and go *whence thee* came, back down Brushfield Lane to Lamb Street and up Broadgate".

As they found themselves being swept backwards by the surge of people fleeing, Sarah cried out, "Oh no", distraught they would now surely miss the barge should anymore of the signs be blown down in the strong wind. A paralyzing fear began to spread through her body.

Sarah was shouting to Jabez, telling him not to let go of his bundle as they were swept along by the human tide, when she heard the voice of the dust-covered man shouting reassuringly, "You'll make good time that *aways*, perhaps twenty minutes or so".

The dirt roads around the dock were churned into a quagmire of mud and filth as Sarah and Jabez picked their way through, carefully keeping to the edge where the going was firmer. A high sided cart loaded high with bricks and sawn planks was being hauled away from the dock by two heavy drays hitched in line. Harnesses jangled as one of the overworked beasts snorted and stumbled as they were urged on by their heartless carter. Ahead of them solitary horses with sad looking faces pulled lighter loads of grain and vegetables brought in from the countryside. Other beasts, closer to the dock, nuzzled the ground as they waited patiently to be loaded whilst the full spectrum of London's humanity milled amongst them.

The rigging *atop* of ships towering main-masts came into view. Relieved to see them, Jabez paused to pat the huge head of an old mare, shuffling its heavy hooves as it waited anxiously to be rid of the day's work and looking forward to being bedded. Sarah had also relaxed a little on reaching the dock and she too stopped to stroke the beast's long mane.

The pair had still not fully caught their breath and their breathing was heavy as they reached the Upper Pool and stopped to ask a seafaring man if he knew where the *Mildred* was moored.

"You'll find her moored against the quay in Butlers wharf", the rosy-faced man told them, as he pointed the way and *bade* them good day.

They *proffered* their thanks for his help and picking up their bundles of belongings for what they hoped would be the final time, they breathed a mutual sigh of relief and made their way towards the wharf where they hoped they would find the barge.

Jabez relaxed and as he did so he became more aware of the sounds and smells of the river. In front of them was the old bridge of London, with the rows of tiled-roofed shops built above its many arches. On either side of it, hundreds of ships crowded around the labyrinth of wharfs which bordered the river whilst other vessels, with their sails furled, were moored and anchored across the river itself. In places they were so many a man could cross the wide strip of water without getting his feet wet merely by stepping from the deck of one vessel to that of another. Further down river, skiffs weaved in and out the lines of tall-masted sailing ships, each one bringing oysters and herrings from the estuary and the east coast. Amongst the jumble of craft and forest of bobbing masts, red-sailed barges and small lighters were bringing cargoes ashore from the larger ships moored further down-river. All around was a cacophony of noise. Seagulls screeched as they swooped and competed for any fish which was carelessly dropped on the granite cobbles and in the tangle of seafarers and lightermen, traders called out the wares, whilst in the narrow alleys bordering the docks, whores were screaming insults at each other whilst they too, tried to sell the wares they had to offer.

"We looking for the *Mildred*", Sarah anxiously reminded her son, as they walked quickly along the quay, peering at each of the names painted on the bows of the long line of moored barges.

Some of the barges were nearly eighty feet long, already loaded with cargo and preparing to get underway; their ruddy-red sails being hoisted by the two-man crew, heaving a cats-cradle of ropes threaded through huge wooden blocks and pulleys. In the meantime more slow moving barges with their main top sail cloths already lowered and rolled, were preparing to come alongside.

"*Where you for?*" the arrivals called lustily to the departing bargemen.

"*Where you from?*" they hollered back, after giving the name of the place *whence* they came.

Close by, large, fat-bellied pigs bound up in netting, squealed in frustration as they tried in vain to escape their tangled captivity whilst alongside, tightly packed into woven baskets, dozens of black and white chicken clucked contentedly, seemingly unaware of their eventual fate. The couple had just hastily passed a huge heap of horse dung piled up on the quayside, no doubt waiting to be transported to the farmers to spread on their fields. A myriad of flies were hovering in the clouds of steam rising from it, enjoying its warmth, when a sharp-eyed Jabez spotted the *Mildred* already loaded with its cargo and laying low in the water

.

"Mistress Sarah?" the bargemaster enquired, as she approached the barge's gang-plank. The man's hands were black with the dust of the coal stowed under the mainsail's mast in the deep hold. Sarah noticed his red, salt-engrained cheeks and immediately recognised he was a man of the sea. She wondered if he remembered bringing her here over twenty years past, probably not, she thought.

"*Yoom* two leaving London town then?", he said, looking at their bundles of belongings, more in conversation than enquiry. He did not ask the reason why nor did she give one. Starvation and death were common enough to warrant any explanation.

She reluctantly proffered her hand as the man extended his dirty fingers to help her aboard.

"Thank you, sir", she said, grateful they were now nearly on their way to Rochester, her soft voice being lost in the noise of mayhem that was going on around them.

Even if Joe Haycock wasn't there to meet them, she thought, it was only twenty-eight miles to Southwell from Rochester and they could easily walk that far. It would take two days if they slept under the hedges and foraged for food on the way. As the weight of her bundle pulled on her arm, she realised it would take them more like three days, if they were lucky.

In front of her, as she tried to keep her balance on the gently rocking vessel, a ferocious looking dog was stretched out on the deck. On seeing her, the *cur* quickly raised its head and started eying her suspiciously as she began to make her way towards the back of the flat-bottomed barge.

As the dog rolled its lip and snarled, the mate stopped pulling on one of the thick hoisting ropes and shouted, "He won't hurt *thee*, not unless you're a *night plunderer* or one of those thieving river pirates and you've crept onboard to steal the cargo". He was still chuckling as Sarah gave him and his dog an even wider berth.

"When we break out of the river and into the open sea there will be some heavy weather which no doubt will keep us two busy". The master nodded towards his mate. "If *thee needs* to take some shelter, you can go in the forecastle". Sarah gave him a quizzical look. The man laughed as he explained, "*Tis* the space below the deck up in the bow".

The westerly wind gusted filling the barge's huge main sail and as the vessel groaned, heavy with its cargo of coal, it left the murk of the dock and began to make its way downstream. Jabez, had spent all of his life in the weavers loft, much of it amongst his books and he watched almost spellbound at the sights crowded on the river bank as the lumbering craft was skilfully tacked into the wind, skewing its way slowly towards the sea. At first, the bank was lined with continuous walls of wharfs, each with a jetty protruding from it, but after the barge rounded a sweeping bend in the river at a place the mate called Rotherhithe, the buildings were gradually replaced with lush fields and grazing cattle.

The young man tipped his head back, soaking in the wind and spray, as the barge began to lurch and roll as it entered the vast, blue expanse of the estuary. He had never seen such a huge body of clear water in his life and delighted in the experience as the *Mildred* was navigated through the ominous looking shallows and sandbanks. It was as if the giant fingers of sand were trying in vain to grasp the vessel and turn it into one of the many wrecks which lay marooned there.

Large, seabirds carried by the off-shore breeze wheeled overhead in the bright blue sky, calling to each other with their plaintive cries that there were fish to be found in the boat's frothy wake.

Mother and son watched in wonder as the force of Mother Nature drove the barge through the under tows and into the open sea, cleaving the waves and cresting the breakers, its raw power seeping into every pore of their bodies.

With his weather-lined hands on the rudder, the master steered his craft skilfully past the Hoo peninsula and the ancient naval dockyard of Sheerness and into the calmer waters of the Medway. As the huge barge rode the tide and was edged past the turreted castle of Upnor, almost hidden by surrounding acres of broadleaf woodland, the two men readied themselves to lower the main mast to go under Rochester Bridge and to berth at the Blue Boar wharf, less than a mile down river.

The noise of the activity going on around the small dock began to drift on the lessening wind and the barge's triangular mizzen sail began to flap limply as the high buildings which were appearing on either bank of the river, shielded what little breeze there was to be had. The wooden vessel slowly nestled against the stone quay and as the tide ran out, it settled onto the thick mud of the river bed. Sarah and Jabez thanked the bargees for their kindness and as they disembarked from the barge's broad deck, a dozen or so lightermen were already beginning to off-load the cargo of coal from its open hold with shovels so large, that Sarah had never seen the likes before.

Joe Haycock was waiting and patiently sucking on his clay pipe as the pair, clutching their bundles of belongings and both mightily thankful at seeing the waiting man and his dray horse and farm cart.

"A good day to *yee* Mistress Sarah", the genial man said, as he touched the brim of his hat as a gesture of respect. She noticed he was wearing a sacking *surcoat* pulled over his smock, probably to prevent it getting too soiled, she thought. He looked every inch a brawny farm hand with a face weathered by a life working in all weathers, all seasons long. The man's Kentish drawl was broad and thick and in an instant it reminded Sarah of the place she was returning to.

"I'm heartily glad to see you Joe", Sarah replied before adding, "this is my son, Jabez"..

"Master Jabez", the cartman greeted, as he hoisted the bundles of belongings onto the heap of coal being loaded onto his cart. He cocked his head towards the black coal, *"Tis* for the fires of the gentry but if *yee* ask me, what's more important to me and my old nag, is that some of it will be burnt on Gideon Larkin's forge-bed", he explained, chuckling at his weak joke.

Sarah smiled and asked with concern in her voice, "Have you been waiting long, Joe?"

"My memory cannot recall the number of the years which have passed whilst I have waited, wondering if I would ever see you again, Mistress Sarah", Joe replied with his eyes fixed firmly on the road ahead and a croak in his voice.

Sarah reached across and took his hand, "Thank you Joe", she said simply.

"I arrived almost on the *call of ten o'clock*", he replied, almost ignoring what he had just said, whilst he glanced up at the clock face staring out from the tower of the imposing Norman cathedral which stood facing the ruins of an equally old castle, "so not too long, thank *yee*".

With the pair sitting alongside him, the softly-spoken cartman picked up the reins and gave his horse some slack. "Let's get on our way, old fellow", he called out and with the words of command, the horse began to start off with a *slow will*. Joe gave the reins a final flick and Sarah felt the horse ease itself into its harness, as her homeward journey to Southwell began.

"We'll make our way along the old Dover road which will take us across the top of the Downs, it's *aways* to go, it is, and then we'll spur off and go down the lane into the village, shouldn't be too muddy going that way, bumpy mind you", Joe rambled on, more to confirm the route he intended to take to himself, rather than for the benefit of his passengers. The tone of his voice changed as he said grimly with his eyes cast down, "I hear you are going to live in the old Looking Hut".

Sarah remained silent, she was already worrying what they would find when they got there and how in God's name were they going to survive.

The road quickly became narrow with deep water-filled hollows as the small town of Rochester was left behind. Nor did it get any better as they began to pass through the small hamlets and villages along the way.

"With some luck, we won't be meeting too many drovers with their herds of beasts to slow us down too much", Joe mumbled, as his cart bounced along.

As Sarah nodded, she realised how hungry she felt. It had been over six hours since they had last eaten.

Passing coaching inns and a scattering of humble dwellings, some with their straw thatch falling in great lumps from the roofs, the journey to Southwell continued without mishap, until there was a sickening jolt as one of the carts' wheels slipped into a deep unseen rut. Jabez looked at his mother as the load of coal shifted beneath the wooden seat they were perched on.

Joe came to life. "**Go on boy**", he shouted, as he flicked hard on the reins urging his nag to keep pulling, *lest* they come to a halt and sink deeper into the mud.

Sarah smiled knowingly at her concerned looking son as the horse gradually pulled the cart's wheel out of the deep gully and moved slowly on.

"*Tis* the narrow carriage wheels of the gentry which *cut* the road", the carter observed, "that and the Canterbury coach that's ploughing the furrows".

Before either Sarah or Jabez could respond, Joe continued to give his opinion on the state of the road. "Those things and the bloody landowners, begging your pardon Mistress Sarah, but *them* buggers are not doing what the law requires of them".

It was Jabez's head which nodded agreement to what the man had just said. He had enough knowledge of the law to know that the landowners were required to supply a cart, horses, tools and two men for six days each year to work on the roads, but few of them did.

"There Mistress Sarah", the carter said, as he took her hand and helped her down from the seat on the high-sided cart.

"I've no *doubting* you know the way now. Along the track, then up towards Fairfoin Rowens", he added, before saying in a lowered voice, "I hope *thee* can make yourselves comfortable there".

Sarah thanked him and as she hoisted the heavy bundle of belongings onto her shoulder, Joe Haycock reached under his seat and gave her a small sacking bag, "I've put a few *tatters* and *nips* in there, I'm sure your father won't mind".

Their eyes met. They both knew just how much George Bentley would mind and if he ever found out. Joe would be tied to the whipping post and lashed twenty times with an ox whip, his family turned from their humble cottage and he would never find work in the locality again.

They *bade* their farewells to the kind man and Sarah and Jabez began to push their way through the overgrown track. It was difficult going. The nettles and cow parsley had grown twice to their normal height as they fought for what little light that managed to filter through the thick canopy of the overhead trees.

Jabez was exhausted and slowed with the intention to rest his increasingly heavy bundle on the ground.

"Just a little further", Sarah urged gently as Jabez stumbled, "just a few hundred paces or so". She could see his weariness as she advised, "If you must put your bundle down, rest it on your shoes, *lest* your books get wet in the mud…. not forgetting they are wrapped with our bed coverings", she added as an afterthought.

Her heart sank as the hut from her childhood memories came into view. "Oh", she cried out in the shock of seeing its dilapidated state which was far worse than she had ever imagined. She clutched her shawl around her and took a long breath as they waded through the long grass and prepared themselves to enter the open doorway.

The light of the day was beginning to leave the sky as she glanced up at the jumble of sticks and twigs poking out of the short brick stack protruding from one end of the hut and as her eyes faded with disappointment, she sighed "the jackdaws have built their nest in the chimney, if it's blocked we won't be able to light a fire tonight".

One corner of the roof had fallen in leaving the hut open to the elements and in places the daub had fallen off and was laying heaped at the base of the hut's wattle sides.

Neither mother nor son said a word as they carefully avoided stepping on the door which had parted from its frame years ago and lay on the ground, half buried in a tangle of grass and thorny brambles.

Fearful of what they would find, Sarah entered the forlorn-looking hut, her face taunt with anxiety. She gasped in fright as a flurry of glossy-coated starlings flew off in indignation as the unwelcome strangers disturbed them from their nightly roosting place. As she looked down at her feet, she could not help noticing that scattered amongst the sheep's dung littering the mud floor, was also many months-worth of droppings the birds had left behind..

"Well Jabez", she said as she looked around, "it may not be much but it is going to be our home. We need to sleep the best we can in here tonight and then tomorrow, we'll decide what is to be done".

Jabez just stood in the open doorway, not sure what to say and even less, what to do. Strands of ivy had crept from the rich, damp earth and twisted their way through the wattle nearly reaching the sod roof where they could re-root and renew their vigour. Green mould covered the remaining daub like a primeval wall covering. He turned and watched in a mixture of awe and amazement as his mother dropped her bundle of belongings and headed briskly towards the surrounding woods.

"It will be dark soon so we need to work quickly", Sarah said as she once more pulled her woollen shawl round her shoulders and looking at Jabez, said with a voice which was laced heavy with determination, "I'm going to break off some branches to sweep out what muck I can. You can find some rotted boughs that have fallen from the larger trees and drag them back for a fire"

It was the silence that struck Sarah. Other than the wind blowing through the leaves, the only sound that pierced the tranquilly were the distant bleats of the sheep up in Fairforn Rowens and the shrill calls of a pair of *hoot* owls exchanging greetings. Thanks be to God, she thought, that they had left the stink and noise of London far behind them.

With her resolve strengthened, Sarah knelt on the newly swept floor and opened up their bundles, quickly searching for her tinder box, iron and flint. Glancing round the gloomy hut, she began to gather together the pile of dry twigs which had fallen down the chimney from the jackdaws' nests and had collected in the fire's blackened hearth.

Holding the sharp flint tightly in her hand, she struck it sharply on the iron bar, not once but again and again until a spark fell onto the brittle-dry tinder stored in the small box. Nothing! She tried again and undeterred she kept trying until a stronger spark fell and ignited the moss tinder. Carefully, she scooped out a small clump of moss where the mere hint of a flame was hiding and quickly placed it into the middle of the small pile of twigs. Jabez watched as his mother knelt down and with her mouth close to the glowing tinder, she softly blew on it until a small flame burst into life. She waited a few moments until, with her hands cupped, she lifted the small pile of burning twigs onto the hearth and gradually nurtured it into a growing fire by adding larger sticks.

"Jabez", she chided, "Poke the end of the long boughs you've collected into the flames and as they burn away we'll keep pushing them into the fire until they are all burnt away".

With the night descending, the derelict hut begun to take on a rosy glow as the reflection from the flames of the fire danced around its daub--clad walls.

With the rest of her belongings unpacked, Sarah was spreading some of their bed covers on the floor when her son returned carrying a clutch of rusty objects which he had found in a bed of nettles outside.

"Mother, he gushed, "I have found some discarded trivets and some other things but I don't know what that they are for?"

A broad smile spread across Sarah's face. "Jabez", she beamed, "We can make good use of the trivets to stand our cooking pots on and the other things are rush nips. They are used to grip rush lights which we will be able to make once we find the pond where the bull-rushes grow".

She noticed the quizzical expression on her son's face and explained, "We won't be able to afford candles now, not even the cheapest tallow ones but rush lamps will only cost a farthing each for the mutton fat. They burn dirty and don't last long, about thirty minutes or so, but they will give us all the light we need, especially as the winter nights draw in. They will even give enough light to enable you to read your books", she added with a grin.

"Tell me about the old shepherd who lived here", Jabez said as he huddled with his mother enjoying the growing warmth of the fire.

"His name was Gabriel Taylor", Sarah reminded her son, as her childhood memories were awaked and seeped back into her mind.

"He was a kind man with a bushy white beard and bright blue eyes. I never saw him without his black felt hat with its narrow brim pulled down on his head and his heavy woollen smock-coat which reached below his calf. It had a wide, flat collar which went right round the smock, so when the front became soiled, he could turn it round, so the front became the back and for him, his smock looked clean again".

The pale looking young man laughed whilst his mother kicked the end of the bough deeper into the fire with the side of her foot.

"The sleeves of his smock were folded into tubes and the smocking across his chest had been embroidered in a honey comb pattern whilst on the other side it had been stitched to look like rows of sheep and shepherds crooks. He called that his Sunday side", Sarah said with a smile.

"I think we should retire now, there is much for us to do tomorrow", she concluded softly.

"No please mother", Jabez urged, "just finish telling me about Gabriel".

Sarah pushed another one of the boughs into the bright flames before she continued. "He had a rough-coated dog he called Thomas. It was brindled in colour with shaggy hair to withstand the violence of the frosts and the cruel winter winds blowing from the Downs. It also had a look about it that he said was more frightful to the sheep than to humans. At night, the dog would lie down by the fold and guard the sheep till morning. If the sheep were *pent up* in a narrow place, Thomas would run over their backs to turn them. The dog was so *well broke*, he would go before the flock, round it, side it or keep behind it whether this was nearer or further off and with just one word of command from Gabriel, the dog would keep them from straying too far about".

"He must have been a clever hound", the young man murmured, aware that the only dogs he had seen in London were those in the baiting rings and the wild dogs which roamed the streets fighting each other for any rotting flesh they *happened* upon; dogs which were fierce and ugly, with great jowls, snarling and slavering and showing the reds of their eyes. Dogs which would never go tamely to a man's hand. He had been listening intently and looked towards his mother, hoping he had not interrupted her thoughts.

"He was", Sarah continued, "When the sheep were ready to be driven to the fold, the dog would fetch the stragglers together from *near a mile distance* and then drive them *fast* or *leisurely* as the old shepherd commanded. If *leisurely*, the dog would keep behind them and not bark but if *fast was needed*, the dog would bark to *hasten* them. Then when the sheep got to the hurdle gate of the field they were to be *fold in*, he would go before and stop them till Gabriel let the flock in".

Almost absentmindedly Sarah said, "Gabriel would never feed meat to his dog, "*Tis* for us humans" he would say. "He only ever fed it with *pollard*, she explained.

She saw the frown on her son's face and realised, being brought up in London, he did not know what *pollard* was.

"Oh'" she explained, "it's what is left over from the wheat grains after the miller has ground them into flour".

Jabez smiled, it was another thing he had learnt about country ways.

"In the winter, when the snow had drifted deep on the Downs, Thomas could smell any sheep that had the misfortune to be *overblown* by the snow and buried even to a depth of several feet". Sarah looked across at her son and saw he was asleep.

As she prodded the last of the boughs into the fire, she wondered what had happened to Gabriel, did he die, she thought or was he cast out by her father when he was no longer able to work?.

There was a sad look on her face and a single tear started running down her cheek as she thought about the old shepherd, then like her son, she closed her eyes and fell fast asleep.

It was the harsh rasping call of the blackbird which woke Sarah as the sound of the dawn chorus broke out around her. She lay there and listened for the *spotted-bellied throsle* to follow it and sing its tune *thrice* over. Next would come the wistful warbling of the *redbreast* and then, the fast, restless trill of *jenny wren*. As she listened, other birds joined in the orchestra of song and her thoughts once again turned to Gabriel and a little rhyme he would recite-

"The redbreast and the jenny wren

Are God's cock and pretty hen"

Through the hole in the roof she could see a fluffy white cloud gliding across the early pale sky and as it skidded by, it almost hid the fading moon behind it and then, like the tousle- haired woman, the sun woke up from its night's slumber and began to emerge through the hazy sky.

During the night the reek of the bird's droppings and the sheep dung had been replaced by the smell of damp earth and wood smoke and Sarah sighed with relief as she noticed a few embers were still glowing red, almost hidden amongst the grey ash on the hearth, knowing she would not have to use her box of tinder again.

She rose from the floor and leaving her son fast asleep, she went to her belongings and taking the largest cooking pot with her she headed off towards the chalk stream. With the pot filled, Sarah's eyes began to search the hedgerow for the pointed leaves of the sorrel and the purple flower stems of wild sage which she could use to add some flavour to the potatoes and turnips Joe Haycock had given her.

The joy of the early morning began to drain from her face as she realised the vegetables and the dried bread she had brought with them would last for a few more days, if they were careful, but then what?

She knew if they were to qualify for any charitable relief in the village, she would first have to prove to the overseer they had the right of settlement. That shouldn't be a problem, she thought. After all, she was born in the village and she had the letter from her father saying they could live in …. It was then to her horror she remembered she had burnt it. She understood the right of settlement was to stop every vagrant in the district coming to the village to get charity and was confident, if need be, the Parson would help her as the church warden also acted as the overseer. Once the man had accepted they had the *right of settlement*, he would then assess how much relief he would hand over. Hopefully, he would decide to provide i*n-kind* relief and provide them with some money and fuel and perhaps some clothing and a few loaves from time to time. Thankfully, they had no need for *outdoor* relief as they had the Looking Hut to live in and would not be sent to the poor house.

"That's for another day", she mused to herself, as she walked back to the hut enjoying the bird song which filled the early morning air.

The next few days, mother and son repaired the hut's roof with hazel *wands* which they criss-crossed to form wattles before covering the framework with brushwood broken from a stand of nearby birch trees.

Sarah took Jabez to the stream and showed him how to make the *puddle-clay* they would use for the final repairs to the roof and to line the holes in the wattle walls where the daub had dropped off.

Jabez, with his small frame and weak arms, did what he could to help his mother and was increasingly amazed at her knowledge as she turned the Looking Hut into their home. His mother had become a country woman again. The *potage* of herbs they were now dependant on did not lessen the hunger pains they felt as they searched amongst the thickets and brambles for the nests of the song birds in the hope of finding some of their eggs to eat.

Suddenly Sarah held her hand up and indicated to Jabez to keep still as she looked skywards. Soaring effortlessly above them with its broad, rounded wings outstretched was a buzzard. As they watched, the bird hung almost motionless in the air with its large yellow eyes scanning the ground below. Without warning, with its wings half-folded, the bird suddenly swooped down onto some open grassland beyond them.

"Wait and keep still", Sarah whispered urgently.

After some minutes she suddenly took off through the undergrowth like a hunted beast towards the spot where the bird had landed with Jabez close on her heels. In front of them, the buzzard, with its wings *mantling* its meal from the marauding crows circling overhead, was gripping a dead rabbit in its sharp talons and beginning to rip off the animal's skin and fur with its curved beak.

"**Rah, Rah**", Sarah shouted, as she broke cover and suddenly rushed towards the surprised bird.

With a couple of flaps of its powerful wings, the huge bird effortlessly took to the air leaving its meal behind. A broad grin spread across Sarah's face as she picked up the rabbit by its hind legs and held it aloft in triumph.

"At first I was afraid the *hawk* had just found a lark's nest", Sarah confided, "but tonight we can now eat like a king and queen with this in our cooking pot".

Jabez was arranging his precious books on an old apple box which he had found abandoned in the woods and his mother had finished sweeping the mud floor of the hut which had now dried into a hard crust, firm and dry to their feet, when she heard them. The thin ringing of church bells had begun to drift up from the village. As Sarah listened, their sound became louder, then softer, before becoming louder again as the indecisive wind kept changing its mind.

A look of surprise was on Sarah's face as she called out to her son, "Jabez, it must be Sunday. Quickly, we must go the church in the village".

He raised an eyebrow and looked at her quizzically. It was the church where she had probably been baptised but it did not preach the faith of the Huguenots which his forebears had died for and had held dear to them for generations.

"I know what you're your thinking", she replied, as she gently took the book he was holding and placed it carefully on the makeshift shelf before saying softly. "You have read the works of Wesley and Owen and you know both churches follow the religion of the Protestant faith and reject the Roman law of the Catholics. I'm sure we can continue to praise the Lord in our own way without distinction or concern"

Jabez smiled at his mother's words of wisdom as they left the hut together and headed towards the lane.

Mattins had begun as the pair walked through the centuries old lych gate, between the avenue of knarled and twisted yew trees and up the winding flag-stone path towards the church. Reaching its blackened oak door, decorated top and bottom with ornate iron strap hinges, Sarah turned the heavy handle and with Jabez in her wake, cautiously crept inside.

With their heads bowed, they deliberately made for the row of pews at the back of the nave which were empty of the God fearing folk of the village. The Parson was standing in the carved stone pulpit delivering his sermon with the passion he had developed over the many years and the many Sundays he had stood there, when he saw the door slowly open and the latecomers creep into his church. He paused whilst they took their seats causing Sarah to look up with unexpected silence. With a deeply furrowed brow, Parson Lamb peered over the top of his wire-rimmed spectacles to indicate his displeasure at those who showed such little respect to the house of God when, despite her destitute appearance and the many years which had passed, his look softened as he recognised the woman.

With the service over, Sarah placed her arm across Jabez's waist to restrain him from leaving his seat whilst she stared blankly at the cold slabs on the floor and waited for the church to empty of its congregation. She did not wish to be acknowledged by any of the villagers, given her circumstances, but particularly, not having to cast her eyes on her father, should he have been sat in his box pew in front of the pulpit.

"My dear child", the Reverend Lamb held out his hands ready to take Sarah's mud-stained hands into his own as she was about to hurry away from the church.

He gripped them and held onto them tightly, not wishing to let them go.

"God be praised, you have returned safely to us and with such a handsome son at your side", he beamed. His *tidings* were joyful and his rich voice held all the passion of one of his fiery sermons.

"Good day to you sir", Sarah replied politely, "it is my pleasure to see you also".

"*How goes it with you, my child?*", there was now a growing hint of concern showing in the Parson's voice as he looked at her thin woollen shawl and ragged skirt.

He studied her for a few moments but he did not see the dirty and dishevelled woman standing in front of him holding the pitiful thin hand of her son. Instead he was seeing a sixteen year old girl. That was her age when he took charge of the parish and on his arrival everybody told him about Sarah Bentley. He was seeing her as a young, happy blue-eyed girl with hair the colour of ripe flax as it fell to the sickle. He could see a girl, full of life, who used to run down the village street chasing an iron hoop, laughing as she beat it with a small stick, urging it to roll faster. He saw her grow into a beautiful young woman who would take a basket of eggs and freshly baked bread to the old and infirm. Someone who sat night after night holding Mother Taylor's wrinkled hand and wetting her dry lips with elderberry wine as the poor woman awaited her Maker's call.

He saw the Sarah he knew. Somebody, who after her mother's untimely death was worked from dawn to dusk with sadness in her eyes and without a smile on her pale face. Somebody, who had to run away to London to escape from her cruel and uncaring father.

"It goes well, thank you sir", Sarah answered, breaking the cleric's memories, "my father has kindly allowed us the use of the Looking Hut and we are reasonably comfortable there".

Parson Lamb's eyes narrowed and he decided to say nothing in reply. He unbuttoned the bottom half of his long black coat and put his hand in to the pocket of his breeches to retrieve his 'kerchief on which he loudly blew his nose.

"Sarah, my dear Sarah", he said, as once again he caught her hands and held them towards him.

She felt something being pressed into them.

"Good day to you both. When you have need, you must call on me", the clergyman said kindly and with a slight flourish of his hand and a touch of his three-cornered hat, he departed, limping down the flagstone path, through the lych gate and on towards the parsonage.

Sarah looked into her open hand and gasped in astonishment at the two golden guinea pieces lying there.

As the days went by, a confidence returned to her, one which she had lost and thought would never return. The Looking Hut had become their home. Their right of settlement in Southwell had been accepted and the charitable relief they were receiving was sufficient to meet their needs and Jabez was reading classical books again, some of which were thicker than a man's fist, as he delved amongst books he had been given access to at the parsonage. He had never seen such a treasure trove before. There were books everywhere, on the floor, on tables, in neat rows on shelves and stacked in wobbly piles against the walls. All full of knowledge which he consumed with the appetite of a starving man.

"Listen Jabez", his mother said, as she held her ear to the breeze, *"tis a lark pouring out its joyous melody"*.

He listened and bent his head to the sky in the hope of seeing the ascending bird, before saying with a smile on his face, "Hark! Hark! The lark at Heaven's gate sings".

Sarah's brow furrowed and looked at him quizzically.

"*Tis* from Shakespeare", he replied, "William Shakespeare".

She smiled proudly at her son's knowledge.

When Jabez was at the parsonage, Sarah wandered for hours across the chalk grassland of the Downs, sometimes, whilst sitting in quiet solitude, she would think about the happy years she had spent with Claude and how much she missed him. On other days, when her melancholy lifted, she walked carefree, delighting in everything she saw around her.

It was the best time of the year for the pond when the sun shone on its blue water and the song of the robins and warblers rang out from the surrounding trees, thick in their summer greens. Dragon-flies, big and small, skirted the surface of the water, their vibrant colours of kingfisher blues and ruby reds flashing in the sunlight like precious jewels. Around the edge of the pond stood tall bulrushes with stout plush brown heads looking like short velvet coats and in the shallows, rings of pink and white lilies were blooming, their big, bright green leaves lying calm on the crystal clear water.

Sarah and Jabez were in no particular hurry after their walk to the pond at the top of the Downs but with Sarah's urging, they eventually got to work and began to cut a bundle of the thick-stemmed rushes they had come for. Once done and with the rushes soaking in the margins of the spring- fed water, they sat on the bank and enjoyed a late *break fast* of bread and cheese, enjoying the warm breeze and listening to the sound of the crickets serenading each other amorously in the long, sweet- smelling grass.

"We'll leave them to drain for a while and enjoy our food", Sarah explained to her son, as they pulled the rushes from the water and laid them on the bank, "then we can peel off the outer skins to reveal their pithy centres, before we take them home".

Several days passed before the rushes were dry enough to turn into lamps. Jabez watched his mother as she began to dip the rushes, a dozen at a time, in the grease pan full of the melted mutton fat which warmed by the fire.

That evening after the fat had set hard, Sarah pinched the stem of a rush in each of the nips Jabez had found in the nettle bed and lit them. At first, there was a small, uncomfortable looking flame which Sarah feared would vanish in smoke lest the slightest draught caught it, but as the flame took hold and the light coming from the rush lamps grew in intensity, she looked towards Jabez and saw he was already reading a book.

5

Eternity's Box

The old woman was in despair as she looked around at the squalor in her master's bed chamber. Apart from the past few days when she had been so busy and hadn't had the time to notice too much, she hadn't entered the man's room for the best part of twenty years. Other people would be coming into his bed chamber now to see him and what would they think? She shook her head slightly and a shudder went down her spine at the thought of what the people in the village would say, when they were told what had been seen. They would think she was slovenly, a sloth who pocketed the pittance he gave her and had neglected her duties in return. It is not true, she thought sadly but who would believe her when they looked at the room. She felt panic rising in her throat.

The dawn had broken some hours past but the room was still dark and gloomy. Although the windows were small, whatever light was coming in was shrouded by the dust-covered cobwebs which covered them. Wisps of sheep's wool were poking out of the *flock bed* on which the man lay and its linen cover had not been washed for years and was holed and stained. The covers for the bedstead lay in a heap on the floor were little more than a pile of filthy rags. The flustered woman looked at them in disgust and thought how fortunate it was that she had the presence of mind to remove them from the bed before she had washed him. She looked at the drapes hanging around the *goodly-sized* oak bedframe and decided they too could join the covers on the floor. It was then the woman made the decision she would try to tidy the room before she left the farmhouse. Nobody would blame her for delaying what she had to do. Her nose wrinkled in disgust at the empty tankards and wine bottles scattered thoughtlessly on the mud-caked floor as she began to pick her way through them and down the rickety stairs to find a besom and shovel.

She had always done her best to keep the farmhouse clean and respectable but he hadn't wanted it, indeed, he would often vent his anger on her whenever she had tried. Every day she had cooked his meals and not once had she complained, not even on the many occasions when he preferred drinking to eating and had pushed his pewter platter away uttering the most unseemly oaths. He could be difficult, everybody knew that and when he had been in one of his moods, she had even feared for her own safety.

If only the mistress hadn't died things would have been different, she thought, as she closed the door behind her and made her way down the lane towards the village. She wrapped her loosely woven shawl tightly around her and hoped she wouldn't meet anybody on her short journey but wondered whether she should stop at her brother's cottage to tell him the news. She decided she wouldn't as she hurried on her way. She could now hear the early morning blows of the blacksmith's hammer ringing out from the smithy and could smell his wife's bread baking in the forge's oven. Blacksmiths always kept hot embers smouldering throughout the night on their forge's hearth and thanks to their family's foresight, the heat from the embers was sufficient to bake the Larkin's bread each morning in the oven their forebears had built into the side of the forge, many years before.

Hannah Brown was busying herself in the parsonage's kitchen when she heard Mistress Sage's urgent knocking on the oak door.

"I need to speak to the Parson", the breathless woman said as the door was opened. Hannah could see the distress on her face as she ushered the flustered woman into the hall and invited her to be seated on one of the upholstered chairs whilst she fetched the Parson.

Maud Sage sat nervously in the hall, wringing her hands and staring aimlessly at the cracks which criss-crossed the flagstone floor whilst she waited for the Parson to appear.

It was some time later when the bewigged clergyman entered the hall, resplendent in his clerical attire, save his *tricorn* hat, and looking at the diminutive woman, he bid curtly, "Good day to you, Mistress Sage". He was feeling particularly irritable at being disturbed at this time in the morning, he hadn't yet *broken his fast* but his mood softened slightly when he saw how upset the woman was about some matter he had yet to determine.

Maud Sage looked up, wide-eyed like a trapped doe and in her distress burst out without acknowledging the cleric, "My master has died, sir."

"Farmer Bentley is dead".

Tobias Lamb looked blankly at the woman, annoyed at what she had just said.

Farmer Bentley indeed, the clergyman thought indignantly. Some farmer! The man didn't know the meaning of the word. His sheep grazing up in Fairfoins Rowen were unshorn, their fleeces matted and fouled. Their lambs, lame with their feet untrimmed. Ten acres of potatoes and turnips with weeds as high as a man's waist at Two Wrothams and the tangled apple orchards at Trottenfield, four hundred hills of hops un-trained, fields unploughed and……….Tobias Lamb's thoughts were interrupted by Mistress Sage, "The master was *seized by an infliction* for two days past and last evening he had a fit and was dead by six in the morning". Her body was trembling and she had difficulty in keeping her hands still.

"Was he attended to by a physician?" enquired the Parson.

The woman stared at him and wringed her hands seemingly in a futile attempt to try to keep them still.

"No sir, just me. He would never pay sir….never pay", the shocked woman said in a shaking voice. "I've washed him, he would have wanted that and I've laid him out, so he's ready", she added.

"Quite so", the Parson responded, still thinking about the uncared farm.

"There is another thing sir". The farmer's housekeeper was finding it difficult to find the right words. She wrapped her shawl around her as if she was trying to make her true self invisible and bit her lip. She didn't want to say the words she was about to utter but knew they had to be said. Respect for the dead saw to that.

"Yes", the clergyman prompted the woman impatiently.

"Sir, my master directed that he wanted to be buried using the *communal coffin*", she blurted out.

"**The *communal coffin***", Parson Lamb spluttered. He could not believe his ears and raised his eyebrows disapprovingly. "He's not a pauper", he said, his indignation growing by the minute.

"No sir", Mistress Sage agreed, "but that's what he said. On his death bed, almost with his last breath, he said, tell the Parson that I want the communal coffin".

"He is", Tobias Lamb paused to correct himself, "he was a man of considerable wealth and as such, was not entitled to ask for the use of the *communal coffin*".

"Begging your pardon sir, but those were his wishes,", the woman whispered. "He said tell the Parson I want the *communal coffin*.

Maud Sage was a good woman and she sat with hooded eyes, embarrassed with what she had just said and sat in silence as the clergyman walked to the window, deep in thought as he surveyed his garden.

The *communal coffin* was kept for the poor and only the poor. Many a time he would waive his fee and say a few words to the bereaved at the graveside as the body was lifted out of the coffin and lowered into the grave.

He slid his finger under his curled wig and scratched his head. The so-called farmer was certainly mean. He was the kind of man who would *skin a flint* if he thought it would save him a penny but he was not a pauper and not entitled to such charity. He was a man who had a reputation as someone who drove his workmen relentlessly but drove his financial dealings even harder.

The cleric's thoughts turned to Sarah and Jabez and his anger rose as he remembered that George Bentley could not even extend any charity to his own kith and kin

Mistress Sage waited patiently as the minutes ticked by from the tall clock down the passageway.

Eventually the Parson let out a grunt of satisfaction at his decision. He would respect the farmer's dying wish to be buried in the *communal coffin* but on this occasion a fee, a substantial fee will be charged for the use of it which would come from the man's estate. There would also be a burial fee and a fee for the graveside sermon. Finally a parish charge of one pound would also be added to the overall amount to be charged. The woman could not see the satisfied smile which had spread across his face.

"*Ah*", he said quietly to himself, "I nearly forgot the quarterly rent that he still owes for the box pew in the church".

A most satisfactory outcome he thought, as he turned to the diminutive woman and informed her that the funeral would be held on the following day.

"It will be a simple service at the graveside with no fuss", he added firmly, as the woman crept out of the parsonage, the final task for her master completed.

The day brought with it the threat of rain as the great mountains of clouds which were piled up over the top of the Downs started dying, before reforming into different, darker shapes as they drifted over the village.

Sarah, alerted by the Parson's visit to her the previous afternoon, stood with Jabez some way from the freshly dug grave. She had agonised whether it was the right thing to do but despite everything that had happened, she was his daughter and he was her father.

The first heavy drops of rain began to fall as four farm men shuffled up the steep lane towards Dunn Farm with the *communal coffin* hoisted on their broad shoulders. They walked past the open farm gate, held fast in the mud as it drooped from its rotted post, and then through the farmyard which was surrounded on three sides by dilapidated barns and animal pens. Somewhere over the hill, animals were bleating to each other. Feather-pecked chicken and yellow-footed ducks scurried from under the men's feet as they splashed through the puddles and hurried towards the uninviting farm house, shrouded in a sickly gloom.

The mournful sound of the death knell being tolled on the church bell could be heard in the distance.

The bedraggled men, with the rain dripping off their sodden coats, walked through the door, held open for them by a white-faced Mrs Sage, without even bothering to scrape the mud off their boots on the foot-scraper outside the door. They would show the dead man the same respect he had shown them at the Michaelmas Hiring Fair when, along with all the other men and women who were seeking employment, they stood on the platform in their Sunday best, waiting to be hired. Each person carried the sign of their trade. A cook had a big wooden spoon and dairymaids held three-legged milking stools aloft. Men who could drive teams of horses or oxen carried whips, gardeners a spade. Shepherds had a crook or a tuft of sheep's wool half pushed in their pockets, whilst cowmen had wisps of straw tucked in their hat bands and mixed amongst the line of men and women were carters carrying short whips whilst others held broad-bladed Kent axes and billhooks demonstrating they could lay and trim a hedge.

George Bentley had not been interested in the various trappings being displayed; he was only there for one purpose and that was to hire men at the lowest possible rate.

The men shouldering the coffin remembered the contemptuous and withering look he gave them as he judged their strength and fitness.

They remembered their empty bellies and their desperation when they reluctantly had to accept the pittance he said he would pay them.

They remembered the shame they felt when he asked them if they had any *heavy baggage* and when they had answered ,"No", having to deny the existence of their wives and children.

They remembered how the man, who never had a thought of anyone other than himself, had scowled when he sealed the contract by pushing a meagre shilling into their palms, telling them that now it was legal and binding, they would work for him for a year, a full year, he had said.

They remembered how the sour-faced man's *countenance* changed when he reminded them he would pay their wages at the year end and if there was no work during that time, they could expect no pay.

They finally remembered how the old lecher had come to the Fair not for a cook or a dairymaid but how he had lingered, leering at the young girls, should it come into his mind that he wanted some young *frippet* to share his bed.

Two of the men entered the bed chamber and approached the corpse. What little warmth George Bentley had whilst he was alive had drained from his body. He was laying on his back, stiff, his flesh a ghostly pale and his lips bluish in colour. The weather-beaten skin on his face retained a fine meshwork of red threads and the dirt of the farm, remained stubbornly trapped under his finger nails.

The housekeeper had laid him out the best she could. She had closed his eyes before binding his feet together with a linen strip and folding his arms over his chest.

With barely a glance, the men roughly wrapped a winding sheet round the naked body before laying it onto the bare elm planks of the eternity box. There was to be no fabric lining or covering as the bare communal coffin was bumped and scraped down the stairway and lugged across the farmyard and jolted down the rutted lane into the graveyard.

The small flock of sheep, more used to the coarse down-land turf, were silently grazing amongst the graves as the Parson preached his short sermon to hasten the spirit of the dead man on its way and with the rain falling heavily, the farm labourers lifted the body from the coffin and on bended knees, lowered it, without too much care and consideration, into the depths of the grave.

"I am the resurrection and the life", the Parson's voice rang out as George Bentley's body was laid to rest with all his mortal sins upon him.

Sarah stared blindly as the remains of her father came to rest amongst the puddles which had collected in the bottom of the grave. The winding cloth had not been fastened round the body properly and a length of it draped down the side of the grave. She was thinking of the time she had last seen him and what he had shouted as she had walked down the lane. The trickles of water coursing down her pale cheeks were not tears of grief as she stood motionless in the driving rain with her son, George Bentley's only grandson. As the men bent their backs and shovelled the sloppy pile of mud onto her father's body, the length of white cloth finally relented and fell into the grave alongside him.

She watched as the grave was filled and realised there would be no commemorative marker for this particular grave, just a few well-fed sheep walking over it until nature took its course and the bare earth became grazing for them.

Sarah and Jabez were bidding their goodbyes to the Parson and a tearful Mrs Sage when the hollow clop of horses' hooves could be heard thundering along the old drover's road and heading towards the church. The Parson listened and heard the coarse voices of the riders as they dismounted and the sound of a horse whinnying. They only whinny when they have been tethered with the reins too short, he thought knowledgeably, as it was followed by that of another horse pawing the ground with its front hoof.

Percival Lightfoot strode up to the small group at the graveside waving a rolled document in his hand and saying in a coarse and uncultured voice, "I have it here Parson. I have Bentley's last Will and Testament". He carried the arrogance of somebody who had rank and power, someone who was used to getting his own way without exception.

Sarah immediately recognised the man. He farmed a large area of land to the east of her father's farm and had a reputation as a bully and as someone to be avoided. He would whip anyone, man, woman or child who was caught gathering fruit in the hedgerows which criss-crossed his land or picking up firewood. He was larger than she remembered but his aggressive air was the same. His mud-soiled coat flapped open and his corpulent and probably ale-filled belly protruded past the missing buttons of his waistcoat, spilling over the top of his mole-skin breeches.

The man appeared to be just as uncouth and vulgar as he was when Sarah last saw him, over twenty years ago and her stomach churned at the sight of seeing him again.

By his side was his son, tall and muscled like his father. Sarah judged the youth to be around Jabez's age, he was certainly taller and much more powerfully built but in truth, he was three years younger than her son.

Lurking behind Percival Lightfoote, was a seedy-looking and poorly dressed young male, about the same age as the man's son, but who had a spayed left foot.

"You know my son Abel and young Henry Prinn", he said addressing the clergyman, whist ignoring Sarah and Jabez . Almost reluctantly, he nodded his head to acknowledge Mrs Sage's presence.

Indeed I do know them, Tobias Lamb thought. Indeed I do.

The Will *tis* here to be read by *thee* Parson", the pigheaded man continued in a loud voice, "let's get the matter concluded and we can be on our way".

"I will do no such thing", the cleric said firmly, with a look of distaste spreading swiftly across his face, "If *thee* do not wish to show respect to the body lying there with the soil still laying fresh on the grave, you will *abide* to the sanctity of this hallowed ground".

Percival Lightfoote's face was as red as a beet as he started to shout at the cleric, "Blood and thunder, Parson I have not got the time to waste waiting here ".

The cleric turned his back on the man and kerbing his anger, said curtly, "Nor me Mr Lightfoote. Tomorrow, on the strike of eleven o'clock at the parsonage, is when I will read the Will. Good day to you".

As they *gallied* away, Lightfoote turned to his son and said, "Damm that *fratchety pudding sleeve*".

His son grinned, knowing how much his father disliked the Parson.

The day dawned early the next day, catching the village cockerels off-guard but Sarah was already awake and waiting for the time to come when she would have to walk down the lane to hear the Parson read her father's last Will and Testament.

Percival Lightfoote did not wait for Hester Brown to fully open the door and pushed past her, with his wife, son and daughter in tow, even before the flustered woman had the opportunity to announce their arrival to the Parson. She shook her head at such behaviour and in the parsonage too, she thought, as she hurried along the passageway to find her master.

The clergyman peered over his spectacles and without extending any pleasantries to the untidy looking group as they strode one behind each other into his chamber. Sarah looked up and noticed their young daughter had her head hung, as if in embarrassment with her family's behaviour. The Parson waited for Mistress Sage to arrive and when they were all seated he began to untie the red ribbon which bound the document Percival Lightfoote had thrown with disrespect onto the desk.

A silver beam of light streamed through one of the distorted glass mullions in the window as Sarah looked across the polished table at the Lightfoote family. Like father, like son, she thought as she looked at the two men. Lightfoote's frumpy wife sat grinning next to him, bedecked in an ill-fitting satin dress, more suited for a rich merchant's wife going to a social ball rather than a *pudding-headed* farmer's wife waiting for a Will to be read in a country parsonage. It was evident, Sarah thought, the *frippet* paid as much attention to the way she dressed as her husband did to his manners. She shifted her eyes and looked through the dust particles dancing in the beam of sunlight at the pretty young girl sitting next to the woman and as they exchanged the briefest of smiles, Sarah thought no mother and daughter had ever looked so unalike.

Tobias Lamb sat perusing the document for several minutes whilst those gathered around him sat in an uncomfortable silence, broken only by the drumming of Percival Lightfoote's impatient fingers on the table

The Parson cleared his throat before beginning to read the document in a deep and sombre voice, *"We are here to read the last Will and Testament of George Bentley"*. He paused and looked around the table and with his rich voice breaking, said, *"In the name of God Amen, I George Bentley of Southwell, farmer, being in good rememberance, Praise be to God, I make this last Will and Testament. I commend my soul unto the Almighty God my Maker and Redeemer and my body to the earth in a decent manner to be buried when God shall call me out of this life"*.

The Parson stopped to once more to cough and clear his throat whilst Sarah looked at him anxiously.

"Get on with it", barked Percival Lightfoote whilst his wife's mouth spread in a simple, moronic grin.

The cleric ignored the man's rudeness and looked across the table at Sarah with a solemn look on his face and despair in his eyes, before continuing. *"My temporal goods I bestow as followeth"*.

"First, I give to Maud Sage, my housekeeper the sum of ten pounds and bequeath whatever goods and chattels she so desires from my house to be taken without the use of a cart within seven days of my death"

The sparrow-like woman had started to cry, even before the Parson had finished reading the words. She could not believe the man who never gave her anything in life, not even his thanks, thought of her in his final days.

"I do give unto Abel Lightfoote, son of Percival Lightfoote, my brown bay with the tanned muzzle and flanks, together with the sum of twenty-five pounds".

Again Tobias Lamb paused, but this time he looked up at Abel Lightfoote and saw the distasteful, self-satisfied smirk which had spread across the youth's face.

He cast a glance at his father. "This is what we have been waiting for", he said, as he rubbed his rough hands together in expectation of what was to come.

"My house and all acreage of my farm and all things that reside within, together with the remaining monies, goods and chattels, I bequeath to my friend and neighbour, Percival Lightfoote. I further bestow on said Percival Lightfoote my fine herd of fattening beasts which graze on his pastures".

"To my undutiful daughter, Sarah Parlairet", the clergyman looked across to Sarah with evident pain on his face and lowering his faltering voice, he read, *"I give to her no more than one corn of pepper to be paid to her by my executor when she demands it"*.

A silence descended on the room only broken by Percival Lightfoot's hand slapping the table. His eyes glinted with victory. "More than she deserves", he said loudly to his wife, as they rose from their seats and left the chamber, laughing at their good fortune. She replied with a loud, spiteful, cackle.

Sarah's eyes followed them and saw their daughter turn her head towards her. A tumble of blonde hair fell on her young shoulders which gave her warmth, despite the sadness on her freckled face and the tears forming in her pretty blue eyes. You don't belong in a place like this and at a time like this, Sarah thought sadly.

Then, as the iron-rimmed heels of the mens' leather boots clattered across the stone floor, Percival Lightfoote called out to Sarah in a mocking voice, "One corn of pepper indeed, one corn more than you deserve".

His roar of coarse laughter was still echoing down the corridor, taunting her as he strode out of the rectory with a broad smile fixed to his face.

Maud Sage rose carefully from her chair, trying not to scrape its legs on the stone floor and in a voice which was hardly audible, bid an embarrassed goodbye to the Parson.

Sarah never saw the woman leave the room. Her eyes were closed, screwed up tightly as she tried to fight back the tears, some of which had already escaped and were beginning to flow in a salty trickle down her cheeks. She was not bitter at Mistress Page's good fortune. She knew more than anybody how poorly her father would have treated the faithful servant. What she resented was what her father had written in such a hateful manner and she knew from that moment, she could never forgive him.

The emptiness of the room became so palpable; if Sarah had reached out she could have touched it, heard its silence and felt its nothingness. It invaded her spirit and soul as she sat at the table with her head in her hands. Her body twitched as she felt the comforting arm of Tobias Lamb wrap round her shoulder. He had a pained look on his face as he said, "I wish I could ease your distress, Sarah".

She remained silent and just nodded as she pressed her chin tightly against her chest staring blankly at the table.

6

Unexpected Visitors

As Sarah came out of the hut the sun had already risen and rays of light tinted the clouds with blazing colours of red and orange. She looked up into the sky and smiled as she recalled the words of old Gabriel, when he would say ominously,

"Red sky in the morning,

Shepherd's warning"

Not today, she thought, not today. She took a deep breath and held onto it. She had forgotten what it was like to taste the fresh air of the countryside after the years of filling her lungs with the foul stench of London's narrow streets.

She had already breakfasted on a slice of bread and a potato and felt content with what the day had to offer. There was a pleasant breeze blowing and the air was filled with the scent of the yellow woodbine flowers, tangled amongst the towering trees which surrounded the hut. Sarah watched with delight as meadow brown and skipper butterflies started to dance in and out of the tall, swollen seed heads rising from the thick tussocks of grass growing along the track.

Nearby, just a stone's throw from her feet, a *redbreast* had spotted a potential meal amongst the lush vegetation on the track and Sarah watched as the bird flitted from branch to branch, forever getting closer, until he darted out and quickly snatched the wriggling creature he had seen hiding there and then in a blink of an eye, he took flight.

The sun suddenly burst through the thickening clouds and the patches of the bright yellow trefoil flowers with their roots growing deep in the hut's sod roof shone out like beacons announcing another glorious day had broken. As if in a pleasurable dream, Sarah wandered round to the back of the hut and looked up to watch the cloud shadows scudding across the rolling green Downs as if they were racing each other in an attempt to be the first one to reach the top. Whilst time stood still for her, ominous clouds were getting darker by the minute and the bright light of the day was disappearing like a shower of summer rain falling on hot flags

Darkness descended early that evening and the flock of starlings had flown cloud-like into their new roost amongst the spiky branches of a large holly tree, nestling together in an attempt to keep dry from the spatters of rain and perhaps to decide where to go for the next day's foraging. Sarah stood in the hut's doorway watching the rain as it began to fall steadily and Jabez, who, until the light of the rush lamp failed, had been transcribing one of his books into Latin, stood alongside her as they looked at the rain tumbling down. The starlings had stopping chattering and now the only noise was the rain dripping off the leaves, sounding like a hundred ticking clocks.

It was the barking of a dog which Sarah heard first. It was a deep-throated bark, the same bark as she had heard many times before. She shivered. It was the sound of a bulldog, the type of dog they used on the bull baiting field behind the great tower in London and in her youth, even here on the green in Southwell.

She cast a nervous glance at her son and retreated quickly into the hut whilst Jabez hastily propped the door into its frame with a crooked branch, kept close by for the purpose.

In the distance the sound of drunken laughter was gradually becoming louder, interspersed with rough voices uttering coarse language and foul oaths. They were audible now and Sarah's stomach churned when she realised the men were heading towards them. The voices she had recognised were those of Abel Lightfoote and the youth with the deformed foot, Henry Prinn. Her breathing was fast, like that of a creature threatened by danger and she began to feel *shackled* by the fear surging inside her.

On reaching the hut Abel Lightfoote grinned at his accomplice as he raised his foot and with the sole of his boot kicked the door in. Sarah and Jabez had already retreated as far back as they could and had their backs pressed against the wattle wall as the door came hurtling towards them. The scream had hardly left Sarah's mouth as Abel Lightfoote burst into the hut and as he lurched forward, he grabbed a fistful of the frightened woman's hair. The man had the smell of the alehouse about him and as their noses almost touched, Sarah instinctively recoiled as she smelt the stench of beer on his foul breath. Her body began to tremble uncontrollably.

"What *ave* we got here?" he sneered, as he pulled her hair so hard it caused tears to well in her eyes. A smirking smile twisted in the man's narrow mouth.

The cripple grinned and looking towards his friend, threw in the word, "Beggars?"

"No, not beggars Henry. We *ave* done better than that, we have found ourselves two thieving trespassers", Lightfoote said triumphantly.

Despite what she was feeling inside, Sarah raised her chin and looking directly into the lout's eyes, said defiantly, "We are neither beggars nor thieves; my father gave us this hut to live in".

"Bentley", Lightfoote scoffed as he spat on the ground, "that old miser never gave anything to anybody, *lest* of all to *thee*, other than a single corn of pepper". His laughter resonated around the daub walls. "He owned this hut and the land it stands on and he let *thou* live here. That's all and things have changed. The old fool is as dead as a nit now", the thug laughed again, "Before he went to feed the worms, everything was left to my father, as you full know, you bitch".

Sarah could see the raw malice blazing like a wildfire in his eyes.

The man's tone changed and his truculence once more filled the air, as he ranted, "*Thou* are trespassing and are about to learn how we treat trespassers. His eyes surveyed the hut until they alighted on the wooden box where Jabez kept his books. His hand thrust forward towards Sarah. She tried to fend it off but was no match for him. Lightfoote grunted with satisfaction as he dragged her towards the books by her hair.

"Sheep can't read. They will have no use for these", he said with a mocking voice, as, with one Almighty kick he sent the box and all of its contents flying through the air, scattering the precious books across the hut's mud floor.

"Nor us, we can't read", replied his fellow simpleton. His mule teeth protruded even further from his lower jaw as he shuffled towards the book which was nearest to the doorway. He laughed as he kicked it with his spayed foot towards a deep puddle which had formed on the track.

"I beg you not to destroy my books", Jabez pleaded, "they are all I have and I need them for my studies".

"Please don't damage my precious little books", Prinn imitated Jabez's educated voice before returning to his natural rasp.

The smile which spread across Abel Lightfoot's face carried more than a hint of sneer and threat.

Sarah was shocked with the hatred and contempt the men were inflicting on them and the valuable books and pleaded with them to stop the destruction. Lightfoote responded by releasing his grip on her hair to stoop down and pick up the nearest and the largest book. His eyes were wild and his cheeks flushed with anger as he ripped off the book's leather covers and threw the pages into the deluge of rain outside. Like a man possessed by the devil he went on a rampage, throwing books in all directions, tearing them open and ripping apart the stitching which held the pages together. Manically, he scooped up the loose pages which were laying deep at his feet and threw them outside, scattering them like autumn leaves blowing in a gale.

Henry Prinn ran outside with the bulldog on a tether, as the books, or what was left of them rained down, making sure that the thousands of words printed in Latin, English and French, were stamped out of existence, obliterated into the thick, glutinous mud.

Jabez stared in shock at the desolation around him and then as he looked at his mother, beaten and bruised, he came to the conclusion, that his books, his precious books, were nothing but ink on paper. Then, as the orgy of destruction was coming to an end, he realised the one thing the two brutes, who without an ounce of brain between them, couldn't destroy, was his memory of the knowledge they contained.

Prinn hobbled towards Sarah and Jabez to leer at them and as he did so, the dog he was restraining, surged forward trying to break free from its iron collar.

"Hold that cur back", Lightfoote snapped at the *clod*. "I've got a job for that thing to do later", he said, pulling Sarah's head round as he grabbed her hair again.

She could now clearly see the snarling dog that Prinn was holding back on the chain leash. The bulldog had its ears back and a string of slimy drool hung from its open mouth and as Sarah watched, it curled its upper lip and snarled in a most awful manner. She was in no doubt that if the simpleton slipped the lease, the dog would attack and tear her apart. A cold shiver ran down her spine and her tongue stuck to the roof of her dry mouth. She had seen the ferocity of this type of dog many times when they were being used for the baiting of the bulls and she knew the one which was now growling in frustration in front of her, would be no different.

In her mind she could see a bull chained to an iron ring held fast in a large block of stone. She could almost hear the crowd on the village green shouting and betting, the yapping and snarling of the dogs. She could imagine the cruel adolescents in front of her would be the first to wager that their dog would be the one which would bring the bull down first, or which of the other dogs in the pack the poor creature would kill first or if it would kill all the dogs. Either way, the hapless beast would be torn to ribbons because the butchers said the flesh was always better if a bull had been baited first and in any case, it was a sport enjoyed in every village and town across the land. She imagined the bull pawing the ground with its massive hoof and could see a dog, like the one in front of her, latch onto its nose and not letting go until it had pulled the creature down. It would be bellowing and kicking and stamping, trying to stop the other dogs joining in. It bent its neck and brushed the ground with its horns. Sarah could hear the yelping of the impaled dog.

The images in Sarah's mind vanished and she became almost paralysed with fear as Henry Prinn asked his friend, "What job *ave yer* got for the *dawg*?"

A sinister grin spread across Lightfoote's face as he jerked he head towards a pale-faced Jabez. His eyes were ruthless and cold.

The half-wit started to dance a peculiar jig on his one good leg in excitement, "Shall I let the *dawg ave* him now?" the oaf with the narrow eyes, asked eagerly.

It was more than Sarah could bear as she imagined the vicious dog going for her son's throat. With a scream of such intensity it sounded almost primeval, she launched herself at Lightfoote. The suddenness of her attack caught him off-balance and he toppled backwards onto the rain-soaked track. As he rose and regained his balance he raised his hand and hit her with such force it knocked her back into the hut, sending her sinking to the ground with a quiet groan. She automatically touched her cheek to feel if the bone was broken. The flesh around her eye was already swelling and inside her mouth her tongue tasted blood.

Somewhere in the distance, as if she was in a dream, she could hear the two drunken *louses* laughing at the game they were playing and amongst their *chortling* there was the dog's deep, threatening growl. Sarah sensed the dog, which was already as fierce as fire, was being provoked into a new frenzy.

"*Thou* would *grievously* attack me and Henry Prinn whilst we were attempting to evict you and your Huguenot bastard son from my father's land. *Thou* are trespassers". Lightfootes' eyes roamed around the hut, before he continued his rant.

Sarah could hear the raw malevolence in his voice.

"Trespassers who have been stealing his firewood and eating his potatoes" his words spat venom at the woman lying on the dirt floor in front of him. "That is a felonious crime and when you are brought before the magistrate, he will sentence you for transportation to the Americas for seven years".

"Or more", the *dull* added.

The men laughed again contemptuously.

"As for that thing", the puppet master motioned towards Jabez, "he will be tied to the whipping post and flogged within an inch of his life before he is transported for twelve years and if the pair of you ever did try to return, you will both be hung".

The voice Sarah could hear seemed distant but it was clear enough for her to understand exactly what had been said. She knew the kind of justice they could expect from the magistrate, a friend of Percival Lightfoote and who was a fellow landowner. The two men frequented all the alehouses and inns in the vicinity and had a reputation for their drunkenness, gambling and wenching the *game pullets* in the whorehouses. It was common knowledge that with a quiet word from Lightfoote in his friend's ear, a guilty person could be set free whilst an innocent one, particularly if they were poor or if Lightfoote would benefit from their removal from society, were found guilty.

Sarah was in turmoil. What could she do to save her son? She was frantically trying to collect her thoughts but her mind was confused and her face was throbbing. Her left eye had shut tight and she could feel blood flowing freely from her mouth and streaming down her chin. Perhaps if she could hold on to one of the attackers, just for a minute or two, she could save her son. Lightfoote was the closest she judged. Prinn would probably come to his aid and she would shout to Jabez to run, run for his life. Her breaths were coming fast as she had made up her mind what to do.

Groaning with pain and effort, she turned on to her side so she could see Lightfoote's legs and inching closer towards him, she waited for his response. Nothing, the two men had seemed to have lost interest for the moment. She took a deep breath and summoning what strength she had left, grabbed the man round his mud-splattered boots and as she did so, she pushed her shoulder against his legs, heaving her knees against the mud floor to put as much weight as she could to topple the man. At first he remained as solid as a rock of granite fixed into the earth's crust but then as she summoned the last of her strength she felt him totter and as he fell, he let out the most blood-curdling bellow.

"**RUN JABEZ, RUN**", his mother screamed to her son "**GO, GO**" as her consciousness began to fade.

"Henry let the *dawg* go", Lightfoote commanded breathlessly, as he staggered to his feet. "*This'll* be the best bit of sport we've had for many *a' time*, we'll bait the snivelling trespasser like a bull.

Jabez whose eyes had been on his mother, concerned at her condition, heard the awful snarling of the dog and the next thing he knew, the dog was biting and snapping at his legs. He felt his balance go and he fell.

He froze, curled up and with his eyes closed, waited for the inevitable.

Nothing!

For some reason best known to the dog, it suddenly stopped its attack and as the terrified young man slowly opened his eyes, it rolled its lip and sniffing the air , it growled and turned away.

Sarah never saw the vicious kicks which Abel Lightfoote delivered, one to her face closely followed by another to her stomach. She let out a groan and fell silent.

"Leash the *dawg* Henry, we are done here", Lightfoote ordered, his anger spent.

Prinn did as he was told and quickly attached the dog's chain-leash to its iron collar. "Have you done for her?" he asked, without a sign of remorse, as he looked at the woman who lay motionless and bleeding on the mud floor.

Abel Lightfoote's voice regained its threat as he turned to Jabez, who was lying next to his mother and warned, "Ten minutes to leave or we'll be back".

He watched the men as they started to leave, laughing, with the bull dog barking at their heels.

Still in a state of shock at what had happened, Jabez could feel his legs shaking as he scrambled from the ground and without thinking, leapt at Lightfoote. The man quickly side-stepped him and as he did so, he brought the back of his hand against the side of Jabez's face. His head snapped back as he fell to the ground. In an instant Lightfoote straddled him and was reaching for the long-bladed knife which was tucked in his belt.

"You *dog's pizzle*", the foul-mouthed toad snarled as he held the point of the knife to Jabez's throat. Jabez looked up and saw the rage of death in his assailant's eyes.

"**Do for him, Abel**", Prinn was shouting, "**do for him**".

Jabez could see Lightfoote's chest rising and falling as the temper inside him raged. His straggled hair was matted and had fallen like a curtain across his forehead, almost hiding his eyes which were bulging with madness.

"**Cut his balls off and we will use them as pig's fodder**", Prinn screamed out excitedly.

Lightfoote was still breathing heavily as he lifted himself from Jabez's prone body. He slid the knife back to his belt and said menacingly, "Ten minutes to get out or I swear I will do for both of you…if she's still alive.

Jabez's eye was already puffed and he could feel his face swelling up as he crawled on all fours to where his mother lay. Frantically he tried to rouse her lifeless body, gently wiping away the blood which was running down the side of her face, blanched white to a deathly pallor. Overcome with grief he put his ear to hear her breath but there was none. He felt her pulse in vain and talked to her, urging her to respond to his voice. Seconds passed then minutes. Nothing; the only sound he could hear was that of the falling rain and his own pounding heart.

"What have they done?" he sobbed. "What have they done to you?"

The rain was relentless and streamed down the young man's face as he started dragging his mother's body along the track towards the place where it met the lane. His only thought was to get away from the hut as quickly as possible before the two men came back.

The black clouds had been unleashing their heavy load for hours and the puddles along the track had joined together to become a shallow stream and the harder he pulled the body, the more his feet slipped from under him.

The suction of his mother's body on the saturated mud was too strong and he released his grip and involuntary sank to his knees. He wiped away the water running down his face with the back of his hand and rested. What little strength he had in his weak body was gone. He felt dizzy and began to sob softly.

"Mother, mother", he pleaded as he looked at her blooded, mud-strewn face. His words came in gasps as he begged in vain to her prone body, "What shall I do?"

I must keep going. The words raced through his mind as once more he gripped his mother under her arms and started to pull her backwards along the track.

He was spent when he reached the end of the track and caught breath and rested, whilst he frantically tried to decide what to do next.

"Somewhere to hide…..get some shelter…… some help", he mumbled incoherently.

His eyes raced from side to side and into the blackness, looking desperately for the place of sanctuary he knew he must find.

"I can go no further", he whispered fruitlessly to his mother. With what little strength that was left, he took her body into his arms and after several attempts, save her legs, he managed to lift it clear of the ground.

With his arms wrapped round her middle, he dragged her to the side of the track and after some effort, entwined together, he slid down the shallow bank to a spot where the overhanging branches of a yew tree would give him some cover from the hammering rain.

The cold and wet of the night had already sunk deep into his bones and wracked with sobs, he huddled against his mother's lifeless form and waited for death to take him too.

The dark of the night was full of fear for Jabez and as he shivered in the driving rain, a horror gathered about the place he had chosen to be their final resting place.

×

The crowing of the cockerels echoed round the village as they greeted the dawn, each one trying to assert their authority over the others, hoping they would be the one to have the choice of the hens. Nathan was up early and had already carried out the most important task of the day; scraping out the previous day's ashes and clinker from the glowing embers on the forge's hearth and rebuilding the fire in readiness for the day's work. Overnight, the coal closest to the embers had turned to coke and he looked at the small flames and remembered what his father had told him. Within them lay the secrets of the craft which his father and grandfathers had nursed with as much care as they had nursed the flames of their forges and now they were his to keep. He knew the secret of building a hot fire was to turn the coal into coke. Coal created plenty of smoke and flames but not enough heat. He scooped some water from the cooling trough and splashed it onto the coal around the edges of the hearth, knowing that as the day progressed he would gradually rake the wet coal towards the fire and turn it into coke. He knew the process would be repeated during the next hour, the next day, the next month and hopefully for many generations to come.

Gideon arrived having *broken his fast* with some eggs and warm bread and opened the forge's double doors and as he did so, a spear of sunlight pierced through the near darkness outside, carrying with it the torch of a new day. Nathan joined him and watched as the soft amber glow already in the sky, slowly changed, filling it with mighty splashes of red and orange, and just as Sarah had said when she too had seen the sky that morning, his father murmured, "Red sky in the morning, shepherds warning…. Rain is on its way".

"Come on, Nathan", Gideon said abruptly, "you've a reap hook to make and a long walk over the hill to deliver it".

His son looked at him in surprise.

"You've shod your first horse and forged your first chisel now it's time you made your first reap hook". He corrected himself with a grin on his face. "*Leastways*, that's what your grandfather called them before everybody else started calling them *sickles*".

Gideon's smile spread from ear to ear as he walked across the smithy to take his son's usual place on the foot-bellows. Gripping the horizontal bar in front of him, he started to pump air into the back of the fire and watched as Nathan began to collect the various hammers and tongs he judged would be needed. Nathan, with his own leather apron wrapped around him watched the intensity of the fire grow until he was satisfied the heat was sufficient for his needs. With the bellows roaring and a multitude of sparks flying from the fire, he gripped one end of an iron bar, which was about half a yard long, with his tongs and plunged the other end into the heart of the fire.

"Forge the tang first", Gideon shouted, as Nathan started hammering the white-hot metal on the face of the heavy anvil. He grinned, knowing his father was still instructing him into the craft he still had to fully master.

Time after time Nathan heated the metal before quickly withdrawing it from the fire and hammering it on the anvil until he had drawn it into the long, tapering, square point he wanted.

Sweat was running in salty beads down his face as he finally plunged the hot metal into the cooling trough. Through the wet, clammy steam he saw his father's grinning face as he said, "That's the tang finished, now you need to fashion the hook of the sickle", then adding as an after-thought, "always forge a square tang. If it's round, the handle will spin on the sickle and will never hold firm".

His son nodded his head to show he understood.

"I need more heat now", Nathan indicated with a nod of his head to his father, as he gripped the finished tang in the tongs and thrust the un-worked end of the iron bar into the roaring fire.

The blacksmith responded immediately, working the bellows more quickly than before, sending a stronger blast of air into the fire. The fire was hot and fierce as Nathan pulled out the glowing iron and started to beat out the curved shape of the sickle round the fat-nosed beak of the anvil.

Sparks flew off the hot metal and the sound of Nathan's measured beat of his heavy hammer rang out through the forge's open doors. Occasionally Nathan shouted to his father, "More air", or "Less air" when he judged the fire needed more or less heat. It had taken nearly two hours to fashion the hook and sweat was running off in small streams from both father and son alike.

"What next?" Gideon quizzed his son.

"We need to form the bevel for the cutting edge", Nathan answered confidently.

The blacksmith smiled as the fire roared again and Nathan heaped more burning coke over the finished shape of the sickle in readiness to beat a cutting edge around the implement's curved blade.

Nathan's face was grimed with the black scale flying from the hot metal and was relieved he had nearly finished at the forge as he wiped the sweat from his forehead with the back of his hand. The muscles in his arms were not yet as strong as his father's iron bands and he glistened with the sweat of his labour and rested a while as he pulled back some of the un-burnt coke from the simmering fire.

"That's it lad. No need to waste it", Gideon counselled his son as he took the sickle from his hand, "I'll finish it", he said.

Nathan watched as his father carried the half-moon shaped sickle to the whetstone and using the foot treadle to turn the heavy wheel, he held the sickle's forged edge against the face of the grit-stone and skilfully sharpened it into a blade which would cut a fistful of wheat with a single sweep of a man's arm.

"Pull the doors together, Nathan", the blacksmith told his son with a hint of mystery in his voice "this part is not for prying eyes".

With the doors closed and bolted, Gideon knelt on the brick floor and, from under his workbench, he pulled out the familiar box of black powder which was similar to touch as the sand dug out of the parish quarry.

Nathan knew what it was, they had used it when they had made the stone mason's chisel .

"You said you would tell me what it's made from", Nathan said tentatively.

Gideon's face took on a serious look as once again he reminded his son, "You must always protect the skills and knowledge I am passing on to you. *Tis* how we safeguard our livelihood. I'm going to show you something that few people know, because it has been so well guarded by our kith and kin".

 He waited until he was sure Nathan had understood the importance of what he had said. "Fetch me the rasp", he nodded towards the file-like tool on his workbench.

Nathan responded as he was told.

Gideon took it and ran the rasp's sharp teeth lightly across the sickle's newly sharpened blade.

"Look how the teeth cut into the sickle's soft blade, if I had pressed any harder they would have taken the sickle's edge right off and *should it be* left like this, after a morning's work, it wouldn't even cut through a pat of soft butter".

Nathan agreed.

"Let's get the fire hot again and I'll show you the secret", Gideon said with a smile returning to his red face.

Nathan, drenched in sweat, set to work to get the bellows blowing and as the fire began to roar into life again, his father buried the sickle in the glowing coals. Nathan stopped treading the bellows and watched as Gideon withdrew the glowing sickle from the fire, "Just dull red is all we need, if it becomes cherry-red it will be too hot", he instructed his willing apprentice.

He walked quickly across to the wooden box and started to sprinkle a pinch of the black powder onto both sides of the sickle's blade. Little sparks, like glow worms in a night time hedge danced merrily towards him as the powder fell onto the hot metal and ignited. Then, without warning and to the surprise of his son, he plunged the sickle into the water trough and waited until the rising steam dispersed.

"Run the rasp across the blade now", he directed Nathan.

Nathan did as he was told. Once, twice and thrice before saying, "It's as hard as glass now" and as he returned the box back to its secret place under the bench he looked at his father and asked again, "What is it?"

"It's made from the hoof of an ox and fine shavings from its horns, mixed with some crushed coke. My father used charcoal but coke is better. Once that is done, it needs to be finely ground".

A serious look appeared on Nathan's face as he nodded his head to indicate to his father that the secret was safe with him.

Gideon continued, "We use the powder in two different ways. Tools like axes and chisels have to be hardened and tempered through to their cores if they are to do the job they're intended for, but thin blades like sickles, only need their surfaces hardened and that's what we've just done".

Nathan understood but a questioned remained as he asked, "How does the powder do that?"

"It's one of the mysteries of blacksmithing", his father chided him, with a knowing grin across his black face.

It was already mid-afternoon when Nathan set off to deliver the sickle. It was eight miles to Warren farm in Challock which meant taking the lane which wound its way over the Downs or *over the hill* as the villagers referred to it. Indeed some of them had never ventured *over the hill,* almost considering it to be a foreign land and a few had spent their entire lives not even leaving the village.

Above him the dove-grey clouds were thin enough to let some of the fading sunlight through but Nathan remembered his father's earlier words as he looked up at the sky, *"Red sky in the morning, shepherds warning, rain is on its way"* and strode meaningfully up the leafy lane. The trees along the ridge of the Downs had grown bent and twisted from the prevailing wind and on seeing them, he made his way along a barely discernible path which had been cut into the tough down-land turf by the trudge of the men's heavy boots who were trudging to their days labour. The going had been steep up the lane and Nathan was relieved to see the flat pastures spreading out in front of him which had not yet been put to the plough. As the shadows lengthened he looked up and noticed the light was rapidly draining from the sky.

"Good day, Nathan", the rosy-faced farmer greeted the young man warmly as he ran his finger along the sickle's newly honed blade. "Sharp enough to shave the bristles off my face" he said with a smile. "Tell your father I'm much obliged and I trust he will enter the charge on my account in his ledger".

Nathan assured him he would and followed the genial man across the farmyard into a small outbuilding where a number of rabbits and chickens were hanging by their bound feet from a row of hooks set into the wall. "Give him this with my thanks", he said, as he removed one of the dead hens, "and if you're thirsty, stop off at the dairy and ask the dairymaid for a beaker of fresh buttermilk".

Tweaking his forelock Nathan thanked the farmer for his kindness and with the fat hen, its neck freshly pulled, dangling from his hand, he headed off towards the dairy which stood at the end of a long pasture its two, single story buildings, adjoined to each other like nestling birds. The furthest of the lime-washed buildings provided the accommodation for the dairymaid whilst the other was the dairy where the buttermilk from the small herd of long-horned cattle was churned into butter and cheese. One of the beasts, its long horns curving down to its nose bellowed deeply as Nathan made his way through the long grass growing in the lush field. Fierce-looking as the beasts were, Nathan was untroubled, knowing the friendly disposition they had. As he neared the dairy he could see there was a light flickering In its window. He quickened his pace through the herd of grazing beasts and as he approached the small square building, he paused and listened as a sweet voice from within, burst into song.

> *"Come butter come*
>
> *Come butter come*
>
> *Peter stands at the gate*
>
> *Waiting for a buttered cake".*

"It's not Peter, my name's Nathan", he said cheekily, as he peered round the door, "and a piece of buttered cake would be most welcome".

The inside of the dairy was cool but a rare ray of sunshine shone, *slanting in* and lighting the dairy, which for most of the day would have purposefully remained in the shade. As he looked around, he could see two pails brimming with warm, frothy milk standing on the red quarry-tided floor, still attached to the wooden yoke the dairy maid had used to carry them in from the milking shed that morning. Fresh curd floating on watery-looking whey, rested in one of the pans standing on the wide shelves which lined the white-washed walls and next to them were a number of settling pots, each full of buttermilk, waiting for the cream to rise.

The young woman looked up in surprise and stopped plunging the cream in the plunge churn. It was a long job to turn the cream into butter and she had been working to the rhythm of her song. She was about Nathans age and as pretty as a picture with ringlets of hair, the colour of buttercups, tumbling out from under her mop cap. She wiped her hands on her long white apron and smiled at the young man standing in front of her.

"Hello, I'm Clara Clark, who are you?"

"I'm the son of the blacksmith in the village, my name's Nathan Larkin", he said, as he felt his face flush. Something fluttered in his stomach. It was something he had never felt it before and didn't know quite what it was.

She smiled sweetly at him, knowing full well who he was. She knew he was as *well a favoured* man as you would meet in ten parishes and would make a good match for any girl. She had been *gawked* at many times by the farm boys but the young man standing before her, with his sandy-coloured hair flopping over his eyes, radiated everything she desired in a man and she was immediately enthralled with what she saw.

"I haven't got any cake to butter but you can have some curd cheese", she giggled, as she dipped her finger into one of the pans of curd which had begun to *clabber* and would soon be thick enough to be cut into pieces and offered it to Nathan.

He tried not to screw up his face as he sucked her finger and tasted the sour cheese. His heart clenched and he bit his lip as he looked into her bright olive-green eyes. He had never seen such a pretty girl in his life and he *catched* his breath a bit. Mesmerised and ignoring her blushes, he reached out for her hand and as she willingly complied, a broad smile spread across his face. *He'd* never an eye for the girls in the market, though there was *a many* who *looked* at him. Her eyes closed as Nathan leant forward to kiss her. She felt his lips on her cheek and became alive as he whispered, "You're so beautiful, Clara".

She laughed and threw her arms around his neck and standing on tiptoe, returned the kiss with wild abandonment as she mischievously asked him, "Do you mind?"

His face flushed as he stammered, "No" and then as Clara released him from her embrace, he whispered adventurously into her ear, "I love you".

She smiled demurely, knowing his heart had slipped into her pocket and hoped it would stay there safe and sound for many years to come.

Outside a spotted *throstle* had started singing its last song of the day, unnoticed by the pair who had became oblivious of the world around them.

"Oh no", Clara suddenly exclaimed, unaware of the time that had passed, "the butter gathering in the churn will separate into buttermilk and will be only fit for the hogs if I do not *hasten* and attend to it".

A look of disappointment flooded over Nathan's face and he fumbled as he breathlessly, asked, "Can I visit you again?" His heart was all *rent* with love and he knew whether it should beat for another day or a hundred years, it was hers for the keeping.

"Of course you can", she laughed, as she skipped back across the dairy as Nathan bade a reluctant farewell.

It felt like rain was building up in the thickening clouds and Nathan quickened his pace in the hope he would be home before the heavens opened. Despite the threatening gloom his eyes shone bright and his face was flushed with first love. His thoughts were of Clara and rain or shine, he didn't have a care in the world.

He had reached the brow of the hill and was walking down the incline when he felt the first spits of rain hitting his face. The smell of the summer rain was heady and Nathan enjoyed its sweet scent. The moon was beginning to rise and with the light gone from the sky and an eerie gloom descending, any hope he had of it helping him home, disappeared as the dense, black rain clouds descended.

Somewhere in the distance he heard the first low rumble of thunder and he stopped as a jagged bolt of lightning *rent* the air. He paused as he recalled the old saying, *"Beware the oak, it curts the stroke, beware the ash, it curts the flash, creep under the thorn, it will save you from harm"*.

Within minutes, the rain started to drop relentlessly and he pulled his black hood firmly over his head and wrapped his leather jerkin tightly around his already saturated body. Huge puddles jumped into life and the bowed branches of the bushes and trees lining the lane, drooped under the weight of water. He was half-way through the tunnel of trees when, through the noise of the rain and the squelching of his boots, he heard it; a faint whimpering sound. He stopped and listened, nothing, other than the sound of the storm overhead. He walked on, more briskly now and had reached the spot where the track met the lane when he heard the noise again but this time it seemed louder. It sounded like somebody was sobbing somewhere deep in the undergrowth: he stopped and listened again. Once more he heard it, close by, to his left. Dropping the lifeless chicken on the lane, he started to scramble down the bank. He lost his footing on the slimy mud and slid to the bottom, landing awkwardly in a puddle of mud and water. As he quickly collected his senses, in the darkness, under the arching branches of a yew tree, he saw a shadowy figure. Nathan froze. A fork of lightning hit the wet earth close by, followed a few seconds later by the heart-stopping boom of thunder overhead. There was another flash of light and in its brilliance he saw the figure was that of a thin, young man with his head in his hands, hunched over the body of a woman. The man looked up, frightened and *wracked by the shakes*, scared that Lightfoote and Prinn had returned. Nathan recognised him; he lived in the old Looking Hut with his mother. He had seen them in church together and had been told she was George Bentley's daughter.

The drenched young man moved away from the body, his clothes slimed in mud and sat corpse-like, white-faced and motionless. "My mother has perished, they killed my mother, Abel Lightfoote has killed her", he cried out relentlessly, as he stared wide-eyed at Nathan.

The thunder was distant now as the storm began to move further down the valley. Nathan didn't answer. His chest was heaving as he crouched by the woman's side. He held his breath and the noise of the driving rain was no longer beating in his ears as he listened to hear if any sound was coming her body. He felt his knee sink into the water-logged ground as he bent closer to her face and put his ear to her mouth. He could see a congealed stream of blood where it had run down her bruised face and wondered what had *befallen* the woman.

He listened and then listened again.

It was almost imperceptible but it was there.

"**She breaths**", he shouted across to her son. .

"Alive?" the pale-faced young man answered back in disbelief.

Both young men looked at each other, both unsure what to do next.

It was Nathan who spoke first, "We must get her down to the village; my mother will know what to do", he said decisively.

The ground underfoot was *claggy* and waterlogged and his feet *slimed* as he placed his hands under Sarah's armpits and took her weight. As

Jabez followed his example and tried with some difficulty, to lift his mother by her ankles, she moaned and cried out in pain, "No".

"Put her down", Nathan said quietly, as he was thinking what to do next. Quickly taking off his jerkin and placing it over the prone woman, he said decisively, "Stay here whilst I fetch my father, he will be able to carry her".

Jabez tilted his head up and down vigorously and mouthed the words, "Thank you".

Nathan clawed his way up the bank and panting for breath ran back to the lane. Hardly pausing, he clutched the chicken with a muddy hand and raced back down the lane to find his father.

When Gideon arrived, Sarah had fainted *dead away* and as he softly wiped the mud away from her face, fresh crimson blood began to flow again from the corner of her mouth. He placed his strong, gentle hands under her frail body and carefully lifted her up into his swarthy arms as if he was picking up a sleeping baby from its crib.

Hannah Larkin had already placed a *flock bed* by the glowing embers of the forge when her husband walked in, carrying Sarah Palairet's seemingly weightless body, followed by the two bedraggled figures. She held her hands up to her face in shock at what she was seeing. The woman's skirt was torn and caked with mud, one of her boots was missing and her arms and face were cut and blooded as if she had been *trodden* by one of the bulls in the ring.

"Gideon, place her here by the warmth of the fire", she ordered, before looking at Jabez's swollen face. "You can sit on the stool next to your mother to dry out and I will see to you later".

He just nodded in agreement, still shocked by what had happened.

Gently, as Gideon laid Sarah on the wool-filled mattress, he heard her say in a voice which was hardly audible, "Thank you, sir"

Outside, the storm was returning and the noise of the thunder grew louder as Hannah gently applied the yarrow poultices which she had made up to stop the bleeding and cleanse Sarah's wounds.

Hannah turned her head towards her son who was still dripping wet and said, "Nathan, put that chicken down and go outside and pick a bunch of comfrey so I can make up another poultice for the bruises.

Nathan", she said, raising her voice in frustration, "did you hear what I said?"

He hadn't. His head was full of the pretty girl he had just met. He knew she was the one. The one he would want to spend his days with and the one whose laughter would fill his life with joy.

"**Nathan**". His mother's exasperated voice reverberated around the chamber.

A week had passed when Sarah was sitting outside the forge, nursing her wounds, half asleep and enjoying the warmth of the sun's rays on her battered face when she sensed somebody was standing close by. Not knowing who it was and with her heart pounding, she slowly opened her eyes.

It was Daisie Lightfoote. Her sad, haunting face stared directly at Sarah's swollen face, blotched blue and yellow from her beating.

"Hello Daisie", Sarah said to the little girl, whom she had immediately liked when they had first seen each other at the parsonage when her father's Will was being read.

The girl didn't reply, not knowing what to say. Instead she thrust out a small bunch of wild flowers she had picked in the barley field.

"Are they for me?" Sarah asked, as she took the posy of blue cornflowers and bright yellow corn marigolds and held it to her nose?

"Yes" the girl whispered, with evident embarrassment showing on her young face.

Sarah looked at the girl. Could this be her way of saying she was sorry for the violence her brother had so brutally bestowed upon her?

"Thank you" Sarah replied. "They're lovely", she said as she kissed the girl on her rose-pink cheek. She looked into the little girl's pale blue eyes and saw the sadness etched within them. You're too young, too pretty and too decent to carry the heavy burden of guilt for the sins of your family, Sarah thought wistfully.

She detected a faint smile on the little girl's face as, with her head bowed and her eyes riveted to the ground, she slowly walked away.

"Come and see me again", Sarah called after her. She was already thinking what kind of existence could the little girl look forward to, living with a family like hers?

The blacksmith and his family sat huddled round one side of the trestle table facing Sarah and Jabez, whilst they waited for the clergyman. It was the chamber, with its white, lime-washed walls where the family lived and cooked. Some people in the village had started calling this room, their parlour, especially the wealthy, but Hannah remained steadfast and kept to tradition referring to it as the hall. On one side, between the small pantry on one side and the buttery on the other, was a narrow passage which led directly into the smithy. On the opposite side, was a narrow-boarded door leading into a small chamber which was now being used as Sarah and Jabez's bed chamber.

Despite the many applications of Hannah's yarrow and comfrey poultices, Sarah's face still bore the marks of the beating and a persistent pain occasionally tore through her rib-cage if she forgot and turned her body without thinking. Despite the flickering shadows dancing round the room, being cast by the candles, the clergyman could not help but see the glum expressions on each of their faces, as he started to explain what Percival Lightfoote had *conveyed* to him.

It had been only a short walk from the parsonage to the forge cottage but it had been sufficient for Tobias Lamb to consider the words he would use and the manner in which he would deliver them. He had pondered whether he should just speak to Sarah alone, but Gideon and Hannah were now involved in this sorry business, as were Jabez and Nathan, so he had concluded, he would say what he had to say to all of them.

Peering over his glasses, the cleric looked at the silent faces in front of him and explained in measured tones what Percival Lightfoote had said.

"What do you mean he has lodged a written statement with the magistrate, stating Sarah and Jabez had viciously assaulted his son and Henry Prinn whilst they were trying to legally evict the trespassers from Lightfoote's property?" Gideon exclaimed.

The clergyman looked distressed as he decided not to answer Gideon directly but carried on, only this time, he looked directly at Sarah. "What the man has said", he chose not to use the man's name, "is that if you make any accusations that his son and Henry Prinn assaulted you and your son, the magistrate has confirmed that he will commence with the prosecution against you and Jabez".

"The so-called magistrate", Gideon spat the words out in disgust.

Sarah sat bereft and shook her head in disbelief and muttered forlornly, "Is there nothing to be done?"

Before the Parson could reply, Nathan shouted out, "**That is not justice, reverend**".

Tobias Lamb leant forward on his stool and with his arms on the table boards and with his hands clasped together, as if in prayer, he said solemnly, "We must all stand before God to be judged and will each receive whatever we deserve for the good or evil we have done in our earthly bodies".

He noticed Nathan was about to speak and held up the flat of his hand to silence him before carrying on, "The judgement of Christ is such, that each of us may be *recompense f*or our deeds when we will be required to give an account of ourselves to God".

"Amen", Sarah and Hannah said together.

Nathan could hold his silence no longer and blurted out, "Somebody as corrupt as Lightfoote will escape retribution".

The Reverend Lamb smiled at the hot-headed boy and said softly, "Fear not Nathan, justice will be served in a higher place".

A rage swept through the young man's mind. He could not wait that long, particularly for Abel Lightfoote and Henry Prinn, he had other plans for them now.

Working at the forge in the late burst of summer was hot work, even sapping the strength of Gideon and on balmy days like this, if there was no urgent work to be done, at around six o'clock, he would *bed* the fire down for the night and sit in the shade. On these rare evenings Nathan would wander round the village to talk to any of the other young men who had also finished work for the day and weren't bird scaring in the cherry orchards. This evening was different; he had no need to gossip with the farm men, clothed in their woollen smocks and sucking intently on their clay pipes.

The heady heat of the day was cooling and the light of the day began to drain away as the sun sunk lower in the sky. Nathan walked purposefully up the lane and towards the track. Overhead, tiny pipistrelle bats flitted in and out of the heavy, overhanging branches of the oak trees, chasing the moths which were beginning to fly from their daytime hiding places.

He was determined to teach Abel Lightfoote and Henry Prinn a lesson for what they had done to Jabez and Sarah. Three months had passed since he had first met Jabez, laying distraught under the trees with his injured mother by his side and during that time the two had become firm friends. They couldn't have been more different. Nathan was strong and muscular, quick to anger and hasty to act whilst his weak-bodied friend considered everything he did and when he spoke, he said the words with great deliberation.

Nathan reached the Looking Hut and peered inside. Amongst the green, onion-shaped wine bottles strewn on the floor, were jagged shards of broken glass. Just as I thought, he mused, they come here to do their drinking. He stepped back into the bushes and waited. Flies were buzzing around his face and as he moved in the hope of avoiding the annoying insects, he saw what was left of Jabez's books trodden in the ground around him. The setting sun had sent the birds to roost and the only sound he could hear was the hum of mosquitoes. As Nathan brushed them away he saw the first star in the night sky shining its bright light through a break in the trees. It was then he heard them, voices coming along the track towards him. The men had almost reached him when he stepped out of the shadows to face them. The look on their faces told Nathan they knew why he was there. He was there to avenge the beating they had given to the Huguenot woman and her weakling son.

Henry Prinn looked at Abel Lightfoote and grinned, assuming two against one would be an easy and enjoyable contest. "I'll *larn* him", he sneered, then, with his peculiar loping gait and his head down he suddenly charged at Nathan. After a couple of strides he faltered and looked to his side. A look of panic flooded over his thin face as he realised his friend was not with him. Abel Lightfoote had decided to let Prinn deal with the blacksmith himself.

Nathan stood his ground, grinning at his opponent's predicament.

Prinn cursed and rushed forward like a bull, wildly punching out at Nathan with clenched fists. The young blacksmith was ready for him and raised his arms to protect his face from the savage blows. He glanced quickly towards Lightfoote; he had not moved from the spot and had no intention of joining in. At least, not yet!

Nathan steadied himself before punching Prinn hard in the face. The man's head jerked backwards. He staggered back a couple of paces, wide-eyed and breathing hard. Nathan instantly moved forward to finish him but as he did so Prinn came again. Nathan ducked but Prinn's fist found a way through and the young blacksmith felt a sickening crunch to the right side of his face, just above his cheek bone. His head pounded and he dropped to one knee. As he put his hand up to his face to feel the damage to his rapidly closing eye he saw Prinn raise his foot to deliver a kick. It came quickly but before it could make contact, Nathan grabbed the foot and twisted it until the man fell, hitting the earth with a thud. Nathan's rage was such that he leapt on the fallen man and rained blows with savage force, wanting to beat the man into the biscuit-dry ground he was laying on. Prinn threw up his arms as he tried to fend off the attack but he was no match for Nathan's fury.

Panting, Nathan groaned as he rose to his feet and watched as Henry Prinn crawled away on his hands and knees like a beaten dog.

It was Abel Lightfoote's *rage full* scream that pierced the evening air and for a brief moment it paralyzed Nathan's thinking. Their dislike was such that each man wanted the other dead and Nathan could see the black hatred in Lightfootes' eyes. Blow after blow began to be traded. Ducking, staggering, rolling and kicking, the two men fought on, breathless with equal pain rippling through their bruised and battered bodies as neither man gave an inch.

"You *whoreson*, I will wipe you off the face of the earth", Lightfoote lisped almost incoherently through his bloody and swollen lips as he reached behind his back for the long-bladed knife tucked into his belt. He stepped back from Nathan, preparing for one final surge and growled like a feral beast as launched his attack.

Overhead, the light from the slender moon was sufficient for Nathan to see the flash of the recently honed blade and he deftly twisted away from the thrusting knife. Lightfoote snarled and slashed the blade wildly at Nathan's arm. Glancing from side to side Nathan leapt into the briars growing at the side of the track and grabbed a fallen bough which was entangled amongst them. In a flash, he bent down and snatched the bough from the briars. As he grabbed it, with all the strength which was left in his legs, he pushed himself up as Lightfoote came at him again. Nathan cautiously circled him; his heart was thundering in his chest. Gripping the end of the bough with both hands he raised it above his head and brought it down on his opponent's wrist, like a felling axe driven onto a log. The knife fell to the ground as Lightfoote cried out in agony as his wrist-bone snapped. Nathan had the advantage now and clenching his blooded fist, he quickly struck the howling man with an arcing, rib-cracking blow to his side. Lightfoote reeled with the impact and as his knees weakened, he wobbled away from the fray.

Nathan had not finished with the man and he heard the crunch of a bone breaking as he delivered the blow which finally sent Abel Lightfoote to his knees. Without wasting a second, he grabbed a fist-full of Lightfoote's collar and pulled him to his feet. He heard the sound of material ripping as the collar was wrenched from the man's woollen shirt. One more blow delivered with such revenge and retribution was all it took to finish the man who fell backwards into the briars.

The shadows were already dissolving into the darkness of the night as Nathan limped home with the sound of Lightfoote's moaning gradually fading into the distance. With every homeward step he took, his body ached from his injuries and he could taste the blood which continued to flow unabated from his swollen mouth. His face winced as he spat it out onto the road.

Reaching his home, he washed the blood off his face and knuckles in the horse trough and quietly opened the smithy's door and made his way through to the passage which led into the cottage. He hoped his parents were already in their bed chamber to avoid the scolding he could expect and was shocked when he saw a sliver of light shining from under the door.

"**Nathan**", his father's voice was loud and severe and bristled with anger. "Come in here lad, so I can see you".

Gideon had spent a successful evening in the Wheel playing *hazard*. The dice had been kind to him and the *humour* had been good until one of the village men let it slip that he thought Nathan was going to give Abel Lightfoote his *just deserts* that evening.

Nathan walked slowly into the hall where his father was waiting, hoping in vain his cuts and bruises wouldn't be too visible in the feeble light coming from the single stub of a candle burning in one of the iron wall spikes his father had fashioned in the forge.

The air outside had not cooled and the room, heated by glowing fire in the adjoining forge, was unbearably hot and Nathan could feel the sweat running down his back as he *awaited* his father's wrath.

He stood with his back to the open stairs facing the glowering face of his father. This was not the first time he would have to explain why he had been fighting and he hoped that after his explanation, he would go to bed with an angry rebuke ringing in his ears. This time it was going to be different, he could tell that by the look on his father's face.

"You have been brawling with Abel Lightfoote and Henry Prinn, like common thugs in a tavern", his father shouted, with his eyes blazing in anger. "Have you got sawdust in that head of yours?" he said in exasperation, "after what the Parson told you".

The young man stayed silent with his head bowed as he recalled the Parson telling him that justice would be served at a higher place. He bit his lip as he decided not to tell his father that the beating he had just given Lightefoote and Prinn was a bit more than they could have expected in a tavern brawl.

Gideon *glowered* at his son for a few moments before saying, "Have you thought *naught* what I have told you time after time about fighting. Well, this time you can expect Percival Lightfoote to go to his whoring partner, the magistrate in the *morn* and lodge a complaint, accusing you of assaulting his son and causing him grievous injury".

"They deserved it for what they did to Sarah and Jabez", Nathan said lamely, wondering if they could hear his father's reprimands in their adjoining chamber.

Gideon's eyes bore deep into his son's. "I think we can expect the parish constable to be knocking on our door with his staff of office", his father said sharply, "and by this time tomorrow, you'll be shackled and chained in the village lock up". He left his words hanging in the air as he continued to stare at his son.

After a few moments of the angry stare, Nathan sensed his father had finished berating him and with a nod of his head in acknowledgement to what had been said, he turned and slowly made his way up the rough-sawn stairs to his bed chamber, satisfied he had paid his reckoning to the thugs.

However, Gideon hadn't finished with his son and shouted after him grimly, "If you don't learn to keep your temper in check, one day you'll be hanging from the scaffold with your neck stretched and your feet *a kicking* in the air".

His face had paled with the concern he felt for his son's future.

Nathan waited for his father's wrath to cease before he retired to his chamber. Sleep did not come easy that night and Nathan tossed and turned in his box bed but it was not the pain which racked his body, nor was it his father's rebuke ringing in his ears. It was what his new-found love, Clara Clark would say when she heard what he had done.

The next morning neither father nor son spoke and individually busied themselves as they prepared for the day's work ahead of them. Nathan winced with every move he made, wondering more than once if his ribs and knuckles were broken. Occasionally their eyes met, and more than once he sensed his father had looked at the cuts and bruises which covered his face with a look of paternal concern.

The adolescent took a deep breath as he stopped pumping the bellows and turning to his father, asked, "*Feyther*, do you really think the parish constable will be taking me to the lock-up today?"

The blacksmith stopped raking the coke into the forge's growing fire and putting the rake down, he turned to his worried son and folding his swarthy arms against his huge chest said, with a grin spreading across his face, "Do you really think I would let that *ne'er do well* who calls himself a parish constable, take a son of mine away to be chained and fettled?"

Nathan breathed a huge sigh of relief on hearing his father's words. He knew his father carried considerable authority in the village and few men dared to challenge him.

"He may busy himself making sure the gates and hurdles in the enclosures are in good order and everybody attends the church on the Sabbath but locking up my kith and kin is something he won't be doing". It was clear Gideon did not think much of the unpaid parish official.

His son's face lit up and he was smiling when he said, "He also keeps himself busy locking up the men in the village who have fathered a bastard child".

"if that is the case, then he should start by locking up Percival bloody Lightfoote", Gideon replied mysteriously, as he winked his eye at his grinning son. The sound of the men's laughter could be heard by anybody who may have been passing the smithy along the drover's road at that early hour of the morning.

×

The long, hot summer had lingered into the autumn and there was a sickening warmth and stillness in the air. The midday sun was baking man and beast alike as Nathan walked across to the village green to collect the plough horse which had been waiting under the cool shade afforded by the spreading boughs of the horse chestnut tree. It shook its massive head as Nathan slipped on the leather bridle to lead it back to the smithy where his father was waiting and the fire in the forge was already burning. He knew how hot it would become working the bellows as his father shaped the horseshoes round the anvil's beak and looked towards the west in the hope a prevailing wind might blow and bring with it a cloud to shield the sun's burning heat. It was then he noticed a *post chaise* being driven at speed up the winding lane towards the village throwing up a white cloud of chalk dust in its wake from the hard-baked ground. Horse-drawn coaches of such quality were a rare sight indeed in Southwell and Nathan wondered what the occupant's business was in this sleepy village.

"*Feyther*, there's a *yellow bounder* heading up the lane, being drawn by four hacks with a rider mounted on one of the leading pair". He used the name his father called the yellow carriages.

The blacksmith put down the pair of hoof nippers he had already collected from the smithy, ready to start the shoeing. "It's probably heading to go up over the hill and up onto the Dover road", he said as he tied the horse's bridle to the rusty iron ring, hanging from the forge's wall.

They watched with a growing interest as the carriage was pulled to a halt for a few minutes outside the Wheel whilst the postillion ran inside to seek directions before continuing its way towards the smithy where the pair were standing. Nathan heard his father mutter to himself, "Nothing wrong with the horses, perhaps a hoop has come loose from one of the wheels". He was already casting a knowledgeable eye over each of the carriages' four wooden wheels.

Nathan stepped forward and took hold of the lead horse's harness as the liveried postillion leapt deftly from his saddle and ran to open the carriage door for the occupant.

Gideon scratched the back of his head in puzzlement. If there had been a problem with either the horses or the carriage which required his services, the postillion would have dealt with it but if it was not that, what did the occupant want with him? Whoever it was, they were wealthy, he decided. To hire the *yellow bounder*, the horses and a rider would cost over a shilling a mile and judging from the steam coming off the backs of the four horses, they had already been driven a long way.

The blacksmith studied the smartly dressed man as he alighted from the carriage, dressed as he was in a silver-grey coat with matching breeches and a neatly tied white silk cravat tied round his neck. Gideon judged the man's age to be about forty years and looking at his shiny, black-buckled shoes, the blacksmith came to the conclusion he had never walked on a country lane before.

"Good day to you sir", the stranger said warmly, as he raised his black, curled-brimmed hat to Gideon. The man wore no whiskers and as the blacksmith's eyes studied the shape and colour of his face, he could see he was not a man of the land weathered by the elements.

Always looking for an opportunity to improve the family's financial situation, Gideon raised his hand to his forehead and responded by saying, "Good day to you sir, could I offer you a tankard of ale or some cold water from the spring or perhaps I can *refresh* the horses *well* with some oats and water and rub them down?"

Apart from his craft, of which he was a master, Gideon was also exceptionally good at judging horses and men, in that order and he could see the well dressed man now standing in front of him was not an empty-headed peacock but somebody of wealth and substance.

"Indeed I would be obliged if you could take care of the horses and *refresh* the rider with some ale and the end of a fresh loaf with some cheese", the stranger replied. "As for myself, perhaps I could avail myself of some refreshment once I have concluded my business here".

Gideons' eyes narrowed and the hint of a scowl began to form on his face. "Your business is?" he enquired. Nathan had been patiently patting the forehead of one the lead pair and looked anxiously at his father as he waited for the stranger to reply.

The stranger sensed the unease in the air. "I understand Mistress Palairet is accommodated here and I would speak to her if I may", he said, in a soft, cultured voice.

A quizzical look spread across Gideon's face as he questioned, "Mistress Palairet?". His face had changed and it now had a suspicious and troubled look.

At first, he did not recognise the name the man had said, Gideon still thought of her by her maiden name, Sarah Bentley, but after a few moments of frantic thought, he suddenly said, "*Aye* sir, Sarah is here together with her son, Jabez".

Gideon stared at the man with raised eyes for a few moments whilst he collected his thoughts before he instructed Nathan to fetch Sarah. If there was to be trouble for Sarah he decided, it would be nothing he couldn't handle, after all, the man seemed friendly enough, at the moment.

A few moments of uneasy silence passed between the two men before Sarah and Jabez came out of the cottage door and walked cautiously towards them. Sarah blinked as her eyes tried to adjust having come from the dimness of her chamber into the bright light of the summer sun. It seemed at first the man standing smiling at her was as much of a stranger to her as he was to Gideon. It was then, as the well-attired man greeted her, a long-lost smile began to spread across her pale face.

"Sarah, *tis* indeed good to see you again, God be praised that I find you well", the man greeted her with evident affection in his voice as he removed his hat.

Jabez stood as his mother's side and smiled, for he too had recognised the stranger's face.

"Matthew Rosser", Sarah cried out in joy, as she proffered her hand to him. He gave her a slight bow before he took her hand and kissed it.

It was then the reality of the situation suddenly became apparent to her. Matthew was wearing some of the finest clothes she had ever seen; a white powdered wig was on his head and a smile so wide, it nearly disappeared from his face. She hung her head in embarrassment or was it shame, it didn't matter. All she possessed were the clothes on her back, nothing more. Not even a penny in the pocket of her torn skirt. She was dirty and dishevelled; how could she greet such a fine looking man?

She felt his finger gently lift her chin until her downcast eyes were level with his own and as he did so, she turned her head away in shame.

"Hear me out Sarah, I beg you". He was smiling at her, as an equal and as a friend. Her frayed nerves relaxed a little.

Once again he took her hand warmly into his own before putting a protective arm round Jabez's narrow shoulders, saying, "It is so, so good to see you once again, my dear friends".

Hannah Larkin had been feeding swill to the hog in the backyard and hadn't heard the arrival of the stranger. With a worried look on her face she hurried out of the small cottage when she realised something was going on outside the smithy and joined her husband and son. She gripped Gideon's hand as she stood speechless at the reunion which was taking place. There was puzzlement on her face as she wondered who the man was and what did he want with Sarah and Jabez?

Behind her, the plough horse tugged at his bridle rein as he raised his huge head and shook it back and forth to show his impatience at waiting to be shod and his annoyance at being led away from the leafy shade of the chestnut tree. Gideon shot a quick glance at the iron ring to make sure the rein was still tethered securely to the wall.

The smile that lit up Sarah's face was as bright as sunshine as she explained who Matthew was and how he had been such a good friend to her husband when they lived in the Weavers loft in Spitalfield.

Hannah visibly relaxed. "Sarah, Jabez, show Mr Rosser into the hall and I will bring you some refreshments while Gideon and Nathan", she turned towards them and ordered, "unhitch the gentlemans' horses and take them across to the shade on the green where they can be fed and watered".

Her husband and son dispersed as directed whist Sarah and Jabez sat on one side of the table and with Matthew Rosser facing them, he started to explain his proposal to the astonished couple. He paused as the door opened and waited as Hannah entered the hall carrying a tray full of bread and cold meat and three overflowing tankards of porter. She looked at Sarah with questioning eyes, hoping to see any sign which would tell her why the wealthy man had come to visit her. Hannah took the tankards of ale and placed them on the table in front of the three silent people. She was in no hurry to go, hoping to hear a snippet of conversation which would enlighten her. She slowly put the plate of meat on the table and then even more slowly, wiped off the froth of ale which had spilt onto the tray.

Sarah mouthed, "Thank you", and Hannah reluctantly left the room, no wiser as to the purpose of the gentleman's visit.

Matthew Rosser waited until he heard the door catch click shut before he continued. He took frequent sips of the brown ale in his tankard, the ride from London had been hot and dusty and his throat was crust dry.

Jabez listened intently whist he washed down a slice of cold meat with a *gulp* of the porter.

Sarah's top lip was trembling. She didn't move, she didn't respond to what Matthew Rosser had said and ignored the food and drink Hannah had placed in front of her. So much had happened since Claude's death, so much unhappiness and now she felt shocked and bewildered at her husband's friend's generosity.

It was Jabez who spoke first. "Sir", he said formally, "when we left, there was much rioting and mob rule in Spitalfield. Will it be safe for us to return?" He looked at his mother to see if she agreed with him.

Matthew Rosser's voice was calm and reassuring, "I will not pretend the violence *hath* ended. Indeed, three men have been hung for destroying draw looms in the weaving sheds in the last quarter but I have been a good employer always paying a fair wage for a fair days work and Praise be to God, my business has been spared".

Despite the happiness she was beginning to feel in her heart, there were tears of sadness beginning their slow journey down Sarah's cheeks as her emotions were released. She walked across to where Gideon kept his ledger and dipping his quill into the small ink pot, she quickly scribbled a letter. Joining Hannah and Gideon, the look of concern was evident on their faces and as she spoke to them in measured tones, her face was knotted in anguish. Matthew Rosser and Jabez watched silently by her side.

"You have been such good friends to us both", she glanced across at her son for his agreement, "you saved our lives and have protected us from….". She had no desire to speak the names of those who would like to see her and Jabez dead. "You have given us shelter, food and water, love and friendship and have asked for nothing in return but I have always known that we could not impose on your generosity forever".

Hannah lifted her apron to wipe her eyes before reaching across to give Sarah a hug, saying in a voice which was breaking with emotion, "It has been nothing my dear, nothing at all".

Sarah reluctantly extricated herself from Hannah's embrace and continued to explain, "Mr Rosser has the need of a *keeper* of his newly acquired house in Spital Square in London and has kindly offered the position to me and has said that he will provide education for Jabez at the *colleges of learning*".

Matthew Rosser interrupted her with a warm smile on face, "Jabez is an earnest young man with a life stretching out in front of him which is full of promise. It would be a pleasure to help him in any way I can". He looked towards Sarah and said politely, "I'm sorry I intruded on your conversation, please carry on".

Her voice was almost a whisper as she continued, "I have accepted his *kindly* offer". She paused, waiting for a response; instead there was silence. "Please forgive me my dear friends if it appears that I am ungrateful for everything you have done for us", her eyes pleaded for their understanding.

Hannah reached out and took Sarah's into her own and said, "You've got a good heart and a fine *countenance* and you deserve a full and happy life".

Gideon waited patiently for his wife to withdraw her hand before wrapping his swarthy arm around Sarah's narrow shoulders, saying with heartfelt warmth in his deep voice, "We will all miss you, of course we will and Jabez too but we wish you nothing but joy and happiness in London and perhaps one day, God willing, we will all meet again".

"Will you give this to the Parson?" Sarah asked, as she handed Hannah the letter she had just written, "it is to thank him for all his kindness and generosity……all of you have been so ……" Her voice broke and trailed off with emotion.

Nathan, who had been waiting at the door, walked across to his friend and clasped his hand. Unlike Jabez, he was clumsy with words and could not think of anything to say but the expression on his face rendered any words unnecessary. Jabez looked into Nathan's moist eyes and said simply, "You saved my life and I will never forget what you did and how you protected me from…..", he hesitated before finally saying, "Abel Lightfoote". It was a name which tainted Jabez's mouth and would haunt him for as long as he lived.

Such was the intensity of the parting that neither man heard the slow clop of horses' hooves or indeed notice the *yellow bounder* as the postillian brought it slowly alongside them.

Their final leave taking was simple. A last shake of the hand and a look in the eye but nevertheless it left Jabez with a vague feeling of guilt; to be saying goodbye to a friend who had done so much for him.

The mutual sadness in their eyes showed as they both realised they would never see each other again.

Sarah took a deep breath. It seemed like a dream as she stepped into the finery of the carriage with her son alongside her and Matthew Rosser sitting opposite. She raised her hand to wipe the tear which was beginning to roll down her cheek and then kept it raised as she bade a fond farewell to the family who had given them so much kindness. It was both an end and a beginning. It was the birth of hope for them both.

The postillian touched his hat at the small group bidding goodbye and holding the reins, he yelled at his team of four, *"Let's get going boys. Go it, go it"*. The horses flicked their ears back when they heard his encouraging voice and began to pick up their pace.

Gideon stood with his wife standing on one side and his son on the other and together they watched the *post chaise* gradually disappear as it bounded down the lane, off towards the toll-pike to London, the bright yellow flash being swallowed up in plumes of white dust rising from the unmade road.

"Come on Nathan, enough time has been wasted, let's get this old nag shod", he said, with a satisfied smile on his face and a hand in his pocket, as he turned over the three gold coins Matthew Rosser had generously given him.

 Unbeknown to them and pressed into a hawthorn hedge, half hidden from view and with the tree's needle-sharp thorns piercing their back, somebody else was watching the carriage depart. Daisie Lightfoote wiped the tears from her eyes as she watched the woman and her son who, despite what her brother had done to them, had shown her so much kindness, disappear into the distance.

✕

The sky was still dusted with stars and high amongst them the moon shone through brightly as Amos Bridge climbed down from his bed chamber using the ladder he had fashioned from some seasoned ash boughs many years before. His bones creaked with each step he took and as he stepped off the bottom rung he stretched his aching back with a groan. He had long forgotten what it was like to have joints that moved freely, without pain and now at his great age, his aches were his only companion. He was of indeterminate years as nobody in the village could remember a time when he wasn't there. It was still dark when the cock had *crewed*, thin and sweet, and sounding like no earthly bird. Winter had come early and the old man's breath puffed out streams of white vapour in the *glass-clear* air as he wrapped his woollen coat round the smock he had kept on during the night. Dawn was still two hours away, the cold had crept into his clothes and he shivered as he pulled his coat tighter around him. His dwelling was nothing more than a tumbledown shack, leaning precariously against the wagon shed and stables. The winter straw on the dirt floor was damp beneath his feet as he *broke his fast* with a quart of the heavily *hopped*, stout-butt ale, a thick slice of bread and some hard cheese. The bread was stale and he dipped it in the ale to make it soft enough for his gums to manage. A mouse darted out from the round nest it had made in the straw. Amos ignored it, just as he did with the smell of its droppings which hung in the cold air. He had never known a mother's love or the love of a sister and his departed wife's love was but a memory, now he was set in his ways and content with his lot in life.

The land was white with the heavy overnight snow and it crunched beneath his booted feet as he made his way to the stables to feed the horses and break the ice off the water in their troughs. He felt the chill of the winter's bitter breath and hunched up against the wind as he shoved open the stables dilapidated wooden door with his shoulder. His brow creased as he realised it may be another two months or so before the winter released its icy bonds, when the streams could run free again and the grass would begin show its fresh green carpet.

His bruised shoulder reminded him that George Bentley had not been a man to spend money on keeping the buildings in good repair but also, since his death and the Lightfoote's had inherited the farm, things were beginning to go from bad to worse.

"Good girl", he said to the old mare as he threw some hay towards her with his long-handled pitch fork. His twinkling eyes were framed by thick white eyebrows and wisps of white whiskers grew out from his stubbled chin.

Steam billowed from the horses' nostrils as it buried its muzzle deep into the frost-crusted hay. Amos watched it chewing the hay before walking across to a pile of *roots* in the corner of the stable and kicked into them with his boot. *"They be* frozen too, old girl", he said to the horse without turning his head. *"You'll enjoys em* just the same I *dares* say", he said as he shovelled a generous helping of the round vegetables towards the appreciative animal. "Need to get on to see to the *old plough boys*", he said almost apologetically, as he made his way to the four heavy horses in the adjoining stable. The lines round the old man's eyes told of the laughter and warm smiles of his younger days but now they were laced with sadness. His wife had been in her grave for seven long years and his only company were the animals on the farm and the rodents in his chamber and as he worked amongst the animals, he would invariable chatter on regardless. Horses, sheep, geese, it didn't matter, he enjoyed their conversations.

Hoisting a sack of corn chaff on his shoulder he began to make his way along the winding track up to the brow of the Downs where a handful of sheep were waiting to be fed at Fairfoin Rowens. The falling snow had lessened slightly and the large-fluffy flakes had lessened to almost dust but the accompanying icy blast was still there, numbing his face and shining his nose red as he laboriously waded through the knee-deep drifts. His heart sank as he passed the remains of the Looking Hut as he remembered how Mistress Sarah and her son had been brought to the accursed place and how they had suffered at the hands of the Lightfootes. He flexed his fingers as they began to tingle with the bite of the cold and he paused to blow some warmth into them. His lips were tinged purple and as he rubbed life into them with the back of his liver-spotted hand, he *remorsed* that as each winter came, the more likely it was that he would suffer.

"Won't be much longer girls", he mumbled aimlessly to the distant sheep and as he lifted the sack of chaff from the snow, he paused and put the sack down again when he saw three riders in the distance galloping towards him.

Amos squinted in the snow's glare and gradually against the wintery backdrop he began to make out the colours of the leading horses' coats. One was black whilst the other was brown with tan flanks.

"The Lightfootes", he murmured sourly, "with their ill-gotten gain". His eyes shifted towards the trailing horse, "Prinn", he said, as if his mouth had become full of sour tasting ale.

He kept his eyes on the men as they relentlessly pushed their horses through the drifting snow and as they approached he could see, despite the biting cold wind, the beasts were dripping with sweat, their barrel chests heaving with exertion. Percival Lightfoote was the first to arrive and as he did so, he pulled on the reins and in a cloud of loose snow, brought his animal to a wheeling halt.

"Good day to you, *maister*". The old man touched the brim of his felt hat with due deference. His chest was thick with phlegm and as his voice broke away, he decided to say no more.

Ignoring him, Lightfoote rose in his saddle and looked back across the snow-clad fields towards Dunn farmhouse. In the distance the fattening beasts bequeathed to him by George Bentley were *lowing* loudly in their pastures covered by the winter's icy blanket. Without pulling his horse round to face Amos, he said bluntly, "Abel is to run the farm now and will be residing in the house. Daisie will keep house for him".

Amos's jaw stiffened as he nodded his head and as he did so, Abel Lightfoote bounded up and heeled his horse's flank with his sharpened spur, bringing it up behind him. The old man turned round to face him, if Lightfoote's son had something to say, he could say it to his face, he thought proudly.

"Bridge", Abel Lightfoote said sharply, "come Michaelmas, I will have no work for you. I will be getting my labour from the hiring fair….men who are capable of doing a full day's work". With a callous smirk spreading across his face he looked down at the sack of chaff standing in the snow beside the old man and said derisorily, "Look at you. You cannot even keep a sack of grain-chaff on your shoulder".

The horse turned and Amos looked blankly up at the young man's face, pleased it still showed the scars of the beating he had received from the blacksmith's son. He said nothing but thought a more villainous creature he had seldom met. Behind him there was a flurry of snow as Henry Prinn arrived, pulling his snorting mount to a wheeling halt. Amos turned round to look at the grinning *clod*. The snow which had been thrown up by the leading horses had frozen on Prinn's doublet and despite his bravado; he was shivering from the cold.

"Out by Michaelmas", Abel Lightfoote shouted out as he jabbed the bay forward and cantered off, throwing up snow in the face of his father's black gelding which had already started to follow in his wake. The two horses plunged through the snow, snorting steam and throwing up flurries of compacted snow from their hooves. Abel Lightfoote *leaned* into an ever increasing pace as he relentlessly compelled his bay mare on.

He turned and looked back. His father was on his horse's tail.

Following up some distance behind was Henry Prinn."Out by Michaelmas", he mimicked back. "Out by Michaelmas".

Amos watched as the Lightfootes' horses were spurred into a furious gallop and as they disappeared from sight into the folds of the hills, they left behind the wisps of steam which was rising from the horses' bodies.

"The stupid buggers will kill those poor animals", he said sadly, as he lifted the sack of chaff once again onto his shoulder and made his way towards the bleating sheep.

The two leading horses were neck and neck as they approached a narrow gap in a thorn hedge. Percival Lightfoote didn't sense any danger: he had raced his son many times before and he expected him to give way, as he always did and what he was required to do. Abel Lightfoote's face was set hard and he grinned as he leant back in his saddle and with his feet pushed deep into the stirrups, he pulled tightly on his rein so his mount flanked hard into the side of his father's horse. Percival Lightfoote shouted out in alarm and screamed to his son to pull back as the horses clashed together. All the time the thorn hedge was getting closer. The grin on Abel's face widened and turned into loud laughter as he glanced across at his father and saw the look of terror on the man's face as he realised he wasn't going to clear the hedge. The black gelding made a brave attempt but its front hoof clipped one of the thick, top bracing boughs. The horse pitched forward and as it did so it launched Percival Lightfoote into the air .Abel Lightfoote's brown bay rose and cleared the hedge with a foot to spare and as it did so, he glanced back and saw his father and his horse slam into the hard, snow-covered ground in a flail of limbs and hooves.

His whoops of laughter followed him as he rode on.

Prinn cried out in delight as the horse's girth breasted the hedge and as he pulled hard on the reins to avoid the fallen rider, he noticed Percival Lightfoote's broken body appeared to be lifeless.

Spurring the mount on, he shouted out to Abel Lightfoote in the distance, "*Me thinks* Abel, you'll be the squire now".

×

The frost had crusted over the blanket of snow and it sparkled in the bright moonlight as Amos walked carefully down the lane for his nightly visit to the Wheel. He could see the glow of firelight through the green, bottle-glass window panes as he walked up the well-worn steps towards the heavy oak door. His belly was *restless* and he entered as quickly as he could and headed towards the fire to get some warmth back into his body. He held his hands to the flames before calling the serving girl over to order his quart of ale and sweet lamb pie. Not having a *goodwife* at home to cook for him, the pie would nourish him and he always found the cloves and nutmeg mixed amongst the chunks of meat a comfort to his stomach. He eased himself on the narrow settle in the innermost chimney corner of the wide inglenook, as close to the burning logs as he could and as he waited for the girl to return, he watched the sparks racing up the blackened flue. Living in such a damp, soulless dwelling as he did, the cold of the hard winter had seldom left his bones and he relished the warmth of the fire. The light from the tallow candles burning on the wall spikes was bright enough to relieve the darkness and in the dim flickering light he saw a few men sitting round a small table away from the fire, taking turns to throw three bone dice and uttering oaths as the small piles of pennies in front of some of them gradually diminished. Other men stood deep in conversation, with their tankards resting on a long, planked table-top perched on top of two empty butts where the fat-bellied alehouse-keeper served his ale. He knew the men and they all knew him but he chose to keep his own company this evening. The northerly wind suddenly gusted down the wide chimney blowing some sweet-smelling wood smoke from the fire, briefly masking the reek of unwashed farmhands and the strong tobacco they were smoking.

Amos removed his felt hat and with his gnarled, slightly shaking hand, he flattened the fringe of white hair around his mottled, bald head and began to leave his place at the fire. The heat had *set* his back and he groaned as he straightened it as much as he could and shuffled towards the make-shift table which acted as a *bar* to the row of ale butts standing behind. He reached in his pocket and banged his ten pennies on *the counter* for his pie and ale. Never a person to accept under payment from anyone, the uncouth landlord carefully tallied up the coins and as he did so, he let forth a resounding belch. Amos ignored the man and waited patiently for his ale, as he had done so for most evenings in the decades before.

"Amos", grunted the alehouse keeper, as he turned to draw off a quart of ale from one of the oak butts lined up behind him, "have you heard *tell* about Percival Lightfoote?"

The old man waited for his tankard to be replaced on the *counter* before shaking his head.

"Dead!" the inn-keeper said flatly, showing several blackened stumps amongst his yellow teeth.

"Dead?"

"Found laying face down in the snow at the bottom of a thorn hedge down the slopes from Fairfoin Rowens with his neck *broked*, frozen stiff he was", the man continued. "They say his black gelding was standing over him……lost a good customer, I have", he bemoaned. "That is, on the times he paid his bill".

The men standing at the *bar* remained silent but their *countenance* was such that it was clear they had already heard the news.

"Good riddance", one of the dice players observed without raising his head.

Others around him looked up and nodded their heads in agreement.

Amos remained silent as he raised his tankard and buried his top lip into the creamy foam. He took a *long pull* at his ale before wiping the froth from his mouth with the back of his hand. A contented smile spread across his lined face as he lowered his tankard on the *bar* for a refill.

PART TWO

To be what we are and to become what we are capable of becoming, is the only end of life.

Robert Louis Stevenson

7

The Speckled Monster. 1765.

Clara Clark rested her needlework gently onto her lap and gazed at it contentedly. She had been promised to Nathan for nearly ten years and had waited patiently for this day to arrive although at times she had despaired it would ever happen. She had lived in the small cottage adjoining the dairy at Warren farm all of her life and she knew it would be strange to live in another house. Her wage as a dairymaid had not been much, just five pounds a year but that, together with the odd gifts of food the farmer in his kindness gave them, she and her widowed mother had managed to get along reasonably well but now, with her dear mother lying cold in her grave, her life was now hers to own and she lifted the dress she was sewing to her soft lips and kissed it tenderly.

How things had changed in a few short weeks. Her mother buried, a wedding to arrange, banns at the church to be called. Her head was spinning. Outside, the coming of spring breathed life into the countryside and the world around her blossomed. The hedgerows were bedecked with the snow-white flowers of the May and somewhere in the distance a cuckoo was calling its familiar cry. The bird, with its curved beak and piercing amber eyes was neither a songster nor a hawk and Clara held her breath as she listened to its repetitive call. *Tis* said that only the souls of good people are transformed into cuckoos, she thought wistfully, and therefore the birds could pass messages between the living and the dead. The bird called again and Clara smiled warmly when she realised her mother was speaking to her on today of all days.

It was also at this time of the year the mystical birds announced the important events that would happen in the village during the forthcoming year; the births, deaths and marriages. The bird knew it was her wedding day and the soul of her dead mother was telling her to enjoy the day and look forward to the time when she would give birth to her first born. The strange bird called again and a shiver ran down Clara's spine. The bird was the protector of life and could decide how long a person would live. Perhaps it was telling her it also knew when she would die.

She shook her head vigorously to drive the dark thoughts from her mind and looked out of the window. In front of her, standing on the window sill was a jug full of yellow nut catkins which she had plucked from a nearby hedgerow. As she looked at them she remembered what the children called them, lambs tails, she thought. It had not seemed long ago when the apple trees in the orchards had been a tangle of unruly branches but now they were dotted with fat, pink buds ready to burst out. The smile returned to her face as she delighted in the sights around her.

It was the first day of May, a day of celebration and a good day to be married to such a fine man.

She had observed the village tradition and had sent her betrothed the shirt she had sewn for their wedding day with instructions that he must keep it for the rest of his life. She smiled. It would soon be time to walk across the fields and down the lane to the church and she hastily picked up the dress again and with her needle and thread, sewed the last stitch. That's it, she thought, everything has now been done for us to have a long and happy marriage.

"Clara Clark", she began to muse to herself, as she stroked the wedding dress, before saying more loudly, "Clara Larkin". She smiled as she thought how good it sounded. She repeated it again, "Clara Larking…….Mistress Larkin". Indeed, she thought, it sounded good.

A tapping on the window interrupted her musings. At first she didn't hear it or the giggling of the three females outside the cottage. It was not until one of the young women knocked loudly on the door was Clara's attention drawn to it.

"Clara, you're not ready. You can't be late for your own wedding", Ester Tanner cried in mock alarm, as she was embraced by Clara.

"You look lovely", Clara said, as she spun her best friend round to admire her pretty floral dress. Turning towards the other two excited women, she gushed, "Oh, Polly and Martha, you all look so beautiful….thank you, thank you".

The three fellow servants from Warren farm helped Clara to pull the long white dress over her head, commenting how clever she was to sew a light blue ribbon round the hem as a sign of her purity. As she turned to admire herself in the mirror, the three bridesmaids shrieked in unison, "No, no Clara, *tis* bad luck to look in the *glass* on your wedding day, come away".

With the long white stems of sweet-smelling bluebells threaded carefully through the woven bands of white may blossom on their heads, the four women left the dairy cottage and danced and skipped bare footed across the soft green grass of the meadows, singing and laughing as they made their way towards to the church.

"Let's sing the blackbird song", Ester called out and as she did, the others burst into song.

>*"Hello says the blackbird sitting in the chair*
>
>*Once I courted a lady fair*
>
>*She proved fickle and turned her back*
>
>*And ever since then, I'm dressed in black*
>
>*Howdy dowdy diddle dum dee""*

"I will sing the next verse", Clara laughed out joyfully.

>*"Hello says the little turtle dove*

> *I'll tell you how to gain her love*
>
> *Court her at night and court her at day*
>
> *Never give her time to say, O nay*
>
> *Howdy dowdy diddle dum dee"*

"Tis my turn next", Polly called out excitedly, as she began to sing the verse about the leather-winged bat, telling why it flew at night.

> *"Howdy dowdy diddle dum dee"*

"The last verse is mine", giggled the red-haired Martha as she started singing with the sweetest voice of all.

> *"Hello said the woodpecker sitting on a fence*
>
> *Once I courted a handsome wench............"*

The verse was never finished as the happy young women joined hands and danced round and round in a circle. Their laughter rang out even louder. Clara drew in a lungful of woodland air and let the sounds of the birds fill her ears as she skipped towards the church in the distance. She had never been so happy in her life. So ecstatically happy it felt as if God's whisper was in the trees around her.

Nathan was waiting for them together with his parents and the Parson. He stepped forward and took his bride into his arms and as he did so, he handed her a newly-forged horse-shoe, burnished until it was as bright as a silver coin. *"Tis* to bring you luck", he said, with a broad smile on his face.

"I don't think I will need it", she whispered in his ear, "I was *favoured* with all the luck I will ever need on the day when we first met".

A broad grin spread across her face when she noticed the wide-cut shirt she had stitched for him, hiding under the red frock coat he was wearing. The metal buttons were straining in their button holes, as the coat struggled to cover his broad chest and Clara wondered if the coat was the one his father had been married in years before.

The Parson herded the group together and as he began to lead the small procession up the flagged stone path towards the church, the bridesmaids quickly gathered around the bride. Gideon Larking smiled at the girls' superstitious natures in believing that brides were susceptible to evil spirits on their wedding day and how the young women had clustered protectively around Clara so the spirits could not distinguish her from them.

With the ceremony binding the smiling couple forever, the Parson led the small party towards the forge cottage where the wedding breakfast had been prepared.

"It *hath ever* been my wish to have you as my husband", Clara whispered in Nathan's ear. A slow, stealing smile like ripples on water spread across his face as he gently squeezed the small, soft hand of his new bride.

Tobias Lamb beamed as he entered the cottage's small hall and made his way through to the small orchard at the back of the dwelling. Brown feathered chicken were running about his feet whilst the black-spotted hog slept contentedly in its stye. There was no fear of rain on such a day and Gideon had put a butt of ale in the backyard for anyone who came to drink the health of the newlyweds whilst Hannah had laid out horn beakers and platters alongside the veritable feast on a trestle table erected under the blossom-laden branches of an old apple tree. The Parson gazed upon the freshly baked *quartern* loaves, the pats of bright yellow butter and the cheese and preserves. His eyes wandered longingly to the liquid gold flowing from the thick slabs of honeycomb and the piles of dough cakes and gingerbread which had been placed alongside them. Subconsciously, he licked his lips when his eyes next alighted on the platters overflowing with meat; thick slices of ham at one end and *a round* of beef at the other. Gideon did not begrudge the expense and as more people arrived, he filled and refilled their beakers with the amber ale specially bought for the occasion from the village brewer whilst Hannah pressed the *tipsy* throng to have a bellyful of the fare in front of them. The small orchard was filled with the *gladsome* sound of *much merriment* when the cottage door was pushed open and the hall resounded with the music from two smiling fiddlers who stood there with their fiddles pressed tightly to their chests.

Clara looked through the open door and cried out with joy and as she pulled Nathan to his unsteady feet, she gushed excitedly, "They are dancing round the maypole on the village green...let's go and join them". With the fiddlers leading the way, the wedding party, with the exception of the Parson who was happy to stay where he was, made their way to the merriment outside. As they passed, some of the village men, their eyes glazed with drink made *bawdy* remarks to the newly married couple, much to Nathan's amusement and his wife's embarrassment. The three bridesmaids quickened their pace as they walked past the men leering at them before they had a backward glance and whispering to each other, they all burst into a giggling fit.

Bunches of white may blossom hung from most of the dwellings in the village to celebrate the coming of spring. A tall maypole which some of the village men had cut down from the nearby chestnut woods some days earlier, stood erect on the village green. More bunches of may blossom festooned the top of the pole and hanging loosely from it, were long ribbons of red, white and blue.

Clara rushed forward and grabbed a bunch of the streamers, handing one to each of her bridesmaids whilst keeping one for herself. Other girls from the village followed her example and as the fiddlers struck up a cheerful tune, the girls wove in and out in time to the music. Soon, some of the men joined in and as the dancing continued and the fiddlers played faster, the warm spring air was thick with the sound of laughter.

The last light of evening lingered in the sky and the shadow of the maypole was long in the grass when the combined celebration of Nathan's and Clara's wedding and the arrival of Spring came to the end and as the couple walked arm in arm to the smithy, Nathan turned to his wife, "I said I would *sup* a quart with father before we retired, do you mind?"

She smiled the sweetest of smiles, "Of course not". She knew it was something men did, whilst for her, she was the happiest woman in the village and nothing in life would ever change it.

Gideon stood alongside Nathan in the doorway of the Wheel, both enjoying a flagon of keeping ale and turning towards him, said, "You've picked a good one there, son". He winked his eye and with a smile spreading across his face, he added, "as well as a pretty one".

Nathan raised his voice so it could be heard above the raucous noise coming from inside the alehouse and returned his father's smile as he replied, "I know" and then as an afterthought and with a broad grin breaking out on his face, he added, "best I was getting back".

×

Even though the air was warm, almost balmy, a fire was burning in the grate of Dunn farmhouse, not least because the house was so cold and unwelcoming. Daisie Lightefoote sat in her bed chamber dabbing away a tear and breathed deeply as she tried to regain her composure. She had suffered greatly from her brothers' misdeeds over the past ten years ever since their father was killed and she began to feel the familiar shiver of fear run up her spine as she heard the heavy footsteps coming up the stairs. Her heart started thumping in her chest and she swallowed back the terrible dryness in her mouth as the door to her chamber was booted open. Retreating to the corner of the room she held back her fear and tried to smile as she said to her brother in a quavering voice, "Abel, you're back earlier than I expected, I haven't put the fowl in the oven yet". His fist had been the answer, coming out of nowhere and shocking her bleeding mouth into silence.

×

The ancient church of St Mary's, with its pointed spire had commanded a view over the village for five-hundred years, ever since the medieval masons had dug its stone footings deep into the chalk beneath. As Parson Lamb made his way towards its gothic entrance for the start of the Sunday service he paused to look at the crisp-cut lettering on the newly erected grave marker close to the path.

Peering through the glasses balanced on the tip of his nose, he slowly read the inscription,

"In Loving Memory of Hester Anne Brown

Born 1st March 1701

Died 20th February 1765

Beloved wife of Thomas Brown"

"Too soon", he sighed sadly, as he slowly walked away and into the church.

As the congregation filed quietly in he stood impassively in front of the altar watching them, occasionally nodding his head in recognition to those whose furtive eyes alighted upon him. He expected everyone in the village to attend his service, save those on their death beds and heaven help any who were missing. At the age of fifty-five and despite his lame leg, he was still a man of impressive bearing, particularly in his cleric's gown and collar. His eyes narrowed as Daisie Lightefoote made her way up the aisle to take her place in the family's box pew. With her mother now buried alongside her long dead father and her brother more likely than not in a drunken stupor somewhere, the young woman cut a lonely figure as she let the shawl drop which was hiding her face as she opened the door to the pew. The Parson's brow creased as he noticed the marks on the young woman's face. Were they what he thought they were, or was it a trick of the light coming through the stained-glass windows? He adjusted his glasses and looked again. They were black bruises which shadowed the side of her face, darkening to purple as they spread around her eye.

Daisie caught sight of his stare and feeling ashamed, she quickly turned her head away.

He was waiting for her as she tried she leave the church unnoticed, hidden amongst the rest of the departing congregation, her eyes fixed on the ground and her shawl wrapped tightly round her battered face.

The Parson decided not to mention the bruising to her face or to ask how they got there. He could guess. Instead he held her hand and said, quietly, "Daisie, the man is lower than pig's slurry".

She chose not to reply.

The cleric thought for a moment before he looked into her eyes and said, "With Hester Brown now dead, would you do me a great service and come to live at the parsonage to be my housekeeper?"

She lifted her head and mouthed, "Thank you, sir".

A thin, indiscernible smile spread across her face, the first one which had graced her pretty face for many years.

×

The seasons faded in and out. Their changes were slow but never faltered. Spring in Southwell that year gave way to summer which lingered awhile before it blazed into autumn. The village then held its breath as it waited for the haunting beauty of winter.

Nathan sat in the alehouse sipping a powerful draught of apple cider, ignoring the shouts of the men playing cards who were wagering money they could ill afford. Outside, he could hear the hollering of some others who were duck baiting on the village pond. Dog's barked furiously as a duck, made incapable of flying with its wings pinioned, was released on the pond, calling loudly as two dogs were set loose. As the bird dived under the water in an attempt to escape its pursuers a loud shout pierced the air as some of the men started to encourage their animal of choice. One of the hounds would have followed but it was been unable to match the duck's speed underwater and had surfaced, yelping in rage. As Nathan listened, the cheers of the men waned and were replaced by angry voices as some of them who had backed good money on the slower dog, threw stones and handfuls of mud in an attempt to disable the terrified duck to their dog's advantage.

Clara was *quick with child* and Nathan did not need the company of the men gambling inside the ale-house or to enjoy the excitement of the duck baiting outside. Instead he *brimmed* with a mixture of anticipation and nervousness as he lifted the tankard to his lips once more and waited.

The door opened and Nathan looked up as Gideon strode into the smoke-filled room, "Quickly", he gasped on finding his son, "your mother said it's nearly time".

There was a growing look of concern on Nathan's face as he held his wife's hand and smiled at her as she lay huddled on the bedstead, her face dripping with perspiration. Clara clutched blindly towards him. There was pain etched over her face and tears poured from her eyes.

Nathan wiped her forehead with his *'kerchief* and leaning forward, tenderly kissed her moist lips.

"*Tis* best you leave us now", his mother said briskly, "I need to get things ready for the birth".

The couple were living in the small chamber at the back of the cottage where Jabez and his mother had lived and he gently stroked his wife's forehead before making his way back into the hall. He waited and bit hard on his knuckles as he listened to Clara's labour screams as pain tore through her body. He paced the floor not knowing what to think or what to do. His mind raced with terrible thoughts as he made his way into the smithy to try to find something to occupy his mind. It was common enough for a woman to die during childbirth, the graveyard could vouch for that and it was natural for new-borns to be deprived of their first breath. He closed his eyes prayed that the good Lord would grant that he would not suffer such grief.

Suddenly there was silence in the bed chamber. A frightening silence and Nathan shot a questioning glance at his father who was standing alongside him. In a blind panic he raced from the smithy towards the small room where his wife lay.

He lifted the catch and pushed the door open and as he did so, he could see his wife's broken body on the bedstead. She lay there, quite still and sobbing. Her eyes were wide open; staring blankly at the cobwebs festooning the rafters and beside her, their son had come into the world crying lustily. Nathan took hold of his wife's limp hand and stared down proudly at the infant. Picking him up he turned to his father and said, "His name is to be James Gideon Larkin and he is to become a blacksmith as were the generations before him".

For the baby, his first few months had been simple. He had been baptised in the Norman font at St Mary's and had survived the period when mortality for infants of his age was high. He had doting parents who adored his every move and who watched in wonder at the way his tiny fingers curled round the covers on his crib, commentating how tightly he clasped the cloth. Gideon told anybody who would listen, his grandson had already got the grip of a blacksmith. For his part, Nathan never lost an opportunity to leave the heat of the forge to cuddle his son, whilst Clara smothered her new son with kisses whenever she could.

"*Tis* not a good thing to *mollycoddle* an infant so much", Hannah Larkin grumbled quietly one day. Gideon smiled and decided to refrain from answering as he recalled how his wife had done exactly the same thing to Nathan when he was of the same age as baby James.

Clara pulled the lace cap away from the baby's eyes as she marvelled at their sapphire blue pupils remembering how long she had waited to be a wife and mother. She knew in her heart that everything was going to be alright and they were all going to have a long and happy life together.

Nathan squinted into the evening sun as he walked towards the Wheel for his evening tankard of ale. The work at the forge had been hot and the day had been long and his roaring thirst needed quenching. The wide gate to the stabling had been left open and he walked across the courtyard to enter the ale house by its back door. The dirt under his feet was fine and dry. It was turned to dust by the spurred feet of the cockerels fighting to the death during the weekly cock fight and the shuffling of the feet of the village *dolts* who recklessly wagered their wages on the outcome.

Somewhere, coming from within the low-ceilinged building, he could hear the high-spirited singing of some of the farm -men.

"My fair lady, fair lady, throw those costly robes aside

No longer may you glory in your pride

Take leave of all your carnal delight

I've come to summon you away this night"

"*Death of a lady*", Nathan said to himself, as he recognised the song and he quickened his pace so he could join in and as he did so, he started to sing the second verse.

"What bold attempt is this? Pray let me know

From whence you come, and wither I must go

Shall I, who am……………….."

Before he could finish the verse the singing suddenly stopped and a *chaos* of raised voices chimed out from inside the alehouse. One voice stood out amongst the rest. It was the slurred rasp of the alehouse keeper.

"Get out you filthy dog. You'll not be turning my establishment into a *midden*". He was screaming insults as he dragged a man out by the scruff of his neck. Nathan stood aside as the man was thrown out of the door and was sent sprawling onto the ground. He cast a look at the man lying at his feet. He didn't give the appearance of being a common labourer seeking work or someone of *inferior order* desperate for alms, nor did he appear to be *flawed* with too much ale.

Nathan looked towards the alehouse keeper, hoping for an explanation as to the man's condition. The landlord was typical of every inn-keeper up and down the country. He stank of sweat and tobacco smoke and had the belly of someone he had eaten too many fat-roasted fowls. Someone who never missed an opportunity to pour ale down his gullet, the proof of which was the *goodly* red glaze on his puffy face. Nathan had never liked the *ill countenance* of the man and waited for him to explain.

The glutton wiped his mouth with the back of his sleeve and winced as he broke wind.

"Arrived last night he did, seeking lodging for the night...said he was on his way to buy a horse at the Ashden market", the inn-keeper explained. "He paid for some supper, a quart of keeping ale and stabling for his horse".

The man paused to break wind again and to thrust his hand inside his rough woollen trousers to scratch his balls.

"He started eating the cold chicken I had served him and the next thing I knew, he had rushed outside and *flayed* all over the place......he complained that the fowl was bad and went to his room".

Nathan looked down at the stranger who was grinding his head into the dust of the cock-pit, moaning deliriously like a man possessed by the devil. It wouldn't have been the first time bad food had been served in this establishment Nathan thought as his eyes shifted once again onto the alehouse keeper.

"It was in the early part of the *morn* he started up again; coughing, moaning and shouting........woke everybody it did. I told him to shut his *hole* and I didn't hear *no more till but a short while* when he started up again, holding his head and *flaying* all over the chamber.........I'll give you bad food you *cup-shotten* drunk, I thought, so I grabbed him by his neck and threw him out".

Nathan ignored the man's explanation and knelt down to tend to the unfortunate fellow who was still writhing on the ground. The man tried to say something as he tried in vain to push himself up. Nathan could smell the vomit on his shirt as he bent down to touch the man's forehead, only to find it was burning up.

"*Ti*s the *sweating sickness*, I suspect", the man said faintly, as Nathan helped him to sit up. "Either that or the damned chicken I ate".

Nathan nodded his head.

"I would be greatly obliged to you sir, if you could help me to my feet", the man gasped. His breathing was coming in short bursts.

Nathan put his arm round the stranger's waist and hauled him to his feet and waited a while for the man to catch his breath.

"The pain in my head beats like a drum", he mumbled as Nathan supported him under his arm and helped him along to the stable. The horse had been tethered for the night saddled and harnessed. So much for the fee the landlord had charged for doing so, Nathan thought grimly.

As Nathan slipped the nag's rein from the hay rack, he realised the man was so weak he would be unable to pull himself up into the saddle.

"I'll take it outside and you can use the mounting block", he said as he started to lead the beast towards the stone block.

With the assistance of Nathan's strong, muscular arm, the man managed to get up the three steps to the top of the block and as he stumbled, he fell fortuitously onto the horse and after some effort, into the saddle. His body slumped forward and with his face pressed against the horse's black, shiny mane, he slowly trotted off in the direction of Ashden.

The next morning was bright and fine as Hannah left the cottage on her walk to the mill. She smiled as she passed the open doors of the smithy and heard her husband bemoaning about the war in the Americas to a ploughman, whilst the man's horse stood patiently waiting to be shod.

"They *says* Farmer George will lose our colonies to someone they *says* is calling himself Washington", the ploughman said, between sucks on his clay pipe.

Gideon inwardly smiled, knowing how most people referred to the king as *Farmer George* because of his interest in *newefangel* methods of farming.

"He's buggered up the Americas for us the same *ways* as he's buggering up the way we *goes* about our business on the farms", the man scowled. The bowl in his pipe had ceased to glow and Gideon walked across to the forge to pluck out a hot coal with his tongs to light the man's pipe again.

The ploughman nodded his head in appreciation as he began to breathe the rich smoke into his lungs again. He sucked several times on his pipe before he was ready to continue their conversation.

"They are saying the King's madness has returned", Gideon said, as a cloud of tobacco smoke enveloped the ploughman's weathered face.

"Mad King George he's being called now", the man laughed. "I heard t'other day he's pissing green now. *Thrice* they've held the *cupping glass* on his neck and *drawed* off the blood and they've even burnt him with hot pokers to try to drive the *malady* out of him but he's still as bloody mad as a bloody March hare".

Gideon squinted through the smoke curling from the man's pipe and nodded in agreement. "I don't think his son, the Prince Regent, will be much better when his turn for the throne comes around".

The ploughman spat a *glob* of spit on the smithy's floor and tried to remove it from sight by grinding it into the uneven bricks with a heavy leather boot. "The man *tis nought* but a *madge*, spending his time in *molly houses* with other queer fellows like him", he said in derision.

Neither man noticed Hannah as she shook her head in amusement and said to herself, "And the men folk in the tavern call us *tattling* old crones".

It was the first time she had been to the mill for over two months, ever since Clara had given birth to the infant James and now her *lying-in* was finished and she had left her bed. Hannah was looking forward to her walk to buy the much-needed flour and to catch up with the village news from the miller's wife. As she approached the mill red-throated eaves swallows skimmed low over the mill pond after the ever present clouds of midges. She had always envied the peace and quiet of the place after living most of her life next to the constant hammering in the smithy. Here, it was only the creaking of the water-wheel as it was driven round by the fast flowing mill race which was heard, but on this day, not even that disturbed the peace. Hannah looked towards the mill and noticed the shutters were drawn across the windows of the upper floors. It was unusual for the miller to stop the mill, Hannah thought uneasily. Windmills could only grind the corn on the days when the wind blew and therefore, with the vagaries of the weather, they constantly stopped turning, but water was plentiful here to drive the mill whenever it was needed, regardless of *rain or shine*. Perhaps the quern stones needed dressing to keep the furrows on their faces deep and the lands rough, Hannah summised and the miller had stopped the mill to remove them. It was only by doing this on a regular basis could he grind the corn sufficiently fine to make bread flour together with the coarser feed he milled for the farmers.

Hannah ducked her head under the watermill's low door and entered its dusty interior. She thought how quiet it was as she looked for the miller. Normally it was difficult to be heard over the sound of the huge wooden cogwheels meshing together as they turned the millstones in a constant pounding rhyme. Even the crackle of the corn as it was fed into a hole in the centre of the top stone was not to be heard. The miller could never relax and would normally be constantly on the move, regulating the flow of corn down the wooden chutes and adjusting the distance between the stones. His eyes would be looking left to right, up and down, alert for any changes in the rhythm of the machinery and his nose ready for any hot smells which might mean the quernstones were rubbing together. Now the mill was still and quiet, almost deathly quiet.

Hannah left the mill and made her way across the grass to the mill cottage and opening its low door, called out, "Anybody at home?"

The miller's wife hurried from the bed chamber at the back of the small cottage to greet her. Her pallid face was gaunt and dark circles ringed her disconnected eyes. Despite the way she looked she had the usual warmth in her voice as she said "Good day, Mistress Larkin. My husband is suffering greatly with a fever and is *indeed* bedridden. If you have come for flour, I will gladly bag some up, if you would be kind enough to sit with him. *Alas*, I try not to leave him too long", she added, with a hint of desperation.

Hannah made her way through to the bed chamber and gasped when she glimpsed the man lying prone on the bedstead. Although his face glistened with beads of sweat, he shivered with cold. She bent down and pulled another bedsheet over him and as she did so, she noticed the crimson-coloured rash around his mouth. She stepped back in alarm and waited for his wife to return with the flour.

When she returned the woman saw the look on Hannah's face and explained, "He was tormented with the most terrible flashes of pains in his head three days past, ranting and raving he was and then he started vomiting. My poor man has been so troubled but now, as you can see, he lies quite still and has not spoken a word since yesterday *morn*".

Hannah watched as the distraught woman wrung her hands together with worry. "You can do no more than keep him warm and *moist* his lips with some water and perhaps *chumble* a little bread in some ale", she advised.

The miller's wife nodded her head in agreement, "I have been bathing the rash on his face with a fusion of yarrow and using a clove and nutmeg tea on his lips in the hope that the *malady* passes soon".

Hannah bid goodbye and clutching the bag of flour to her chest she made her way home, full of concern about the man's *ailing*. He had good *countenance* and was popular in the village although the farmers and gentry continually complained he over-charged to grind their corn. One sack of flour for every nineteen he gave them back, not much for the poor man's labour, Hannah thought.

"Were there any black crusts on the man's skin?" Gideon asked, on learning about the miller's condition, "or yellow puss in the pustules?"

"No, just a rash round his mouth and a most dreadful fever", Hannah replied.

Gideon thought for a while before answering, "Sounds like the *sweating sickness* to me, either that or *tis cow pox*. They keep a house-cow at the back of the mill and it's probably come from the beast".

Hannah bit her tongue. Cow pox sometimes *inflicted* young dairy maids but not old millers, she thought.

Four days passed and Gideon had not given much thought to what his wife had told him when he saw the Parson walking up the drover's road from the direction of the mill, with his housekeeper, Daisie Lightfoote by his side, their faces *bereft of their usual humour*.

"The miller is dead", the clergyman said bluntly, as Gideon walked towards him to bade him good day. He could not help but notice the look of concern on Daisie's face.

"Dead, sir?" he questioned.

"May God save us all, sir", the Parson murmured, "the man was afflicted with the *speckled monster*".

"Smallpox", Gideon exclaimed as a shiver of cold fear ran down his spine at the *doleful* news. It was not the cow pox, he thought ruefully.

Both men knew what it meant. The *speckled monster* was the most terrible *minister* of death, filling churchyards across the country with the dead, tormenting those not yet stricken with constant fear and leaving those it had spared with the most hideous *traces* of its power.

Over the weeks which followed a black pall of death hung over the grief-stricken village as coffin after coffin was carried into the church. The rows of grave stones in the churchyard stood in silence, like a sea of the dead. Some of the older ones had crumbled with the weathering of time, overgrown and unkempt but others were new, smooth white stone markers untarnished by time. Beyond them, new graves had been dug, patiently waiting their new occupants as the *sore pestilence* spread unabated.

Some days later, Clara saw Hannah's sombre face and held her breath. *"Tis* bad news I bring you", Hannah said in measured tones. "Ester Tanner has become stricken with the monster"

"Has she the *purples*?" Clara asked nervously, knowing if a purple flush had spread across her dearest friend's body, she would be meeting her Maker.

Hannah did not answer at once. "No, but she was *foully abounded* by crops of blisters all over.........."

Clara gasped and she held her hands to her mouth in shock at what she had just heard.

"Is she....?" she asked, not bringing herself to say the word.

Hannah spoke quickly. "No, no, she has been spared but.....", she hesitated, "but it has left its most terrible and most hideous traces on her face".

"Oh no", Clara gasped as she remembered how lovely Ester had looked when she had been her bridesmaid and now she would be the object of horror to all those who ever caught sight of her.

The baby stirred restlessly in his rush crib and Clara hurried to him with tears streaming down her pale cheeks as a result of Hannah's sad news.

Gideon and Nathan were working at the forge when they heard it. It was a cry of such piercing volume and intensity it seemed to well up from the bowels of the earth.

Together they rushed back into the cottage where they found Clara cradling the baby in her arms. Hannah had been in the garden when she heard the scream and was breathless as she arrived at the same time.

"He's dead, Nathan, our baby's dead", Clara cried, as she stared into her husbands' eyes.

Hannah reached forward and took the little bundle into her arms whilst Clara pressed her tear-stained face into Nathan's broad chest, sobbing uncontrollably. His face too had already become wet with tears from his reddening eyes as he stared unbelievably at the limp body of his little son. He wrapped his arms around his wife but they had lost the strength to give her the comfort she needed.

Clara lifted her head and with a distraught voice, she said, "It has taken our son, the *speckled monster* has taken our son".

The following day Gideon left the small group at the side of the grave mourning the death of his grandson to talk to the Parson. "There appears to be no respite from this devil's curse", he said solemnly.

The Parson looked drained of strength and emotion. Together, with Daisie Lightfoote constantly at his side, he had visited the dwellings of the afflicted, ministering what comfort he could to the living and giving the sacraments to the dying.

Gideon looked towards the rows of freshly dug graves and asked, "How many have succumbed?" He had lost count of the number of times he had shown his respect for the dead and had stopped working at the forge upon hearing the church bell pealing the death knell. The sexton tolled the bell in sets; three for a man, two for a woman and single mournful toll for a child.

"Forty-two and I fear it is not finished yet".

Gideon was astonished at the number. *Tis* one in three of the village, he thought grimly.

"It makes no distinction between husbands, wives and infants. *Tis without saying* the hideous traces it has also left behind. Terrible, deep pitted scars and blindness, transforming beauty into beast without distinction………." the Parson's voice trailed off. "*Tis* said that it is caused by foul air but only the good Lord truly knows".

The blacksmith's eyes shifted downwards as he realised the village would never be the same and may not even survive the calamity which had *befallen* it.

Clara's muscles ached and she decided to lie on the comfort of the flock mattress for another hour or two. She had been listless during the two weeks which had passed since James had died and if it had not been for her much-loved husband, life would have lost its purpose.

With the doors of the smithy closed and bolted and the fire laying stone-cold in the forge, the small family clustered round Clara's bedside praying for her recovery. Her feverish temperature and the headaches began to give way to flashes of pain which caused her to scream out in agony. Nathan did his best to sooth her but the pains grew with such intensity they clamped her chest as if it was being held in the blacksmith's vice. She beat her head against the bedstead and screamed so loud that Nathan thought that the devil himself had visited her.

The chamber was dark and as Hannah lifted the candle to mop Clara's sweat-drenched chest, she saw the rash round her nose and mouth had begun to turn to blisters. She moved the bed coverings and to her horror, she saw the foul blisters were beginning to spread over her arms and legs.

The Parson had visited every day and had held Clara's hand and prayed for her delivery from the evil. Once or twice she had lifted her head and opened her eyes a little. A faint smile had even passed over her face, almost like the sun breaking through on a cloudy day which gave Nathan much hope for her recovery.

In the early hours of the *morn,* a single candle was still burning in the chamber when, with a growing fear, Nathan noticed some of the blisters around Clara's mouth were filled with yellow puss. Holding his breath, he held the candle closer to her face and by its flickering light; he saw the pustules had darkened to purple, outlined with rings of red, like burning coals in the forge. A feeling of panic raced through every nerve in his body. His mind raced. Less than twelve months had passed since this room had been their bride-chamber and now it had become……

He buried his head into her breast and prayed to the Lord she would be spared. Minutes passed before he lifted his head and as he did so, he saw crimson blood was trickling from her nose and the corner of her mouth. Waves of grief overwhelmed him and he became lost in time, then as his legs buckled from under him and his knees fell to the ground, he began to weep as if she was already dead.

"Clara", Nathan cried out, and as he did so, he felt her gentle hand grip his own. Her grip was as soft as a mid-summer breeze. He looked into her milk-white face and saw her eye lids briefly flicker before she breathed her last and sank into the wall of pillows in blessed release.

Tears flowed unchecked down his cheeks and dripped from his *unshaved* chin. He was too sad to cry out or wail, he just knelt there as still as a statue while the magnitude of loss swept over him.

In the weeks which followed the speckled monster finished its evil work and moved on to find new towns and villages to *foully abound*. It was said by some that it was the traveller who had lodged at the Wheel who had carried the *infliction,* others said it was caused by the *bad air* which it was said had hung over Southwell at the time.

The one thing they all knew was the long trail of grief and suffering the *monste*r had left in its wake.

8

Where the Mind Goes. 1798.

Daisie Lightfoote sat at the oak-planked table in the parsonage's kitchen waiting for the pots of the fruit preserve to set. The ancient mulberry tree standing on the front lawn had borne much fruit this particular year, so much, in fact there was enough to make the jam and leave sufficient of the juicy, black fruits behind for the blackbirds to feast upon at their leisure. Over the years the tree had become crooked and gnarled and Parson Lamb would jest that he was similar to the tree, both in habit and age. Daisie smiled at the thought and left the table to look out of the window towards the garden. Thomas Brown had long since left this mortal coil and now a young man named Stephen Thatcher had replaced him to tend to the Parson's dwindling hives of bees in the glebe field, his horse in the stable at the back of the parsonage and the graveyard sheep. Together, with his ten year old brother, Thaddius, or Tad as he was called, Stephen did his best to maintain the garden to meet the Parson's pleasure but both the brothers knew, try as they might; they would never replace Thomas Brown in that respect.

No two brothers could have been so unalike. Although Stephen was a full six years older than his brother, he was a weak, sickly looking youth, never free from some malady or another, winter and summer alike and glum and sullen in face. Meanwhile, Thadius, who towered above his brother, was broad in the chest and strong in the arm and enjoyed a quick and ready wit.

As Daisie watched the elder of the brothers remove the *full blown* rose blooms in the hope new ones would bud and burst forth before they were *smitten* by the winter's frosts, she spotted the Parson fast asleep on his favourite seat under the rose arbour. The old man's head had drooped forward with his chin pressed firmly against his chest, bobbing gently in time with his breathing. Every so often he was awoken by his snoring, causing him to straighten up momentarily, before his head dropped to his chest again.

Daisie looked at the old man who had been so kind to her and marvelled at his great age. At eighty seven he was now the oldest person in the village. He could still ride his horse around the parish collecting the tithes and had never missed taking the Sunday services, save once or twice, thirty or so years ago when Southwell was scourged by the dreadful *speckled monster*. Her mood darkened as she recalled the grief and suffering it had brought to the village.

She had been just twenty years of age when she had come to the parsonage and had always done her best to serve him as well as she could, particularly in the preparation of his meals which was something he valued greatly. That was until two winters *past* when the sickness came and turned his insides to water. She remembered how the pain had *clawed* at his bowels and how the rich meats and wines he had enjoyed for most of his life had now become a source of pain rather than pleasure, but he had *roused* somewhat since then, and even last week had commented on how much he enjoyed the morsels she had cooked for him.

Daisie's mind wandered and turned back to her family. Her memories of her father were not something she wanted to recall and instead her thoughts turned to her mother. She had just been a country *doddy poll* before she became betrothed to Percival Lightfoote, when her head was turned by his power and influence and the *fripperies* in life became increasingly more important to her than caring for her offspring.

Her hands went up as she suddenly remembered the pots of mulberry preserve needed covering before they were taken to join the other pots of preserve lined up on the shelves in the pantry store and she quickly turned away from the window and from her memories. She paused and brushed away a wayward lock of fair hair which had fallen across her blue eyes. Over the years she had attracted a lot of attention from some of the *menfolk* and had a number of suitors but it came to nothing. Even at the age of fifty-three she knew she was still considered by some of the men in the village to be an attractive woman. Her look darkened. No, she thought, it all came to nothing and it always would, thanks to the threats to the men's lives from her brother Abel. She sighed at the thought of his name and wondered, as she had so many times before, why he despised her so much. Even as a child the hatred was in his heart and try as she did, it never moved. Many years ago, soon after she had come to the parsonage she had spoken to the Parson about it and she recalled his words to her.

"Child", he had said, "It is not just you that he hates. You must remember that evil is born and not made. Most people are born good and will always fight off the bad. Others are born into light and fall into darkness". She remembered how the kind man had held her hand as he finally concluded, "*Ala*s, there are some like your brother, who are born into darkness and despite everything, will never see the light".

She knew what the Parson meant, the devil had claimed her brother as one of his own and its evil presence had long resided within Abel's mind. His life had now become a downward spiral of strong ale and gambling and of course, violence. Always short of money, he had squandered what money and land their father had left behind. Together, with the equally evil Henry Prinn at his side, he stalked the neighbourhood with his long-bladed knife pushed in the leather sheath hanging from his belt, threatening to skewer anyone who opposed him. Sometimes he would disappear for months, making rich pickings in the back alleys of London and amongst the homes and pockets of the rich. He did not have the skill to pick locks or was clever enough to clip off the edges of gold coins. Instead he just saw what he wanted and took it knowing he was well armed and strong enough to go up against anyone who opposed him. Then he would return to the village and in the drunken stupors which followed, he would boast of the low life he had mixed with in the bawdy houses and the fist fights and robberies he had indulged in, and yet, with his age now reaching over sixty years, he and Henry Prinn, had somehow managed to escape the *hempen* rope of the scaffold.

✗

Blown by autumn's chill wind, a faint odour of wood smoke drifted over the churchyard from one of the tall chimneys of the nearby parsonage. The wind did not have the wintery blusters which were to come but just a nip sufficient to show the village that a new season was dawning upon it. The thickets of bracken clinging to the folds in the Downs were already yellowing and soon the dogwoods and spindle berries on the lower slopes would be aflame with a riot of red and gold.

Showers of leaves had already begun to dance down in their final flight. They were beautiful but dead, their life was over. As Nathan threaded his way through the grave stones in the churchyard his face was set as hard as the ancient stones. His stride never faltered as he headed towards one stone in particular. A bough from a nearby beech tree had drooped low and a finger-thick branch snagged onto the pocket on his jacket. He pushed past it and cursed with *unbridled* anger in his voice but as the branch tried to break free he heard the sound of ripping yarn as the side of his pocket was torn apart.

It only took a dozen or so more strides before he stopped and helped by the weak rays of the sallow sun, stared at the eroded lettering on the stone. His eyes were red and his face was already wet with tears. After all the years which had passed, the pain he felt was *liken* to an open wound, forever raw by something which couldn't be undone. His finger tenderly traced the outline of the name which the mason had cut into the limestone thirty-three long years before.

"Clara", he whispered, as his finger pushed against the cold stone

He reached out and embraced the headstone with both hands, as he had done during their final moments together

He remembered looking at her and holding her hand as if it was yesterday. Huddled on the *flock bed* like a wounded bird, she was panting as the air drained from her body. Her eyes were looking at him with a soft, unseeing look as she took farewell of all in life that was good. Nathan's face was stern and unforgiving as his thoughts turned to the ugly red, festering pustules which had covered her beautiful face and how they had gradually turned into black, puss-filled crusts. His lip curled as he recalled the rage he had felt on that terrible day, and on every single day ever since.

He looked haggard, worn down by the years which had passed as his eyes turned to look at the small marker close by. He shifted his position and once again his finger traced the lettering. It was smaller this time in keeping with the size of the stone.

"James Larking", he read, "beloved son of Nathan and Clara". The ghosts of so many dashed hopes flittered across his tear-filled eyes. He shook his head to vanquish them from his mind fearful that the grief he was feeling would never leave him.

Some time passed before shifted his position. His leaden feet ploughed through the thin blanket of fallen leaves which coved the ground. He paused to look at two more stones, skirted by pools of autumn gold, snuggled together as their occupants had been in life.

"Gideon Larkin, died 5th July 1780 aged 68 years"

Nathan turned towards the other stone and read, "Hannah Larkin, wife of Gideon, died 18th August, 1782 aged 67 years.

The day was growing old and the fainting sun still had some way to go when Nathan's large, calloused hand gently touched the top of each stone and then after a few moments of reflective thought, he slowly made his way from the graveyard back to the smithy.

Shadowed faces loomed out of the half light in the alehouse but most of the village men averted their eyes from the solitary man staring into his flagon of ale, fearful of trouble. They remembered the nights when they had been jostled and punched, when tables had been over-turned and good ale spilt. Even the two flighty serving wenches who busied themselves amongst the taverns other customers, laughing and joking, knew better than to approach him. Tonight the flagon was his only friend. His drinking partner was probably nursing a headache under a hedge somewhere, *cup shotten* from the day before. Abel Lightfoote wiped away the foam around his mouth with the back of his dirt-engrained hand before lifting the flagon to his lips once more.

The flame of the solitary tallow candle burning on the *counter* held *steady* and was bright enough to relieve the darkness in the large, smoke-filled tavern. Watched by a group of unwashed *clodhoppers*, two men were sitting at a small table playing a game of *three mens morris*, each one taking their turn to lay one of their three pieces on the place where one of the six lines they had scratched on a wooden board intersected with the others. Their faces were etched with concentration as they tried to outwit the other and win the coins which lay on the table in front of them.

Abel Lightfoote ignored them and drained the flagon. His scowling face looked even more sinister as the flames from the logs burning in the tavern's wide grate, reflected on the patchwork of red and blue veins which flecked his weathered jowls. His pockets were empty and as he looked into the bottom of his empty flagon, he bristled with anger as he spat out the name of the man who was now farming his father's fields.

"Farmer bloody Bithnell", he mouthed, with an undisguised threat rumbling from deep down in his belly. The bitterness in his voice rose like bile into his mouth and he spat into the straw which covered the brick floor.

His blood began to boil as he remembered how Samuel Bithnell had bought his father's farm, to the east of Southwell, at auction when his own mounting gambling debts forced him to sell and how the same man had bought most of the land surrounding Dunn farm for a *knock-down* price for the same reason.

"One day I will flay the *hog grubber's* hide and he will pay *hearty* for this", he vowed, with raw malice in his voice.

Without lifting his head, he slowly raised his eyelids and through the slits of his bloodshot eyes he saw Henry Prinn approaching with his peculiar loping gait and spayed foot. The man was ragged, dirty and unshaven, with his damp hair hanging lankly to his shoulders. His waistcoat was stained with *ale-tears* and all manner of other filth: his breeches torn and gaping at the knees. The sleeves of his woollen shirt had been roughly cut off at the elbows and despite the cold evening air gusting outside, he was coatless. As he made his way towards Lightfoote, his restless eyes darted furtively around the alehouse, anxious to see who was inside.

Lightfoote did not acknowledge his presence and looking at his empty flagon, growled, "Have *yee* got a *bender,* I need a *sup*?"

With the ever present vacant look on his face, Prinn hastily searched the pockets of his breeches for one of the soft silver coins. He fished out the sixpence and with a sense of relief showing on his face, handed it to Lightfoote, saying, "That's the last of the *shiners*, Abel. I *aint* got nothing left other than some *fiddlers money* and I'm *gut foundered,* I *aint* eaten since Tuesday.

Lightfoote spun the coin in the air and said in a low voice, "That being the case, Henry, tonight *thou* and I will go *a'thieving.* His eyes were cold and ruthless as he snarled "and I know the very place".

The inn-keeper watched the men with a wary eye as they left and skulked off into the night. Those two *cloyers* have broken enough bones in here, he thought thankfully, as the sound of Lightfoote's hob-nailed boots disappeared into the distance.

×

The *long case* was striking *eight of the clock* when a beer-soaked farm *clod* staggered towards the open doorway of the alehouse as Nathan Larking strode in. There was a sickening thud as the two men collided. Nathan snapped as the rage which had been simmering all day boiled over. His eyes flashed with anger as he raised his fist to strike the man. The *clod* straightened his back ready to confront the blacksmith but a glance at the anger blazing in his eyes confirmed what the final outcome would be. The blacksmith was ready to half kill him and the *clod* quickly backed away and made his way home.

Nathan looked haggard as the serving girl brought him a tankard of apple cider. The pain of Clara and the infant's death was as raw as ever and he knew it would never ease. He had taken solace in the alehouse most nights since the last of his parents had died and now his only friend was the bottom of a tankard. The *speckled monster* had taken his wife and child and now, due to the events unfolding in the country, he was beginning to lose his livelihood.

"A master of iron", he scoffed to himself. "What use is it when there are fewer people who require my services and no son who can learn the secrets of our craft?" Every word he muttered, stung him to the core, fuelling the fire burning inside him.

The girl brought another tankard and as she did so a man wearing a heavy woollen smock pulled up a stool and without a word being spoken by either man, sat opposite Nathan. Neither spoke, both sipping their drink, unaware of the noise around them.

It was the *youkell* who broke the silence. "Evening, blacksmith", he said, eager for some conversation.

Nathan stared into the golden liquid swirling in his tankard. He had no need of company tonight of all nights and ignored the man.

"The ground's soft over *top of hill*", the man went on, not waiting or indeed wanting Nathan to comment. "Farmer Bithnell says *we's to* use the new plough *on the morrow*", the man persevered, having changed his mind and now hoping to have some congenial company.

Nathan felt his chest tighten as the words the ploughman had just uttered resonated within him. He had not forgotten that Bithnell owed him twelve days money for the work he had done on the turn-wrest plough: money he desperately needed to survive the lean times during the winter months. The serving girl passed by and noticed his empty tankard and as she went to take it away, he slapped another four pence on the table for it to be filled again. His head was beginning to spin.

"Mister Bithnell is calling it his *Rotherham* plough. It's the first time one of *'em* has been made this far south", the *youkell* continued.

Nathan nodded his head.

"It was you who shod it with iron?" the man said. "Never in my life have I *sees* a wooden plough being clad with iron plates…..nor has anybody else for that matter", he added.

Nathan nodded again as he remembered how surprised he was when he had helped the ploughwright to manhandle the wooden plough into the smithy and how the man had told him what Samuel Bithnell wanted. He remembered the concerned look on the ploughwright's face when he asked if Nathan thought the days of the wooden long-plough were over. He felt the rage rising again as he recalled the work he had done for Samuel Bithnell and still no payment had he received. Twelve days it had taken him. Twelve days of hard labour for one and sixpence a day, Seven days had been spent shaping and beating the iron to cover the time-honoured oak-wood plough-share and mouldboard and another five days forging the coulter cutting blade and the hitch irons. Anger blazed in his eyes.

"Bithnell expects me to plough an acre a day with the thing, by myself and a team of two!" the smock-clad man added.

Nathan came to life. "An acre a day, by yourself!" he exclaimed, with a voice which was becoming increasingly slurred. An image of a field being turned with a wooden long-plough came into his mind, One man walking backwards, leading a team of four drays or oxen, yoked side by side, occasionally striking them to urge them on. Behind the wooden plough, holding onto its long handles was the ploughman whilst a third man followed behind with a spade, turning over any ground the plough had missed. Three men and four beasts to plough half an acre, he thought, and now, with the iron-clad plough, one man and two beasts will be able plough twice as much.

"The cost of corn is rising and *whens* I have ploughed all that *needs it*, the farmer *says* he will hire the plough out at two shillings and sixpence a day", the man continued, unaware of Nathan's rising anger. "The new plough is not the *ends* of it. He said *t'other* day the time is not very distant when a thing they *calls* a steam engine will be what matters on every well conducted farm of three or four-hundred acres, perhaps even less".

Nathan's mind was racing as he tried to calculate how much land Bithnell now farmed. He had bought Warren farm a few years back which had considerable acreage as well as buying Lightfoote's farm and then he had bought most of the land which had belonged to George Bentley's farm, after the old fool had bequeathed it to the Lightfoots.

"He *says, the steam thing* will be used for threshing and dressing the corn for the use of his stock as well as crushing oats and cutting the roots". The man looked at Nathan as he drained his tankard. "That's not the end of it; the steam in the thing's engine will afford the means for boiling the potatoes for the swine and the hens in a *cheap manner.* Wouldn't be at all surprised if the thing doesn't wipe our arses when *the needs be*", he added as an afterthought

The rage rising in Nathan was faster and more destructive than he had ever known before. What could he expect from life now with his wife and child lying in their cold graves for many a year and with no one to pass on the skills of the blacksmith, which had been passed from father to son for generations? He was lonely and short of work and short of money.

His mind was becoming more *befuddled* with the drink and his father's voice was beginning to echo round and round in his head, *"One thing is for certain",* it was telling him, *"nothing will ever replace the horse and the plough and if you master the skills and protect our secrets, you'll always be able to enjoy a plate of cold meat and a quart of ale under the roof of your own home".*

You were wrong, father, he thought bitterly, you were bloody wrong.

A sneer formed on the *youkell's* face as he leant forward, his eyes bearing straight into Nathans. "They say that I *drove* the straightest furrow in these parts but the day is coming my friend when there will be no need for the horse and plough", he paused to spit into the straw on the floor before finally taunting, and the likes of old fellows such as *thee* and me".

Nathan's hands twitched and he could feel a vein pulsing in the side of his face. His fists were clenched as he exploded with rage.

"**As God is my oath, no man cheats me out of my rightful due**", he shouted and as he tried to rise to his feet, his leg became entangled with the stool he had been sitting on and he kicked it viciously to one side. Men around him left their seats, alarmed at the commotion but their faces were but a blur to Nathan. As he went to move forward his leg failed to take his weight and he sprawled across the table in front of him, scattering the card players and spilling their ale. They cursed at him and pushed him onto the floor. They had no time for anyone who ruined their card game and spilt their beer, *lest* of all, a *flawed* blacksmith, who had spent the evening crying into his ale.

Nathan glared at them as they searched the floor for the scattered coins which had been strewn across the floor and with a threatening voice, shouted out, "**If the man does not pay me what he owes, I will take it in kind**".

As he staggered up and towards the doorway the inn-keeper blocked his way, saying, "Go home Nathan and sleep it off".

He ignored the man and tried to push past him.

The man briefly stood his ground as he put a small carved tinder box into Nathan's hand. "It dropped out of your torn pocket when you fell to the floor", he said, relieved the troublemaker was leaving his establishment.

Without a word, other than a drunken grunt, Nathan snatched the tinder box from the inn-keeper's hand and without a thought, stuffed it back into the torn pocket.

With the moon lighting his way, he stumbled and fell several times as he made his way to the stable behind his cottage. The nag stood patiently as he bridled and saddled it, only objecting slightly when he buckled the girth strap too tightly. His *ale-fuddled* mind was made up; he would take vengeance against the man who was going to bring so much misery to Southwell. It was a case of where the mind goes, the man follows.

"*Ave yer* got your *sharps and flats*", Abel Lightfoote questioned his companion.

The two men had made their way up the steep lane, passing Dunn farmhouse on the left and after going over the brow of the hill, they began to make their way across the pastures where Samuel Bithnells' sheep were grazing contentedly in the moonlight.

"*Got me* knife", Prinn answered with a grin; "it's more than enough to skin one of Bithnell's *woolly birds*". He raised his head in the direction of the full moon. "See that, Abel?" he said with a chuckle.

"I do indeed, Henry", Lightfoote replied, understanding Prinn's meaning, "*tis* the hunters moon, a good omen if I ever did see one". He held his hand up to silence Prinn's *beef-headed* chortling and cocked his ear to the wind. "Quick, under the hedge, there's a *galloper* heading this way", he ordered.

The night air was cold on Nathan's face as he urged his mare on towards Warren farmhouse and his confrontation with Samuel Bithnell.

The two men pressed their bodies flat to the ground and backed under the thorn hedge as the sound of a horse's pounding hooves grew closer. It was becoming apparent the man was riding close to the hedge and Lightfoote beckoned to Prinn to keep himself well hidden. As the *galloper* thundered by, Lightfoote lifted his head to catch a glimpse of the rider before his eyes became filled with the dust churning up from the horses' hooves.

"*Tis* Larkin", he said, and barely before the words had left his mouth, something was thrown from the galloping horse and bounced along the ground in front of them.

Prinn broke cover and crawled through the dust storm to retrieve the object. Holding it aloft, he shouted in glee, "*Tis* Larkin's tinder box....it will be worth a pretty penny when *wees* sell it".

Lightfoote said nothing; instead he looked across the moonlit landscape, his gaze being drawn towards two straw-topped ricks, standing side by side in the distance. "*Methinks* Henry, we will not be skinning one of Bithnell's *woolly birds* after all", he said cunningly. "This could be our lucky day", he spluttered as his laughter began to drown out the sound of the horses' hooves cantering off into the distance.

Lightfoote snatched the box from Prinn's hand and examined it. "There's no mistaking it at all", he said as he looked at the carved lid, "It's even got a bloody horseshoe nicely carved on it".

Nathan pulled up his mount with a sharp tug on the reins and leant forward in the saddle. He stroked the horse's sturdy neck and despite the brisk wind which was blowing; he felt the sweat running down into the thick, black hair covering the horse's broad chest. The ride up the hill had been hard and fast and he had not spared the beast and it whinnied and stomped as it caught its breath. He sat up in the saddle and ahead in the darkness he could see the flickering light of the candles burning in the lower chambers of Warren farmhouse. His head throbbed uncomfortably, almost painfully and the need to vomit rose in him. His hands slipped from the reins and dropped limply by his side. He felt worn down by the events of the day and gratefully filled his lungs with the cold night air. The anger which had raged inside had burnt out and now all he was left with was a sense of loss: a loss of everything he had once cherished. What is happening to me? he thought, as he lifted his eyes to the heavens and stared into the star-studded sky. Moments passed and it was sometime later when he steered his horse round and slapped the reins.

"Home girl", he said quietly, "it's time to go home".

Henry Prinn's spayed foot determined the speed he could travel and he had a job keeping up as he trailed behind Abel Lightfoote's fast pace across the freshly reaped clover meadow towards the towering ricks.

"What have *thee* a mind to do?" he asked breathlessly as he limped behind, mindful it was *long years* since he had been in the *flush of youth*.

Lightfoote waited for him to catch up and with a grin fixed on his face, said, "Larkin has been *nought* but a thorn in our flesh for many a long year". He laughed a hideous laugh. "The time *hath* come Henry, to remove that thorn once and for good".

"They're certainly big buggers", Prinn said, with a vacant look on his face, as he looked up at the clover ricks.

"The bigger the better", Lightfoote replied.

"*Tis* said it's been a good year for the clover and rye, so that accounts for their size", Henry Prinn *prattled*.

Lightfoote ignored the *dull swift* and walked round the largest of the ricks, sizing it up. Up to its conical top its height was at least that of three tall men and it was probably twenty feet or more across. Some sheep that were enjoying a little shelter alongside it paused their grazing and looked up at the wild looking man who had suddenly appeared and as they sensed danger, they followed their natural instinct and ran off to safety.

The wet spring and early summer had indeed made the clover grow lush and thick and it had laid more than ankle deep in the meadow after the reapers had done their work. Building the ricks had been a back-breaking task which had taken over a month of hard labour. At first, the sweet smelling hay was brought armful by armful by the men and women toiling day-long in the field and passed up to the two ploughmen who were tasked to build the ricks. When the distance became too far to reach, hay carts piled high with the sun-dried hay were used, drawn by slow plodding drays. Slowly, as the stacks gradually grew higher, the rick builders tramped the hay down with their heavy leather boots, before they finally capped the top with a cone-shaped, barley straw thatch.

Prinn watched as Abel Lightfoote pushed his fist into the rick before saying with growing satisfaction, "*Tis* as dry as an old bone".

The slow-witted *dolt* suddenly realised what was about to happen and he visibly shrunk away from his friend. "If we are *undone* by this, we will be for it. *Tis* a felonious crime for sure and many a man has already been *scragged* for *doing such*", he said nervously.

Lightfoote laughed. "Don't be so *light timbered* Henry, we *aint* going to get caught. Once I've fired it, I'll drop the tinder box *whence* it can be found and then *hoof it*. That *diseased dog*, Larkin, will be swinging for this before the week's out", he said, with unconcealed loathing in his voice. In the moonlight, Prinn could see the man's eyes were as cold and ruthless as he had ever seen them in more than sixty years.

Lightfoote opened the tinder box and took out the jagged flint and iron bar. He struck the flint hard onto the bar and watched as a lifeless spark dropped onto the moss and rag tinder. Again and again he struck it, his anger rising with each strike, until a spark caught and a small flame miraculous appeared almost from nowhere. It was insignificant at first but quickly grew into a life of its own. He raked out a handful of hay from the rick and carefully lit it from the burning tinder before placing it back whence it came. Slowly the side of the rick began to yield to the small flame. Its light was feeble at first but as the fire grew in strength and its shadows danced in the moonlight, the men's faces became distorted into grotesque masks. Within minutes, tongues of fire began to lick round the girth of the rick and higher up the side until the barley thatch on top was ablaze. The wind increased and as it did so, it began to take the whole of the rick into its roaring flames. As the men watched, almost mesmerised by the ferocity of the fire, the size and shape of the clover rick was becoming lost in molten, white flames.

"*Tis* a picture of hell itself", Prinn whispered nervously, as he became increasingly aware of the enormity of the crime they had committed.

The flames, fanned by the wind, began to lick the second rick until within minutes, it too was ablaze, causing the two men to step back from the ever growing heat and as they did so, they became enveloped in the thick clouds of white smoke which was rolling around them. Prinn breathed in a mouthful and began to cough loudly.

"Shut up you fool", Lightfoote barked, as he looked cautiously around.

There was no sound, other than the roar of the flames as the burning hay started to fall inwards, sending up clouds of grey ash from the sullen, smouldering fires. They had been good solid ricks but as Lightfoote and Prinn watched, they were all but gone, other than mounds of fire within their cores..

"Look Abel", Prinn called out with panic rising in his voice, as he saw black figures running towards the red light of the fires. Through the swirling smoke, he could see people running towards them from the direction of Warren farm.

"Best we then look smart, Henry, it's time we weren't here. They'll be alerting the constable in no time and he'll be organising a *hue and cry*", Lightfoote said, pleased with their night's work.

As the two men started to race away, Lightfoote suddenly stopped, "I nearly forgot", he said, with a grin on his face as he laid Nathan Larking's tinder box on the steaming ground, just back from the smouldering ruins where the clover ricks had once stood.

✕

Samuel Bithnell's face was stricken with the horror as he stood looking in disbelief at the sea of smouldering embers. The man's mouth gaped open and his chest heaved at the sight in front of him.

"How am I going to keep the animals fed this coming winter without the fodder to feed them?" he mumbled in horror.

His face and clothes were smeared with black ash and his parched throat longed for a mouthful of water as rivers of sweat ran down his face from the great heat of the fire. He could only watch, rooted to the spot as three of his farm-men, almost oblivious to the heat, started to dig their pitchforks into the heart of the burning piles in an attempt to save any of the clover hay which had not already burnt.

Gradually, the farmer's shock at seeing his burning ricks turned to seething anger, "Whoever did this will be hanging from the gallows *afore* the month is out, as God is my witness, I will see to it", he vowed ruthlessly.

Nathan was nursing a sore head as he raked out the coke smouldering in the forge's fire, getting ready for another days work when there was a loud banging on the smithys' double doors. As he pushed the doors open the man stepped back, his blackthorn staff of office gripped firmly in his hand.

Nathan recognised him. He was a tenant farmer from over the hill, appointed at the last vestry meeting to be the parish constable for the year.

"Good day to *thee* Jonas", Nathan said warily.

There was no smile on Jonas Sedge's face as he said, solemnly, "I'm here to bring *thee* to justice, Nathan". He only had two months left to serve as the village constable and then somebody else would be given the thankless task. The two shillings he had already earnt in delivering the evidence to the magistrate would supplement his meagre income he *gleaned* from the stony land he farmed and then there would be the shilling he would get for locking Nathan in the village round house but he would willingly *forego* it all, rather than helping to send the blacksmith to the gallows.

The smile on Nathan's face rapidly disappeared as he stared in astonishment at the man's un-blinking eyes. "What do *thee* mean.......what for?" he stuttered as he began to step forward.

The constable held his ground. "*Tis* said that last night, you *fired* the clover ricks belonging to Samuel Bithnell".

"I did no such thing". Nathan's voice rose in indignation, before his heart began to pound as he remembered where he was last night. He had been close to where the ricks stood but the anger which had been in his eyes had blinded him from seeing them. It was then a terrifying thought flashed across his mind. Had he in his drunken stupor set fire to them?

"There are witnesses who were in the Wheel last night who heard you make threats against Bithnell and his property", the constable said calmly.

Nathan slowly nodded in agreement as began to recall the threats he had made in the ale house.

"Best come with me to the lock-up", Jonas Sedge said quietly as he took Nathan's arm and led him along the lane towards the small, stone building with the barred, slit window and the studded oak door, hanging on its heavy iron hinges.

Sleep had not come easily that night and Nathan was already awake when he heard the rumble of cart wheels coming along the drover's road from the direction of Ashden. His mouth was parched dry and with his searching tongue, he tried to get some saliva to moisten it. He was cold and the iron fetters had chaffed his wrists and ankles. As he struggled to get to his feet he winced as he felt the pain they had caused. He listened, wondering what would happen next, as the key turned in the rusty lock and the heavy door creaked open. The pale light of the early autumn morning flooded in and standing alongside a stern looking Jonas Sedge, Nathan could see the toothless grin of a shoddily dressed man who was nearly as wide as he was tall.

"This is the gaoler from Ashden. He's here to take *thee* to the Assizes", the constable said quickly, almost pleased to rid the words from his mouth. The tone of his voice had changed overnight and Nathan sensed the farmer had already judged him as guilty.

The gaoler took hold of the chain attached to the double fetters and pulled Nathan towards the cart. "You're a big bugger, aint thee", he said, with a sickening grin on his pock-marked face. "You won't need your *legs a pulling*". He was still laughing as he chained his captive to the floor of the cart. "Go on", he shouted at his horse and as he did so the cart jolted forward causing Nathan to fall heavily on his back. The man laughed again, "Many a good man has been *scragged* from the back of this cart, as *thee* will be finding out".

Nathan tried to ignore him and pressed his back against the side of the cart in an attempt to make himself more comfortable.

"The Assizes are in session and they say you'll be tried tomorrow and hung on Friday", the man informed Nathan over the noise of the cart wheels. "Only two sentences on felons who burn down clover ricks……they either turn '*em* loose or they hang *em*. He chuckled as he concluded, "As I *say*, you'll be *hanging* on Friday".

Daisie Lightfoote had pondered for some while what to serve the Parson for his midday meal before deciding she would offer him a bowl of *pease* soup with some oatmeal added to it for the sustenance it would provide. She was thinking it was a good choice and that the elderly cleric, mindful of his troublesome stomach, should be able to manage, when the kitchen door was suddenly pushed open and Stephen Thatcher burst in, his white face seeming to be even whiter than usual.

"Mistress", the young man blurted out, "they've taken the blacksmith in chains to the Assizes. He's burnt down farmer Bithnell's clover ricks. They say the farmer had not paid him for work that had been done and the blacksmith has taken his revenge".

Daisie held her hands up and covered her face in horror as she gasped, "My dear God, they will hang him". Her face drained of colour. She walked to the window and deep in thought, stared blankly at the garden whilst the young gardener waited, unsure what to do or what to say.

Moments passed until she remembered the Parson would need to be immediately informed of the dreadful situation which had arisen.

Her first few knocks on the chamber door had been soft and unassuming *lest* she startled the old man from his morning sleep. She lifted the latch and entered the room. A low fire was burning quietly in the grate and the rank smell of stale tobacco smoke hung in the air.

"Excuse me sir", she said softly, as she roused the clergyman from his slumber, aware he was now in the eighth decade of his life.

Tobias Lamb pulled himself upright in his chair and looked blankly at Daisie as she explained the situation. At first, he remained silent as if he was still half asleep or in shock or perhaps he hadn't understood the full significance of what he had just been told. Daisie was unsure of which and remained silent as the old man gradually regained his senses. He wanted to know more than she could tell him and she suggested that they should summon Stephen Thatcher. The Parson waved the suggestion away with a flourish of his hand and remained silent in thought.

"*Tis* the work of the devil", he murmured at last. He rose slowly from his chair, saying, "Ask Stephen to saddle my horse whilst I find my riding boots and my thick woollen coat". His voice was slow and he somewhat stumbled over his words.

Followed by his young brother, Stephen Thatcher led the mare out of the stable and across the cobbled yard towards the mounting block as the cleric prepared himself to climb into the saddle. Pain was the old man's constant companion and he winced as he pulled up his lame leg and placed it clumsily into the stirrup. With each movement there was a creak of his bones.

"I may be some time before I return", he said, , "but rest assured, I will do what I can for Nathan". His voice was laboured.

Daisie stood next to Stephen and Tad Thatcher and watched the Parson, who despite his great age, sat erect in the saddle and with a voice, shaking with exertion, said, "Go on old girl", as he gently spurred his horse towards the lane and over the hill in the direction of Warren farm.

Daisie turned and walked slowly back into the parsonage. A feeling of guilt began to haunt her for asking so much of her elderly employer but there was no one else she could have turned to. All she could do now was to wait and pray.

9

The Greenless Tree.

The earthen floor of the gaol at the Assizes felt cold and damp and as Nathan lay looking up at the heavy planks of the fortified ceiling, he could feel every beat of his heart as it pounded against the hard ground beneath him. Somewhere in the heap of straw piled up in the corner of the small, square cell the rats he had heard scurrying about during the night were going about their morning's business. He listened. They were real enough. Outside, the solitary morning star which had escaped the darkness of the night was also real enough, as was the air of the despair Nathan was feeling. I have been such a fool, he thought, as his father's words came into his mind. Over forty years had passed since his father had spoken them but he remembered the words as if it was only yesterday.

"If you don't learn to keep your temper in check, one day you'll be hanging from the scaffold with your neck stretched and your feet a kicking", his father had told him after his fight with Abel Lightfoote.

The grimness of the place made him feel sick in his belly, not helped by the smell wafting from his unwashed cellmates who cowered away from him in the corner. The other prisoners had ignored him since he had arrived the day before and had kept their distance. They too were all awake and looking warily at him, fettered and chained like an animal, knowing he was a felon and fearful what he may have the presence of mind to do to them.

Nathan adjusted his position on the floor in the hope he could lessen the weight of the iron shackles which *cuffed* his wrists and ankles and as he did so, another acrid stink reached his nose. It was stronger this time. He looked towards the rotting pile of straw and was pleased he had avoided using it for his bed, suspecting all kinds of defilement lay buried within it. He struggled to his feet and as he did so, he wrinkled his nose in an attempt to lessen the *assault of the stench*. His chains were bolted to the wall and as he attempted to get closer to the small barred window, his face grimaced as the links tightened, causing the shackles to cut deeper into his wrists.

The early morning air was fresh and cold, taunting him to go outside and taste it. He shivered and regretted he had not thought about putting on his leather jerkin when the constable had arrested him. Not that it mattered now. His mind raced and panic began to rise from the pit of his belly as it started to replay the terrible thoughts which had haunted him during the long night. His throat was crisp dry and once again he felt the weight of the iron chains as he tried to raise his hand in an attempt to loosen his shirt collar, already imagining the noose tightening round his neck.

He raised his head and listened. His ears had become as sharp as a fox, alert for any sound which would signal his inevitable journey to the scaffold. Suddenly and without warning, the serenity surrendered to the harsh scream of rusted hinges as the cell's door was roughly pushed open. Nathan's breathing became more rapid and he could feel his heart hammering inside his rib cage as the gaoler came into the cell carrying a metal scoop hanging in a pail of murky-looking water and a fistful of dry bread.

"Bread is sixpence, if you have the money to pay for it", he said, as his eyes roved suspiciously round the small group of prisoners.

Nathan knew *guests* of the gaolers up and down the land had to provide their own food or pay for what they were offered and chose to remain silent.

A small waif of a girl broke free from the comforting folds of her mother's skirt and inched towards the man with a thin, outstretched hand. Nathan looked at her and wondered what crime she was accused of. Pick-pocketing, he thought, or perhaps from the look of her, stealing food, either way, it would be transportation to the colonies for seven years, if she was lucky.

The gaoler looked contemptuously into the begging girls' eyes and said sharply, "That'll be sixpence". Her head dropped with disappointment, knowing she would spend another day with her belly desperate for food.

Nathan fished in his pockets the best he could for one of the small coins he hoped were still in them. He wasn't surprised at the slovenly man's demand, knowing he benefited considerably from the money he made from his wretched prisoners. The man took the coin with a grin spreading across his unshaven face, content in the knowledge that the rest of the coins he had heard jingling in Nathan's pocket would be in his own by *the sunset of the morrow*.

Nathan took the slice of bread and handed it to the girl who snatched it from his hand before running back to the safety of her mother's arm.

"That's all you'll get offered today", the man said to Nathan, as he rubbed his hair vigorously to ease the itching of the lice which resided there, "that's all felons get offered, convicted or not".

Nathan didn't reply but nodded his head blankly, as if he knew what to expect.

The man looked Nathan up and down with more diligence than he did with the rest of his prisoners checking his iron shackles were in place and secure, before saying curtly, "The Sessions always start two hours after *the break of day*. The Judge likes to conclude his business quickly so I expect I will be taking you for a short ride in the back of my cart soon after".

The door slammed shut and Nathan heard the man's laughter as he shuffled back to his dingy cottage adjoining the festering gaol.

Five hours had passed before Nathan was dragged into the Courtroom like a dog on a chain leash. This was the moment he had been dreading and unknown hands pushed and pulled him into the place where the accused were required to stand. Everything was a blur as he blinked his eyes in disorientation at the number of people crowded into the cavernous room. He shuffled uneasily from foot to foot and after taking a deep breath, glanced around. Gradually as he became more aware of his surroundings, he saw he was facing a central aisle which was mostly free of gaping faces belonging to the crowds of people standing either side of it; most were men but mixed amongst them were some women and children. Their piercing eyes seemed to be penetrating his very soul. To his right, the jury sat looking dispassionately at him. Many of the men had been in the jury seats many times before and they knew it would be the role of the Assize Judge to pronounce the verdict on the prisoner and leave it to them to decide the sentence. That was the way it was done but this Judge was different. He had already decided that if he found the dishevelled and villainous felon standing in front of him guilty, there would only be one sentence and he would be the one to decide it, death by hanging.

Nathan stared back at the grim-faced jury and didn't like what he saw. These men in their frock coats and be-wigged heads weren't men who toiled from dusk to dawn for their masters and knew what it was like to be cold and hungry, worried about the changes which would threaten their jobs. These were freehold farmers, tenants who farmed their land by lease, copyholders and traders. They were gentlemen who would welcome any changes which would reduce the cost of labour making them even richer and scornful of anyone who might threaten it.

To one side of the jury, sitting behind an oak desk, raised on a high platform was the Judge and as Nathan nervously lifted his chin from his pounding chest, he saw the sombre looking man was peering over his wire-rimmed spectacles studying him. In the shaft of sunlight coming through the wide mullioned windows, the man's cold-blue eyes gleamed like frozen pools of water. Hidden for many years from the rays of the sun, his pale face was framed by a well-trimmed white beard which softened the lines furrowed deeply around the rest of his face. On his head, a full-bottomed wig hung down beyond his shoulders which did little to lessen his grim countenance. A black scarf was wrapped over his flowing scarlet robe, whilst a *casting hood* of a similar bright colour hung down his back. All of his judicial finery added to his look of menace.

The man coughed slightly before saying in a deep, rich voice, "You, Nathan Larkin, are capitally indicted for feloniously setting fire to two clover ricks belonging to one, Samuel Bithnell".

He paused to adjust the two rectangles of white linen tied at his throat before continuing, "It is a charge of such heinous nature that if you are found to be guilty, it is without holding the slightest hope of a reprieve". His eyes were stern and unforgiving as he glared at Nathan in his dishevelled state.

A murmur of surprise rippled through the crowd as they suddenly realised the gravity of the charge and they looked accusingly at the shackled, pale-faced man standing alone before the Judge.

Nathan glanced at the people standing to his left and saw a familiar face which lifted his spirits and he raised his eyes in the hope Jonas Sedge would see him. It only took a fleeting second for him to realise that the man was here in his position as village constable and would be giving evidence that would damn him and there could be others in the crowd with the same intention. A feeling of despondency swept through his shaking body.

The Judge's voice cut through the foul air in the courtroom, "Will the village constable step forward".

Jonas Sedge edged his way through the shoulders of the crowd and faced the bench. It was the first time he had been in this situation and was unsure what to do next.

"Come on man", the be-wigged Judge urged impatiently, "say what needs to be said".

Sedge noisily cleared his throat.

"Two nights ago, at around *ten of the clock,* Mr Samuel Bithnell, farmer at Warren farm was awoken by his man-servant and told that his clover ricks were ablaze". He hesitated, unsure whether he should continue.

"Get on with it man", the Judge ordered.

"Together the farmer and his man-servant ran across the fields and had the misfortune to find both ricks were burning with the flames bursting out of the top of the barley straw thatch. Other workers from Mr Bithnell's farm came to *assistance* with pitch forks and the like, but both ricks were totally destroyed, apart from a cart load of the clover hay and a bushel or two of the barley straw".

The learned Judge leaned forward, his crimson clad arms folded on top of the oak desk in front of him. "Was the accused man found at the scene of the crime?" he asked the constable.

Nathan took a deep breath and waited.

"No, your Honour, but he was in the alehouse *not an hour before*, much agitated he was and expressing vengeance against Mr Bithnell".

"Are their witnesses to this effect?"

Nathan averted his eyes and moved awkwardly from foot to foot, not knowing what to expect.

"Yes sir............I mean your Honour. There were many but the keeper of the inn.........". The man's head turned as his eyes searched for the alehouse keeper who was hidden somewhere in the crowd.

Nathan watched as the repulsive man emerged from the crowd.

Judge Parr removed his wire-framed spectacles and looked the man up and down, before asking, "Did you hear the accused make threats against Mr Bithnell?"

"He swore an oath sir, and then said no man would cheat him out of his dues. *Thence* he crashed across a table and scattered the cards and the players, saying, if the man does not pay him what he owes, he would take it in kind, those were his very words........I will take it in kind", he said.

The Judges' ice-cold eyes flashed from the alehouse keeper to Nathan who caught his gaze and swallowed hard.

Why in God's name did I do such a thing? he thought remorsefully.

"What happened next?"

"I told him not to be a bloody fool and go home and sleep it off. I then gave him the box he had dropped and he staggered off".

"What is the box you speak of?"

"A tinder box, sir, with a horse-shoe carved in its lid".

The Judge adjusted his position on the high-backed chair and stared directly at Nathan. "Did you make the threats the witness has described?" he asked in a clear judicial voice.

"Yes your Honour".

"And the carved tinder box he has described. Is that yours?"

"Yes sir, my father gave it to me many years ago", Nathan answered truthfully, as his manacled hand fruitlessly searched the torn pocket on his jerkin for the box.

"Where is the box now?" the Judge questioned, as he turned once again towards to the village constable.

"I have it your Honour". Jonas Sedge replied, as he held the box aloft for the Judge to see. "I found it by the burnt-out ricks".

An all-knowing gasp emanated from the crowd.

The Judge held his hand up and stroked his chin as he considered what he had just been told. A silence descended on the Courtroom as he studied some papers in front of him before saying, "There is another witness, I believe".

"Yes, your Honour", Sedge answered.

Nathan gulped and his face visibly paled as he saw a swath being cut through the crowd, not unlike standing barley falling to the sickle. A face appeared and to his horror, Nathan realised the man who was pushing the people aside with no regard, was none other than Abel Lightfoote.

At first the Judge said nothing as if he was deep in thought as he studied the man smirking in front of him. Abel Lightfoote stood boldly with his hands on his hips before he turned his head towards the blacksmith and grinned. How long have I waited for this, he was thinking?

When the Judge eventually spoke, his voice was quiet and his words precise. "What did you see?" he enquired.

He emphasised the word "you"

Lightfootes' eyes shifted around the room, unable to keep them focussed on the man who just asked the difficult question. "I was.... I mean, Henry Prinn and me *was* above Fairfoins Rowen on Samuel Bithnell's land when we heard a *galloper* coming up from the village, so we *ducks* under a hedge and as he passed, we saw it was Larkin heading towards the clover ricks".

Judge Parr remained silent as he digested the words until Lightfoote, who was keen to make his point, interrupted his thought, "It was Larkin we saw, no doubting it, we............" The Judge raised an eyebrow and hushed him with a wave of his hand, before asking, "What pray, were you doing on Mr Bithnell's land at that time of night?"

Abel Lightfoote's voice faltered as he struggled to answer. His eyes scanned the room in the hope of seeing Henry Prinn, so he could offer him some support. "I......I mean we......we *was* just out walking before we headed back to Dunn farm.... where I live", he said lamely. "*T'was* the next morning we heard the ricks had been *fired* so we *wents* to the constable and told him what *wees* saw....."

The Judge's voice cut across him and he turned his attention to Nathan, his face was set hard with a question. "Is that man telling the truth?"

Blood pulsed through Nathans' veins and his heart began to hammer as he began to realise all was lost. He had made threats against Samuel Bithnell and his property. It was his tinder box which was found by the burning clover ricks and he had ridden from the village in a foul and drunken temper towards them.

"Yes your Honour". Saying the words stung Nathan's dry lips as if they had been smeared with a foul tasting acid. "It is true that I did ride towards Mr Bithnell's farm and I did utter the words which the alehouse keeper has relayed to you, but as God is my witness, I did not burn his ricks nor did I go near them".

Judge Parr's eyes creased at the corners as he knotted his brow.

Nathan turned and stared at Abel Lightfoote. The smirk on the man's scarred face told him how much the brute was savouring the moment. There had been decades of hatred between them and now as resignation settled coldly inside him, Nathan knew he had lost all.

He didn't hear the hollow hoof beats which clattered on the granite sets outside the courthouse nor did he hear the whinnying of the horses as the riders pulled on the reins to bring the beasts to a wheeling halt.

Although he was over sixty years old, the younger of the two riders deftly swung his leg over the saddle and quickly dismounted and lost no time to walk round his sweating horse to help his elderly companion. The horses had been ridden hard, with steam rising from their thick, matted coats and white foam already dribbling from their mouths. The older rider was lying forward in his saddle, exhausted by the days' events and as he took his foot from the stirrup, he almost fell into the other mans' arms.

Nathan heard a commotion to his right and looked towards the entrance door of the Courtroon and saw a large man with a time-weathered face forcing his way through the crowds. As the crowd regained their places, a shorter man wearing a three-cornered, curled brimmed hat pushed them *asunder*. The Judge had caught sight of the men and his face tightened with impatience at the interruption to the proceedings.

"Forgive me your Honour but I have something of the greatest importance to say", said the breathless voice of the man who was still trying to shove his way the crowd.

Nathan recognised the once-rich voice. It belonged to Parson Lamb.

Slowly, with his familiar limp, he approached the Judge. Nathan had seen the Parson age with the passing of the years but was nevertheless surprised at the man's appearance. His aged face had the resigned look of someone whose life had stopped giving and was now only taking away and it was clear he was in some kind of pain. The old man was muffled in a heavy coat; his face was deeply lined but his eyes, framed by thick white eyebrows, still twinkled as bright as ever.

"Your Honour", the elderly clergyman addressed the Judge in a feeble voice, "I have brought Samuel Bithnell with me, whose ricks were *fired*".

He waited for the Judge's approval before carrying on. The Judge sensed his hesitation and nodded his head for the cleric to continue.

"This morning Mr Bithnell and I visited the scene of the crime. There was still much clover hay smouldering there and many footsteps surrounding it, no doubt from the men who tried to save the ricks". His voice broke away whilst his chest heaved as his old lungs demanded air.

Samuel Bithnell stepped forward. "*M'lud*", he said, "amongst the *traces* we saw were those made by someone wearing hobnailed boots with rounded heel rims". The farmer paused before adding, "The unusual iron rims were not of a type worn by any of my men".

Tobias Lamb interrupted him. "I believe Mr Lightfoote wears boots with iron rims nailed to their soles". A wave of gasps spread through the crowd.

"Damn you Parson", Abel Lightfoote snapped, as he exploded with anger, "may God burn your miserable soul for saying such a thing".

Judge Parr stroked his magnificent curled wig and allowed himself an inward smile as he ruminated that the least likely person in the courtroom to have their soul burnt in hell would be the good Parson.

It did not go un-noticed by the Parson who realised that even Judges had emotions realising they were probably better in hiding them than most ordinary mortals.

Lightfoote calmed and continued, "It's a *cock and pie* story you're trying to tell Parson, "many *mens* in Southwell wear *nailed* boots". His eyes bore into those of his accuser.

"Maybe so", the Parson said quietly, "the point I am making is that the blacksmith wears smooth-soled boots because he does not work the land. He carries out his craft on the worn-brick floor of the smithy where hob-nails and iron heel rims would be of little use". He paused and raised his voice slightly as he looked towards the Judge, "Indeed, if he was to wear boots of that nature, I fear they would cause him much inconvenience, slipping about on the hard floor".

The Judge pursed his lips as if to comment but thought better of it and remained silent. After a few moments of silent contemplation, he signalled to the Parson to continue.

The clergyman's voice was becoming strained. "Next to the boot *traces* which Mr Bithnell has referred to, were smaller *traces,* where the left foot appeared to be spayed out".

A wave of voices, some louder than others, rippled around the Courtroom as rows of heads turned to look accusingly at Henry Prinn. Prinn stared back at them in a mixture of shock and horror. The Parson's eyes narrowed and hardly pausing, he continued to speak, not giving either man the opportunity to respond. "Your Honour", he said, "could I have your permission to ask the constable a question?"

The Judge indicated his approval with an almost indiscernible nod of the head and Jonas Sedge stepped forward.

"When Mr Lightfoote and Mr Prinn came to you at *first light* after the fire, did you notice anything unusual about them?. How they looked, how they smelt?" the Parson enquired, almost nonchalantly.

The constable thought for a moment before answering, "It was soon after dawn when the pair of them came to see me and I noticed they smelt of smoke". He hesitated and looked at the Judge before he continued, "It was not the rich, seasoned smell you get from wood smoke, more like the damp, sticky smell of green weeds in a bonfire", he added ominously.

"Or clover hay?" the Judge prompted.

"Green weeds or clover hay, your Honour", Jonas Sedge, replied in a low voice, aware of the implications of his evidence, "that was the smell".

The Judge learnt forward and with an unmoving gaze, looked directly at Abel Lightfoote. He had been a man of few words throughout the trial, all of which had been keenly weighed, but none more than what he was about to say.

"Mr Lightfoote", his voice was solemn, "you did not tell me you had been at the scene of the fire. You have testified only that you saw Mr Larkin galloping towards the clover ricks and that when you heard of the crime, you reported what you had seen to the constable the following morning".

The learned Judge had not finished and glanced towards the jury, before his cold eyes confronted Abel Lightfoote once more.

"This is no time for your *prevarications* and I will allow you time to refresh your memory, should you................".

Henry Prinn's panic-stricken voice suddenly drowned him out.

"Tell him Abel it was you who found the blacksmith's tinder box and fired the ricks or else I am done for".

Lightfoote's eyes blazed as they searched for Prinn amongst the crowd and when they alighted upon him, he growled, menacingly, "Damn your eyes Henry, if you say anything more about me, I swear I will do for you".

"*Hang* you Abel. I *swear* to the Judge, I would wish that my right arm drops from my shoulder blade if it is not the truth that I'm telling to you".

A hum of astonishment swept through the crowded Courtroom. The Judge's head turned and beneath his bushy white eyebrows, he glared at the crowd, daring just one of them to cross him.

"QUIET", he commanded in a loud, irate voice. He faced the jury who had already turned their heads to those alongside them, as they discussed what they had just seen and heard. "I have heard enough to satisfy me that the defendant is innocent of the felonious crime he is accused of and through the admission of Henry Prinn, it is clear to me that those guilty of the crime are Abel Lightfoote and his accomplice, Henry Prinn".

Nathan, with his broad chest pounding against his rib cage, stared at the Judge, stunned and relieved. It was then hell itself erupted.

Abel Lightfoot's voice boomed above the general noise, "You bloody *cur*, I'll kill you", he screamed out at his partner in crime.

Through the sea of heads, Nathan saw Lightfoote was already frantically pushing his way through the crowd to get to Prinn. Within minutes the two men were trading blow after blow amid shouts of encouragement from the crowd and amongst the mayhem was the gaoler, closely followed by Jonas Sedge, heading towards the pair and yelling fruitlessly at them to stop. Lightfoote's chest was rising and falling as he grabbed Prinn's shirt and lunged towards his throat, intent on killing the man. Using the advantage of his bulk, it was the gaoler who reached the sprawling pair first and grabbing Prinn, who already had bright red blood pouring from his nose by the scruff of his neck, he threw him forcibly aside. Lightfoote's anger was so great he was like a lunatic in a mad house and before he could be stopped, he pounced on Prinn again, gripping him by the throat and started to throttle him. The gaoler bellowed like a bull in the ring as he, with Jonas Sedge's assistance, struggled in vain to restrain the brute until they were aided by a man who came out of the crowd and together, after much scuffling and a blow from a club, they took hold of Lightfoote and pinioned his arms behind his back.

"*Fetter* these men *hastily* and *commit* them to the gaol. I will sentence them *on the morrow* at *the hour of nine*", the Judge ordered calmly. He ignored the threats of violence being directly at him by Lightfoote as he and Prinn were being hauled away and instead, turned his attention to Tobias Lamb.

"Parson", he said, after pausing for thought, "could I prevail upon you to visit the culprits at *first light on the morrow* in the hope they see sense of their situation and show due repentance for their awful sins, in the hope they will enter the Kingdom of Heaven?"

"I will, your Honour", the cleric replied, less than enthusiastically, hoping instead for a longer rest in his bed chamber in order to rest his aching bones.

The Judge nodded his head in appreciation and turned his attention to Nathan. "Mr Larkin, I am inclined to find you guilty of *proffering* threats to Mr Bithnell and to his property and will...", he paused and Nathan held his breath. "I will speak to the good farmer and seek his opinion before sentencing you; in the meantime you may return to your smithy until the *morrow*".

Nathan mumbled, "Thank you, sir" as he drew a long-ragged breath.

It was before the dawn of the day when Nathan rode south-east to Ashden, descending a snaking, wooded bend before climbing the long hill which wound its way to the market town. The road showed signs of the animals and fowls which had been driven along it to the market. Bright moonlight was trying to break through the rain-heavy clouds, silhouetting the roadside trees as Nathan urged his mount on through the darkness. He had slipped through the grasp of deaths long fingers and now as he rode on, he was wondering what the Judge's sentence would be.

When he arrived, the light of day had dawned and crowds, swelled considerably by those who had come to the weekly market, were already milling outside the packed Courthouse, waiting in anticipation for the entertainment to begin. They had expected there would be a hanging to be enjoyed but a double *scragging* and a market to attend was something not to be missed and they milled about excitedly for the gaoler's cart to arrive. Nathan began to push his way through into the Courthouse to await the arrival of the scarlet-robed Judge and as he did so he was much relieved to see the strained but friendly face of Tobias Lamb.

"Good day to you my friend, are you refreshed from your night's rest and are not unduly fatigued?" the cleric enquired as he approached Nathan.

Nathan gave him a weak smile as he shook his hand warmly but he could see from the Parson's pale face and hooded eyes that it was him who could have done with the respite of a good night's rest. The poor man looked half-dead from weariness.

The two men made their way to stand in front of the Judge's bench and waited. Judge Parr entered the Courtroom and sat silent, his cold eyes boring into the noisy crowd in front of him, demanding their silence before he spoke.

At last, turning his attention to Nathan, he spoke, "Mr Bithnell has accepted that *monies* were owed to you and has said he *believes* you to be a good, honest man, driven to anger through grief and drink. Neither he nor I for that matter *believe* you played any part in *firing* his clover ricks. I therefore am of a mind to dismiss the case against you, other than to say you are to present yourself at my lodgings in Beaver Street at *seven of the clock* this evening".

Nathan expelled a huge sigh of relief and some moments passed before he raised his head to question the need to attend the lodgings but the words died on his lips as the Judge impatiently waved him away.

As he made his way to join the muttering crowd, Nathan heard the sound of rattling chains and shuffling feet as Prinn and Lightfoote, manacled together, were pushed towards the Judge. Glancing round, he saw that Prinn, his head bowed, was nervously clutching the nightcap which was perched precariously on his head whilst Abel Lightfoote stood in a determined manner, his *countenance* unchanged from the day before.

"Parson Lamb", Judge Parr said, in a clear commanding voice, "what say you?"

The cleric stepped forward a pace from where he was standing. "Your Honour", he paused as his eyes turned towards the manacled prisoners.

From a distance, Nathan studied the hunched old man's pale face and noticed, that despite the clerics obvious fatigue, he could still see the familiar lines etched around his eyes, telling of the laughter, warmth and affection he had enjoyed in years past.

"I have prayed with the prisoners, telling *to* them that when Jesus died on the cross he gave the gift of salvation for anyone willing to accept it. In the case of Prinn, the wretched man appeared to be duly penitent and is resigned to the fate that awaits him".

The Parson looked towards the gaunt-faced man before continuing, "He knows with true penance, he will go from the gallows today to the glory of heaven and has therefore accepted his fate".

The Judge's expression remained emotionless, as if his face had been set in stone.

"With regard to Abel Lightfoote", the tone of the Parson's voice changed, "his heart was *little affected* by my council, rendering him callous to the situation his enormous crime has placed upon him, other than frequently expressing that it was Prinn who *set the fire*…………but no matter".

"No matter indeed sir", the Judge repeated, as he reached for the square of black silk which lay on the desk in front of him. A silence fell over the Courtroom as he slowly and deliberately placed the cloth on the top of his curled wig and in a low voice which seemed to echo in his throat, said, "Abel Lightfoote and Henry Prinn, you are condemned to die, repent with lamentable tears and ask for the mercy of the Lord for the salvation of your souls".

Prinn's head dropped in resignation whilst Lightfoote shouted out defiantly, "Damn your soul" at the Judge, as the dignified man slowly rose from his chair and departed the Court.

Even before Nathan left the confines of the Courtroom, he could hear the near-deafening noise which was resonating from the bustling market place outside. Beasts were bellowing, pigs squealing and the shrill bleating of nervous sheep drifted on the breeze as a butcher and his boy herded them away. Despite the din of the animals, it was the whistling of the drovers and the barking of the wild dogs at their ankles which cut through the putrid air. It was like bedlam. Hawkers were crying out their wares and ringing bells which mingled with the roar of drunken laughter spilling out of the open doors of the many alehouses bordering the paved square. High-sided wagons and riders sitting upright on frisky mares competed for space with others who were straddled across the sagging backs of old farm nags. All of which helped to clog the narrow streets. The smell of ankle-deep filth and horse-dung hung pervasively in the air. As Nathan made his way out of the courtroom the bewildering scene in front of him momentarily confused his senses and he stood rooted to the spot as lines of squalid and ragged people pushed their way in the direction of *whence he came*. Market days in Ashden were always busy affairs but today the crowd was swelled *thrice-fold* by the people coming to watch the hanging, not just a hanging but a double hanging. Around him were people of every class. Well-to-do farmers, butchers, drovers, thieves, vagabonds all jostled together in a dense mass, whilst young children were laughing and shouting as they chased each other in and out of the seething thong. Men and women who had swilled too much drink, staggered aimlessly out of one alehouse and into another, before being thrown out onto the crowded streets by bloated, red-faced landlords.

Nathan moved forward the best he could, his nose following the delicious aroma drifting from a stall piled high with meat pies.

"Only tuppence", the man in a blood-stained apron said, "best savoury mutton pies in the market. *Them be* flavoured with thyme and onions with a generous pinch of nutmeg".

Realising how hungry he was, Nathan thrust his hand into his pocket and dropped two coins in the man's open palm.

"Never seen a double *scragging* before", *a cup-shotten clod* slurred, bumping into Nathan as he stood enjoying the pie. "They *says* it's the first time in Ashden…..First time it's *'appened* in living memory", he repeated, as he attempted to wrap his arm around Nathan's shoulder.

"They're coming, they're coming", the cry went up as the melancholy procession began to *cleave* its way through the jeering crowd towards the heathland where the gallows stood.

Nathan roughly pushed the man's arm away and began to make his way through the baying crowds, grateful his frame was such that he soon got a better view. Even at the age of sixty-one he still had considerable strength in his body. Through the sea of heads he could see Abel Lightfoote and Henry Prinn hunched up in the back of the gaoler's cart. He shouldered on until he had a clearer view. He saw the look of defiance on Lightfoote's face whilst Prinn, who curiously still had a nightcap on his head, appeared to be shaking with the fear of what was to become. Walking behind the cart was Parson Lamb reading from an open bible. Nathan assumed the Parson had offered the prisoners to *partake of* the holy sacrament but doubted whether Lightfoote would have accepted it. As he crested a small rise Nathan looked out over the rough heath land on a landscape which was bare and empty in every direction, save the double beam gallows standing forlornly in the morning air.

When the cart reached the scaffold, the large *assemblance* of spectators surged forward taking Nathan with them, much in the manner a pebble is thrown by a powerful wave. He watched as the gaoler walked round to the back of the cart and hauled the two men to their feet. One by one he pinioned their arms behind their backs before removing their fetters and chains. With the skill of a man well practised in the art of execution, he quickly pulled down the ropes from the protruding beams of the gibbets and looped them round the men's necks like the halters hanging from the necks of the cattle which were still bellowing in the market's *wattle* pens.

Nathan could feel the anticipation of the people around him, whilst others who were closer to the gallows started to hurl anything they could find at their feet. Mud, animal dung and rotten fruit, all started flying through the air in the direction of the condemned men.

As the running knot of the noose was adjusted round the back of Prinn's neck he turned to the gaoler and asked if he could address the crowd. His earnest voice carried high on the air as he said in a shaking voice, "I truly repent the crime I have committed and ask for the Lord's forgiveness". His face was gaunt and rigid with tension and as Nathan eased his head he could see the man's' legs were shaking uncontrollably. "I have frequented ale houses", Prinn's voice faltered, "broken the Sabbath day, uttered many profanities and……..". His voice was drowned out by the cheering crowd. Knowing the time was *nigh* he turned and said something to the gaoler who nodded and pulled Prinn's night-cap over his face.

He didn't want the crowd to see the grotesque contortions on his face as the noose tightens around his neck, Nathan thought grimly.

The gaoler moved from Prinn towards Lightfoote and as he did so, the man lunged at him in a final act of defiance. The crowd saw it and cried out and shouted encouragement to the condemned man, hoping there would be more drama to come before his neck was finally stretched.

Gripped Lightfoote's arm the man roughly pulled him closer to the rope, grinning as he carefully adjusted the noose so the slip knot was snug against the side of the Lightfoote's neck; he didn't want the man's neck to break too easily. He had decided that this particular man wasn't going to meet his Maker too bloody quickly.

Lightfootes' eyes roved across the crowd as the gaoler dropped the back-board of the cart and walked round to take hold of the horse's bridle. Unlike Prinn, the unrepentant man showed no sign of remorse for his crime and as the gaoler slapped the horse's flank, it appeared to those closest to the scaffold that Lightfoote deliberately took a lungful of air. The crowd quietened as the two men were dragged off the back of the cart and left hanging from the *hempen* ropes. As the nooses tightened round their necks and their heads twisted round, a huge cheer of delight rose from the crowd like a wave in the ocean. Nathan watched the grisly scene being acted out in front of him with a mixture of disgust and horror. Prinn jerked on the rope and his legs started kicking as the breath was being slowly being choked out of him. Minutes ticked by until the crowd started cheering as a thin, narrow-faced man ran from amongst them and pulled down hard on Prinns' legs to hasten his death. Two more hard yanks were needed before he hung still. Once again the crowd cheered. "One down", a voice shouted. The narrow-faced man turned his attention to Lightfoote, anxious to end his suffering. Lightfoote swung on the rope and brought his legs up, angrily booting the man away; he wanted no help in the manner he had chosen to die.

Nathan had seen enough and turned away. They deserved to be hung ten times over for all the crimes they have committed over the years, he thought, but this is an awful way for any man to meet his end. As he walked back across the heath towards the town he did not hear Lightfoote gasping for breath, nor see his bulging eyes, nor his face turn purple as his neck was gradually stretched. What he did hear in the distance was a group of chattering children who had started chanting the greenless tree rhyme.

"How dismal is the lot of those what we see

Poor guilty sufferers hanging on the greenless tree

Warned by their fate, their crimes o let us shun

Lest we, like them, transgress and be undone"

The gaoler pushed a woman aside who had run from the crowd to touch the men's bodies believing it would bring her good fortune. He had not finished and still had work to do. He hastily begun to free the bodies from the nooses and then, once he had loaded the lifeless forms onto the cart, he began to cut the ropes into small lengths. As he did so, some people who had been close to the gibbet gathered around him, all clambering for a piece of the rope as a keepsake of the hanging, knowing it too would bring them good luck.

He laughed and started shouting, "Penny a piece, penny a piece" and as the first of many pennies dropped into his open palm, he said to himself, "Superstitious fools, *tis* money for old rope". He laughed before repeating, "t*is* money for old rope, *tis* is".

The sun was setting behind the heavy clouds in the west when the spectacle ended. Numerous pipes of tobacco had been smoked and many more beakers of ale drunk dry. Drunks staggered into the alehouses looking for one last drink. Children played happily amongst the crowds, dogs barked at the beasts still tethered in the market. Tavern keepers counted their profits and two men had been hung.

 All around the gallows, people began to disperse with the same jollity as they did when they left a summer *fayre* once the entertainment had finished for the day. Some were heading jovially towards the alehouses whilst others were reluctantly going back to their chores, all ignoring the gaoler with his heavy cart bumping across the heath, his work done until the next time.

10

The Judge's Lodgings.

Nathan found the house without any difficulty. It stood on one of the widest streets in Ashden, far from the paved market square and its incumbent stench and rowdy, uncouth populous. A few furlongs on, the wide street narrowed as it wound its way through fields and woods to Canterbury and as Nathan stood at the foot of the wide stone steps leading up to the front door, he could hear the unmistakable sound of a pair of owls as they started their nights hunting. It was quite dark now and he felt the autumn's chill wind through his thin linen shirt and he pulled the front of his jerkin together by tightening its leather lace.

He had wandered aimlessly round the small market town after leaving the hangings, looking for no particular reason at the wares the traders were selling and avoiding the alehouses. He had been such a fool and was in no doubt he would not be in the situation he found himself in, had it not been for his *ale- fuddled* brain two evenings ago. How ashamed Clara would have been that her well respected husband would have come within an inch of having his neck stretched and now was about to walk up the steps of the Judge's lodging house to see what further penalty awaited him. He could see the dancing flames of the fires burning in the grates of the two chambers standing either side of the wide door. There were shadows coming from the fire burning in the darkened room to his left and in its illumination, Nathan could see a silver candelabra, which had a tall candle flickering from each its five arms standing proudly on a high bookcase heaving with the weight of old volumes.

He took a deep breath before rapping his broad knuckles nervously on the iron studded door and subconsciously cast a knowledgeable eye over the forged strap hinges whilst he waited. Minutes passed as his knock remained unanswered. He put his ear to the wooden planks to listen for any forthcoming footsteps from within and then stepped back onto the flagged path and waited. No one came. Perhaps he was early he thought, not having the means to tell the time. Time in Southwell was determined by the crowing of the cocks in the farmyards and back gardens of the cottages or by the light that was left in the sky, not by the time pieces standing on the mantelpieces of fine houses. He approached the door again and knocked louder. The heavy door rattled in its iron hinges.

Minutes passed before the door creaked open and a clerk's beady eyes peered out beneath thick, black eyebrows which were nearly hidden by a fringe of hair of a corresponding colour. A black linen robe was wrapped tightly round the man's shoulders which gave him the appearance of a large beetle whose wing-case would suddenly burst open and after a couple of quick flaps, would fly off into the inky night.

For a moment Nathan thought the man was going to slam the door shut as he visibly recoiled at the sight in front of him. The clerk knew the Judge was expecting someone but…….his nose twitched as it caught the familiar smell of the town's gaol. He raised the chamber stick he was carrying to get a better sight of the man standing on the other side of the door. In the feeble, yellow light of the candle he could see the villainous looking creature towering above him but strangely, and despite the man's size, was staring nervously at him. He was large and powerfully built, perhaps sixty or more years old with at least two days growth of white stubble covering his grimed face.

The clerk was about to slam the door shut on the face of the intruder and was already thinking he would additionally bolt it, when Nathan spoke," My name is Larkin, Nathan Larkin. I appeared before the

Judge today and he summoned me to *attend him* here at *seven of the clock"*.

The beetle-like man hesitated. He was fully aware that there were many felons who would wish to do his master harm and could this man be one of them? He pondered. Nathan waited whilst the manservant considered his decision.

Slowly the heavy door was fully opened and Nathan had scarcely stepped into the small inner hall before the man snapped almost angrily, "Wait here" as he disappeared through another door in front of him. Nathan looked around. The room was small and uninviting. Shadows flitted across the lime-washed walls as the draught which was creeping through the loose-fitting door caught the flames of the candles burning in the wall spikes but doing little to lift the gloom.

 The door opened and the black-robed manservant appeared again. Without saying a word he ushered Nathan into an uncomfortably large room. The tall candelabra he had seen through the window commanded attention on the bookcase, holding five smooth beeswax candles whose burning wicks were devoid of the foul smelling smoke of tallow. Under his smooth-soled boots he could feel the woven floor covering which nearly reached to the outer edges of the dark, polished wood floor. Glancing down, Nathan noticed how clean it was, free from dirt and any defilement brought in from the streets outside. Above his head, designs of fruit and flowers were carved into the plaster mouldings which ran around the top of the walls, which to Nathans' eyes, could have been of any hue, he couldn't tell in the flickering candlelight.

"You are to wait here and to remain standing", the man ordered as he noticed Nathan was looking at the upholstered chairs placed round the fireplace.

Nathan had forgotten how soiled his breeches were after lying in the filth on the prison floor and understood immediately what the man meant.

 "And do not touch anything", the clerk added sternly, before he disappeared once again.

Almost immediately he re-appeared again to add as an afterthought, "It is customary to address a Judge of this land by his full title".

Nathan froze. He had heard the Judge's name mentioned in the Court but it had not stuck in his mind and he shot a questioning look at the man.

"If you need to speak to his honour, his name is Justice Parr", he reminded Nathan somewhat impatiently. He had taken a dislike to the man standing in front of him, having seen many felons during his years of service with the Judge, most of which had been hung.

Nathan watched the man leave before he edged towards the fire roaring in the grate and looked at its glowing embers. The heat reminded him of his forge and he suddenly longed to return back to it and put an end to the nightmare. He was still deep in thought when the door opened and the Judge walked in. Without his judicial finery the man looked much smaller than he did in his Court. Without his magnificent curled wig, his head was shorn and free of hair, contrasting with his clipped white beard. Nathan recalled being told once that most lawyers shaved their heads to prevent the lice from the rabble they dealt with in the courtrooms, breeding in their hair.

Nathan's large frame contrasted sharply with the diminutive looking man whose facial expression was set in stone as he studied the blacksmith standing in front of him. His scarlet robes had been replaced with a black, swallow-tailed coat and knee breeches of the same sombre colour. Nathan suddenly became aware of his dishevelled appearance as his eyes saw the Judge's white silk stockings and the black, silver buckled pumps on his feet.

Nathan's demeanour was evident as he stood with his back to the fire, his head bowed and his hands clasped in front of him. The minutes passed by slowly before the Judge eventually spoke. It appeared he had been deep in thought. His strong voice echoed round the chamber. "What were the circumstances which brought you before my Court?" he asked.

Nathan cleared his dry throat before he tried to reply. What did the man want him to say? he thought as memories raced through his mind. "I was angry" he started to say in a faltering voice, "I had been to my wife's grave..." He froze again as he realised he had already forgotten the Judge's name.

"Your wife's grave?"

"Yes, sir and my son's grave...they both died when the speckled monster swept through the village", Nathan replied.

"Smallpox! When was that?" The Judge's voice had softened and he seemed surprised at what Nathan had just said.

Nathan thought for a moment before answering, "Over thirty years ago. It was brought to the village by an itinerant horse dealer and over the months which followed it spread like a heath-land fire. There was no escaping the monster. Many suffered dreadfully and died, whilst on others, it left its hideous traces"

The Judge adjusted the double-tabbed linen bands hanging from his neck before responding, "The curse of smallpox has travelled the length and breadth of the land and has left thousands of dead in its wake, young and old, men and women but thankfully, those who were left in grief, have not stood before the Judges of our land, such as you, accused of a felony".

"No sir", Nathan answered ruefully.

The Judge had not finished, "Nor did they utter threats against those who *did them* injustice".

"No sir".

"Nor did they try to drown their sorrow by pouring ale down their throats in self pity".

"No sir".

The Judge turned away, holding his hand in the air as if he was impatient with the conversation and looked out of the window into the ink- blackness of the night.

After, what seemed to Nathan was an hour, the Judge said, almost vaguely, "It occurs to me that not once have you correctly addressed me".

Nathan swallowed hard and waited for the words to form in his mouth as he stared blankly at the man's back. "Begging your pardon sir", he stuttered, "but in truth, I have forgotten………"

He was interrupted by the Judge, who slowly turned to face him again.

"*Tis* of no consequence……. tell me about the man who was hung on the gallows this afternoon. The man called Lightfoote".

"Over the years he caused much suffering to many people in the village and beyond, as did his father before him". Nathan relaxed a little as he carried on, "The evil of the father was passed to the son. Abel Lightfoote bullied and stole and took whatever he wanted from whoever he wished for his own evil ends, ably assisted by Henry Prinn".

"Why did the man hate you so much that he wanted to see you hung for a crime you didn't commit?" The Judge was a man of few words but each one was keenly weighed.

Nathan thought for a moment before answering, wondering whether it was wise to tell the truth "Many years ago I gave him a beating which he never forgot nor forgave", he said, deciding not to go into too much detail.

The Judge remained silent and deep in thought whilst Nathan anxiously waited for him to question him further. Eventually the diminutive man turned and slowly walked towards a small, dignified-looking desk, piled high with stacks of papers all tightly bound with bright red ribbons.

Nathan watched anxiously as the man swept his coat tails aside and sat down. Taking a sheet of paper from the top drawer he slowly lifted his quill and started to write. The eerie silence which had descended on the chamber was broken by the grating noise the pen nib made as it travelled in flourishes across the coarse paper.

"Can you read?" the Judge asked, as he handed the carefully folded the sheet to Nathan.

"Well enough, sir", Nathan replied, as he nervously took the document. With a slightly shaking hand he opened it and looked down at what the Judge had written.

The man watched as Nathans heavy eyelids widened as he stared in disbelief at the bold hand of the Judge's pen.

He froze into silence.

Lifting his eyes he surveyed the man in astonishment. Beyond the shaved head and the bush of facial hair, Nathan began to see a different face slowly appear. It was like looking into a misted mirror as it slowly cleared.

"I have written my name so you will not forget it so easily in the future". The voice Nathan was hearing seemed distant, as if it was in another room.

He stood stock still as he gaped at the man in front of him. .

"We are older than before", the Judge said cryptically, before adding, "it's been over forty years".

"Jabez Palairet", Nathan muttered disbelievingly, refusing to believe the words which had just left his lips..

"*Tis* indeed me", the Judge replied, as his stern face broke out into a rare grin, half hidden by the bushy, white growth on his face.

The quizzical look remained locked on Nathan's face, his wide eyes seeking an explanation.

"I changed my Huguenot name many years ago to the more english sounding name of Parr", he explained as he walked across the chamber to grasp his long-lost friend's hand.

A knock on the door interrupted further enlightenment between the two men as the black-cloaked manservant entered the chamber.

The words, "Dinner is served, your honour……", were already coming from the man's lips as he stopped and stared at the sight in front of him; a learned Judge of many years standing, shaking the filthy hand of a felon. The look of shock on his face mirrored the one which had been on Nathan's face moments earlier.

"Thank you, Wheeler, we will come through immediately; we have much to discuss", Jabez replied calmly, fully aware of his servant's shock. "Come Nathan, I am sure you could enjoy a good meal".

The man backed away and held the door open as Jabez put his hand onto Nathan's back and ushered him back across the small hall and into the parlour. The room was filled with a smoky scent. It was dark. Darker than the one they had left but the arcs of brilliant gold shimmering from the candles helped to lift its blackness. A long mahogany table stretched out in front of them, already laid with polished silver cutlery, *heavy to the hand* and shining in the candlelight. At each of the three places stood an empty wine glass standing next to a beautifully folded napkin. All that is missing is the food, Nathan thought ruefully.

As his eyes adjusted to the changed light he could see a figure of a man sitting in a high-backed chair close to the burning fire. The roughly hewn logs in the wide grate were crackling and popping as the flames slowly ate them away. The man sitting in the chair had heard the door open and stopped looking at the wisps of curling silver-grey smoke as they tried to escape the gentle pull of the chimney. He slowly turned his head towards the door. "A good evening to *your good self,* Nathan", he said, in a voice *cracked* with age and fatigue.

Nathan's head was still swimming with everything that had happened but he recognised the voice immediately. "Good evening, Parson", he said, in surprise.

"I feel much relieved that this frightful business has been brought to a close", he said to Jabez, before turning to look directly at Nathan, "as I am sure you do, my dear friend".

Jabez's expression hardened as he said solemnly, "Many years ago the good Parson said that justice at a higher place would be served on Percival Lightfoote".

Nathan nodded his head as his mind drifted back and he remembered the words the Parson had spoken more than four decades ago.

"I have been told that he was hastened to his end by the most heinous of crimes committed by his son", Jabez continued.

The elderly cleric interjected, "There is no doubt that Abel Lightfoote was culpable of the crime". He paused and shook his head almost in horror of what he was about to say. "It is hard to imagine such an evil act; surely there can be nothing on God's earth more serious than parricide…a son killing his own father".

The conversation paused as the manservant brought a large platter of beef surrounded by roasted potatoes and bright green cabbage to the table. "It's roasted sirloin, m' lord", he said, proudly as he placed the meal before Jabez for his approval.

The Parson looked ruefully at the food, regretting the days had long since gone when he could do it justice. "I do not have the appetite I once had", he said as the man was about to serve the food, "a mere morsel will suffice if you please…..oh and could I have some water to add to this fine claret". He tapped the goblet in front him as if to apologise for having to dilute the ruby-coloured wine of such obvious fine quality.

Jabez Parr looked at Tobias Lamb for several moments before he turned his gaze to Nathan and said, "Nathan, my friend, it is appropriate that we raise our goblets and toast the good Parson. What we both owe him is indeed incalculable. Without his benevolence in allowing me to use his library at Southwell, I doubt I would have ever become a Judge and without his efforts during the past few days in proving your innocence, you may have finished up with your neck stretched".

Nathan solemnly nodded his agreement.

The two men stood and raised their goblets to the old man. With his face beaming with pleasure at what had just been said, he remained seated and replied by saying simply, "God bless you both, my very good friends".

The men were already enjoying the meal when the manservant returned with the water. "Shall I leave the platter, should you wish to serve yourselves?" he said to his master. Jabez glanced across the table at Nathan who was obviously enjoying the *fare* and nodded his approval to the man. "*Tis* a white pot pudding with a brown sugar topping to follow, your honour", the servant added, as he left the room.

"Enough of this melancholia, *what say you* Nathan?" the old Parson said, as he tried to shift the conversation to something the blacksmith would feel more at ease with. The old man turned to Jabez. "It is a matter of interest to me as to how you came to be a learned Judge?" he asked.

Jabez indicated his approval to the question by a slight judicial nod of his head and gently rested his bone-handled knife and fork on his plate. "It seems such a long time ago when my mother and I left Southwell with Matthew Rosser. He was a good man and true to his word he *progressed* my education at his expense and I learnt quickly. Eventually I entered the Inns of Court and entered the bar which gave me access to the court circles where I was able to expand my social acquaintances and greatly advance my status".

Nathan looked at his old friend as he sat in his finery and marvelled at his change of fortune. Jabez caught Nathan's gaze and said, "When my mother and I lived at the smithy, little did you realise how I marvelled at your mastery of iron and how you held the knowledge of your ancient craft so close to you".

"It is something which has been handed down in my family for generations", Nathan replied. He paused, knowing he was the last of the line and the secrets of the forge would now die with him.

Jabez peered perceptively at him through his wire-rimmed spectacles as if he knew what Nathan was thinking. "You must pass your skills and knowledge on Nathan. When the time comes and the good Lord calls you, your skills are too precious to be buried with you in the rich soil of Southwell".

Nathan nodded his head thoughtfully, unsure how to respond.

It was Tobias Lamb who broke the silence. "I have someone in my employment named Thaddius Thatcher. He is a sturdy, energetic young man and has a good nature and a strong arm. I am sure he would apply himself to your noble craft if you would care to teach him".

Nathan's eyes brightened. He knew Tad Thatcher and the Parson's *notion* immediately appealed to him.

Jabez smiled as he continued to answer the clergyman's enquiry, "It was some years later when Matthew Rosser and my mother married in La Neuve Eglise, the Huguenot church in Spitalfield and they lived the rest of their lives in supreme happiness".

He rose from his chair and stood behind Nathan and the old Parson and rested each of his hands on their shoulders. "Nathan", he said with a wicked grin spreading across his face and a twinkle in his eye, "the times are changing and without as many horses to be shod or sickles to be forged, this may be the time to tend some neglected pastures and over-grown orchards". He paused before saying, "Perhaps at my mother's old home, Dunn farm, I hear tell that the new owner, Daisie Lighfoote could do with some happiness in her life and the love of a good man".

The door opened as Wheeler entered to clear the table and as he left with the three plates piled up on the empty platter, Jabez clapped his hands together and said, "It is now time to enjoy the white pot pudding we are about to be served and raise our goblets and drink to our friendships". He helped Tobias Lamb to his feet and as he turned to face Nathan, he raised his goblet and said, "My dear friend, perhaps our paths will cross again one day".

"I hope not", Nathan replied, as he embraced his laughing friend.

Nathan Larkin married Daisie Lightfoote six months after his trial. The service was conducted by their mutual friend, Tobias Lamb. The couple lived happily together for another eighteen years.

The Parson died peacefully in his sleep at the grand age of ninety-two, five years after the wedding. Daisie Larkin was at his bedside. He bequeathed his library of books to Jabez Parr and to Nathan Larkin he left his collection of fine wine and butts of ale.

Whenever Judge Parr presided at the Ashden Assizes, he took the opportunity to visit Nathan and Daisie at his mother's old family home at Dunn Farm and enjoyed many a happy meal with the couple.

Despite the continuing mechanisation of the farms in the vicinity, Tad Thatcher made a good living as Southwell's blacksmith, as did the three generations of his family who followed him. Until his death, Nathan Larking would often stroll down the lane to the smithy to ensure the fashioning of iron and the keeping of the forges' secrets were to his liking.

La Neuve Eglise, the Huguenot church, still stands on the corner of Fournier Street, close to Spitalfield market.

Printed in Great Britain
by Amazon